if lions could speak

and other stories

other books by paul park

Available from Cosmos Books:
Three Marys

Available as e-books from ElectricStory.com:
Soldiers of Paradise
Sugar Rain
The Cult of Loving Kindness

Coelestis
The Gospel of Corax

if lions
could speak

and other stories

paul park

COSMOS BOOKS

if lions could speak
and other stories

Published by:

Cosmos Books, an imprint of Wildside Press
www.cosmos-books.com
www.wildsidepress.com

For more information, contact Wildside Press.

Hardback ISBN: 1-58715-512-5
Trade Paperback ISBN: 1-58715-508-7

acknowledgments

"The Tourist" first appeared in *Interzone*, February 1994.

"The Breakthrough" first appeared in *Full Spectrum 5*, Bantam Books, 1995.

"A Man On Crutches" first appeared in *Omni*, January 1994.

"Get A Grip" first appeared in *Omni Online*, February 1997.

"Untitled 4" first appeared in *Fence*, Spring/Summer 2000.

"Tachycardia" first appeared in *Fantasy & Science Fiction*, January 2002.

"Christmas in Jaisalmer" appears here for the first time.

"Self Portrait, With Melanoma, Final Draft" first appeared in *Interzone*, May 2001.

"If Lions Could Speak" first appeared in *Interzone*, February 2002.

"The Lost Sepulcher of Huascar Capac" first appeared in *Omni Best Science Fiction One*, 1992.

"The Last Homosexual" first appeared in *Asimov's*, June 1996.

"Bukavu Dreams" first appeared in *Interzone*, November 1999.

"Rangriver Fell" first appeared as part of the novel *Soldiers of Paradise*, Arbor House, 1987.

These stories are dedicated to Lucius Lionel
and Miranda Caspian, in hope that they might
like this sort of thing some day.

contents

conTenTs

the tourist

Everybody wants to see the future, but of course they can't. They get turned back at the border. "Go away," the customs people tell them. "You can't come in. Go home." Often you'll get people on TV who say they snuck across. Some claim it's wonderful and some claim it's a nightmare, so in that way it's like before there was time travel at all.

But the past is different. I would have liked to have gone early, when it was first opened up. Nowadays whenever you go, you're liable to be caught in the same pan-cultural snarl: We just can't keep our hands off, and as a result, Cuba has invaded prehistoric Texas, the Empire of Ashok has become a Chinese client state, and Napoleon is in some kind of indirect communication with Genghis Khan. They plan to attack Russia in some vast temporal pincer movement. In the meantime, Burger Chef has opened restaurants in Edo, Samarkand and Thebes, and a friend of mine who ventured by mistake into the Thirty Years War, where you'd think no one in their right mind would ever want to go, said that even Dessau in 1626 was full of fat Australians drinking boilermakers and complaining that the 17th century just wasn't the same since Carnage Travel ("Explore the bloodsoaked fields of Europe!") organized its packaged tours. They weren't even going to show up at the bridgehead the next day; my friend went, and reported that the Danish forces were practically outnumbered by Japanese tourists, who stampeded the horses with their fleets of buses, and would have changed the course of history had there been anything left to change. Wallenstein, the Imperial commander, didn't even bother to show up till four o'clock; he was dead drunk in the back of a Range Rover, and it was only due to contractual obligations that he appeared at all, the Hapsburg government (in collaboration with a New York public relations firm) having organized the whole event as a kind of theme park. Casualties (my friend wrote) after seven hours of fighting were still zero, except for an Italian who had cut his finger changing lenses—an im-

11

provement, I suppose, over the original battle, when the waters had flowed red with Danish blood.

And that period is less traveled than most. The whole classical era barely exists anymore. First-century Palestine is like a cultural ground zero: nothing but taxi cabs and soft-drink stands, and confused and frightened people. Thousands attend the Crucifixion every day, and the garden at Gethsemane is a madhouse at all hours. My ex-inlaws were there and they sent me a photograph, taken with a flash. It shows a panicked, harried, sad young man. (Yes, he's blond and blue-eyed, as it turns out, raising questions as to whether the past can actually be altered in retrospect by the force of popular misconception.) But at least he's out in the open. Pontius Pilate, Caiaphas, and the entire family of Herod the Great are in hiding, yet still hardly a week goes by that Interpol doesn't manage to deport some new revisionist. It's amazing how difficult people find it to accept the scientific fact—that nothing they do will ever make a difference, that cause and effect, as explicative principles, are as dead as Malcolm X.

Naturally they are confused by their ability to cause short-term mayhem, and just as naturally they are seeking an outlet for their own frustrations: Adolf Hitler, for example, has survived attempts on his life every 15 minutes between 1933 and 1945, and people are still lining up to take potshots even since the Nazis closed the border to everyone but a small group of Libyan consultants—now stormtroopers are racing back in time, hoping to provide 24-hour security to all the Fuehrer's distant ancestors. Who wants to explain to that crowd how history works? Joseph Stalin—it's the same. Recently some Lithuanian fanatic managed to break through UN security to confront him at his desk. "Please," he says, "don't kill me." (They all speak a little English now.) "I am a democrat," he says—"I change my mind." These days it requires diplomatic pressure just to get people to do what they're supposed to. It is only by promising the Confederate government $10,000,000 in new loans that the World Bank can persuade Lee to attack at Gettysburg at all—"I have a real bad feeling about this," he says over and over. "I love my boys," he says. "Please don't make me do it." Who can blame him? He has a book of Matthew Brady's photographs on his desk.

And in fact, why should he be persuaded? What difference does it make? People hold onto these arbitrary rules, these arbitrary patterns, out of fear. Not even all historians are able to concede the latest proofs—confirmations of everything they feared and half-suspected when they were in graduate school—that events in the past have no discernible effect upon the present.

That time is not after all a continuum. That the past is like a booster rocket, constantly dropping away. Afterward, it's disposable. Except for the most recent meeting of the AHA (Vienna, 1815—Prince Metternich the keynote speaker, and a drunken lecher, by all reports), American historians now rarely go abroad except as tourists. They are both depressed and liberated to find that their work has no practical application.

That's not completely true. It certainly changed things, for example, when people found out that the entire known opus of Rembrandt van Rijn consisted of forgeries. But that's a matter of money; it's business contacts that people want anyway, not understanding. So everywhere you go back then are phalanxes of oilmen, diplomats, arms dealers, art collectors, and teachers of English as a second language. Citibank recently pre-empted slave gangs working on the pyramid of Cheops, to help complete their Giza offices. The World Wildlife Fund has projects (Save the Trilobites, etc.) into the Precambrian era—projects doomed to failure by their very nature.

Of course the news is not all bad: world profiles for literacy and public health have been transformed. In 1349 the International Red Cross has seven hundred volunteers in Northern Italy alone. And the Peace Corps, my God, they're everywhere. But nevertheless I thought I could discern a trend, that all the world and all of history would one day share the same dismal denominator. Alone in my house on Washon Island, which I'd kept after Suzanne and I broke up, I saw every reason to stay put. I am a cautious person by nature.

* * *

But that summer I was too much by myself. And so I took advantage of a special offer; there had been some terrorist attacks on Americans in Tenochtitlan, and fares were down as a result. I bought a ticket for Paleolithic Spain. I thought there might be out-of-the-way places still. Places pure and malleable, where I could make things different. Where my imagination might still correspond in some sense to reality—I might have known. My ex-inlaws had sent me postcards. They had recently been on a mastodon safari not far from Jaca, where they had visited Suzanne. "The food is great," they wrote me—never a good sign.

I might have known I was making a mistake. There is something about the past which makes what we've done to it even more poignant. All the brochures and the guidebooks say it and it's true. It really is more beautiful back then. The senses come alive. Colors are brighter. Chairs are more comfortable. Things smell better, taste better. People are friendlier, or at least they were. Safe in the future, you can still feel so much potential. Yet the town I landed in, San Juan de la Cruz—my God, it was such a sad place. We came in over the Pyrenees, turned low over a lush forest, and then settled down in an enormous empty field of tarmac. The hangar space was as big as Heathrow's, but there was only one other commercial jetliner, a KLM. Everything else was US military aircraft and not even much of that, just five beige transports in a line, and a single helicopter gunship.

We taxied in toward His Excellency the Honorable Dr Wynstan Mog (Ph.D.) International Airport, still only half built and already crumbling, from the look of it. For no perceptible reason the pilot offloaded us about 200 yards from the terminal, and then we had to stand around on the melting asphalt while the stewardesses argued with some men in uniform. I didn't mind. The sky was cobalt blue. The air was hot, but there were astonishing smells blown out of the forest toward us, smells which I couldn't identify, and which mixed with the tar and the gasoline and my own sweat and the noise of the engines into a sensation that seemed to nudge at the edges of my memory, as if it almost meant something, just in itself. But what? I had been born in Bellingham; this was nothing I recognized. It was nothing from my past. I put my head back and closed my eyes, while all around me my 19 fellow passengers buzzed and twittered. And I thought, this is nothing. This feeling is nothing. Everybody feels this way.

The men in uniform collected our passports and then they marched us toward the terminal. They were not native to the time and place; they were big, fat men. I knew Dr Mog had hired mercenaries from all over—these ones looked Lebanese or Israeli. They wore sunglasses and carried machine pistols. They hustled us through the doors and into the VIP lounge, an enormous air-conditioned room with plastic furniture and a single plate-glass window that took up one whole wall. It appeared to lead directly onto the street in front of the terminal. Certainly there was a crowd out there, perhaps a hundred and fifty people of all races and nationalities, and they were staring in at us, their faces pressed against the glass.

One of the uniformed men moved to a corner of the window. A cord hung from the ceiling; he pulled down on it, and a dirty brown curtain inched from left to right across the glass wall. It made no difference to the people outside, and even when the curtain was closed I was still aware of their presence, their sad stares. If anything I was more aware. I sat down in one of the molded

14

chairs with my back to the curtain, and watched some customs officials explain two separate hoaxes, both fairly straightforward.

There was a desk at the back of the room and they had spread our passports onto it. They were waiting for our luggage, and in the meantime they checked our visas and especially our certificates of health. I was prepared for this. The region is suffering from a high rate of AIDS infection—almost 25% of the population in San Juan de la Cruz has tested HIV positive. The government seems unconcerned, but they have required that all tourists be inoculated with the so-called AIDS vaccine, a figment in the imagination of some medical conmen in Zaire, and unavailable in the US. Nevertheless it is now mandatory for travel in large parts of the third world, as a way of extorting hard currency. I work in a hospital research lab and I had the stamp; so, apparently, had someone else in our group, a thin man my own age, deeply tanned. His name was Paul. Together we watched the others gather around the desk, and watched them as they came to understand their choice—to pay a fine of $150 per person, or to be inoculated right there on the premises with the filthiest syringe I'd ever seen. It was a good piece of theatre; one of the officials left to "wash his hands," and came back in a white smock with blood on it—you had to smile. At the same time one of the others was handing out bank booklets and explaining how to change money: all tourists were required to exchange $50 a week at the State Bank, for which they received a supposedly equivalent amount of the national currency—three eoliths, a bone needle, six arrowheads and two chunks of rock salt. An intrinsic value of about 40 cents, total—this in a country where in any case dollars and Deutschmarks are the only money that anyone accepts.

* * *

Paul and I lined up to buy our currency packs, which came in a convenient leather pouch. "It's ridiculous," he said. "Before time travel they didn't even have domesticated animals. They lived in caves. What were they going to buy?"

He had been working in the country for about five years, and was knowledgeable about it. At first I liked him because he still seemed fresh in some ways, his moral outrage tempered with humor and a grudging admiration for Dr Mog. "He's not a fool," he said. "His PhD is a real one: political economy from the University of Colombo—the correspondence branch, of course, but his dissertation was published. An amazing accomplishment when you consider his background. And he's just about the only one of these dictators who's not a foreign puppet or an adventurer—he's a genuine Cro-Magnon, native to the area, and he's managed to stay in power despite some horrendous CIA intrigues, and get very rich in the process."

Someone wheeled in a trolley with our luggage on it. The customs men spread out the suitcases on a long table. Paul and I were done early; we both had packed light, and were carrying no modern gadgets. The others, most of whom were with a tour group going to Altamira, stood around in abject silence while the officials went through everything, arbitrarily confiscating cameras, hairdryers, CD players on a variety of pretexts. "This is a waste of our electrical resources," admonished one, holding up a Norelco.

But by that time Paul and I had been given permission to leave. We had to wait in line outside the lounge to get our visas stamped, and then we made our way through the chaotic lobby. I allowed Paul to guide me, ignoring as he did the many people who accosted us and tugged upon our arms. He seemed familiar with the place, happy or at least amused to be there. Outside in the heat, he stopped to give a quarter to a beggar he appeared to recognize, and conversed with him while I looked around. I was going to get a taxi and find a hotel and stay there for a night or so before going on into the interior. I haven't traveled very much, and I was worried about choosing a taxi man from the horde that surrounded us, worried about being overcharged, taken advantage of. I put on my sunglasses, waiting for Paul, and I was relieved to find when he was finished that he expected me to follow him. "I'll take you to the Aladeph," he said. "We'll get some breakfast there."

He was scanning the crowd for someone specific, and soon a little man broke through, Chinese or Korean or Japanese—"Mr Paul," he said, "This way, Mr Paul." Then he was tugging at our bags and I, untrusting, wasn't letting go until I saw Paul surrender his own daypack. We walked over to a battered green Toyota. Rock and roll was blaring from the crummy speakers. The sun was powerful. "We've got to get you a hat," said Paul.

A long straight road led into town, flanked on both sides by lines of identical one-story concrete buildings: commercial establishments selling hubcaps and used tires, as well as piles of more anonymous metal junk. Men sat in the sandy forecourts, smoking cigarettes and talking; there were a lot of people, a lot of people in the streets as we passed an enormous statue of Dr Mog, the Father of the Nation with his arms outstretched—a gift from the Chinese government. We drove through Martyr's Gate into a neighborhood of concrete hovels, separated from the narrow streets by drainage ditches full of sewage. People everywhere, but not one of them looked native to the time—the men wore ragged polyester shirts and pants, the women faded housedresses. Most were barefoot, some wore plastic shoes.

We passed the Catholic Cathedral, as well as numerous smaller churches of various denominations: Mormon, Seventh Day Adventist and Jehovah's Witness. We passed the headquarters of several international relief organizations, and then I must have dozed off momentarily, for when I opened my eyes we were in a different kind of neighborhood entirely, a neighborhood of sleek highrises and villas covered with flowering vines.

The cab pulled up in front of a Belgian restaurant called Pepe le Moko, and we got out. Paul paid the driver before I could get my money, and then waved away the bills I offered him; he had said nothing during the ride, but had sat staring out the window with an expression half rueful and half amused. Now he smiled more broadly and motioned me inside the restaurant—it was an expensive place, full of white people in short-sleeved shirts and ties.

"I thought we'd get some breakfast," he said.

We ordered French toast and coffee, which came immediately. I spooned some artificial creamer into mine and offered the jar to him, but he wrinkled his nose. "I'm sure it's all right," he said.

"What do you mean?"

He shrugged. "You know the United States government pays for its projects here by shipping them some of our agricultural surplus. It's a terrible idea, because it makes the population dependent on staples that can't be grown locally; at any rate, Dr Mog sells it, and then uses the money, supposedly, to finance USAID, and famine relief, whatever. Well, my first year there was a shipment of a thousand tons of wheat, which they packed in the same container as a load of PCV's, which was being sent to some plastics factory. When it got here, the customs people claimed the wheat was contaminated and couldn't be sold. They sequestered it in warehouses while the US sent a scientist who said it was okay. But as they argued back and forth, the wheat was sold anyway. And then the raw PCV's began to show up also here in San Juan, in some of the poorer restaurants. It's a white powder, it's soluble in water, and it's got a kind of chalky, milky taste, apparently."

"Thanks for telling me," I said.

"That's okay. It was a shambles. The Minister of Health was fired, before he came back last year as the Minister for Armaments. Somebody got rich. So what's a blip in the leukemia statistics?"

He smiled. "That's horrible," I said.

"Yeah, well, it's not all bad. And what do you expect? It's got to be like that. People don't understand—they think it's every country's right to be modern and industrialized. Mog's been to college; he knows what's what. You and I might say, well, they're better off living in caves, chipping flint and hitting each other with bones, but who are we? Mog, he wants an army. He wants telephones. He wants roads, cars, electricity. Who can blame him? But if you can't make that stuff yourself, you've got to get it from the white man. And the thing about the white man, he doesn't offer you that shit for free."

Paul was looking pretty white himself. "What do you do?" I asked.

"I work for Continental Grain. We've got a project in the bush. Near Jaca."

I looked down into my coffee cup. "Do you know Suzanne Denier?" I asked.

"Yeah, sure. She works for an astronomy project in my area. Near the reservation there."

I closed my eyes and opened them. I asked myself: Had she been to this restaurant? Where did she sit? Did she know the story about the powdered milk?

"She's with the Cro-Magnon," I said. "Is that the only place they live? On reservations? I haven't seen a single one since we've been here."

"You'll see one. In San Juan they're all registered. It's one of Mog's new laws. You can't kick them out of business establishments, and all the restaurants have to give them food and liquor. So they're around here begging all the time. You'll see."

In fact, shortly after that, one did come in. She stood in the doorway and watched us as we ate our toast. She was almost six feet tall, with delicate bones, a beautiful face, and long, graceful hands. She had no hair on her head. She had green eyes and black skin. At ten o'clock in the morning she was very drunk.

* * *

After breakfast I spent most of the day with Paul. We had lunch at the Intercontinental and then went swimming at the Portuguese Club. Soon I began to find him patronizing.

In those days I was sensitive and easily annoyed. Nevertheless I stayed with him, my resentment rising all the time. I allowed him to get me a room, as he had mentioned, at the Aladeph—a guesthouse reserved for people on official business. I think it amused him to demonstrate that he could place me there, that he could manipulate the bureaucracy, which was formidable. I was grateful, in a way. Jetlagged, I went to bed early, but I couldn't sleep until a few hours before dawn.

"Suzanne," I said when I woke up. I said it out loud. I lay in bed with my throat dry, my skin wet. At six o'clock in the morning it was already hot. White gauze curtains moved in the hot breeze.

I lay in bed thinking about Suzanne. I thought of how when she was leaving I had not even asked her to stay.

It's not as if our marriage wasn't difficult, wasn't unsatisfying, and I remember my cold anger as I listened to her reasons why she should take a job so far from home. Later she had written and told me that even then, if I had just said something, anything, she would have stayed with me. Lying in bed at the Aladeph, I remembered her walking back and forth next to the dark long living-room window of the island house while I sat in the chair, half watching her, half reading. I remembered how her face changed as she made up her mind. I saw it happen, and I did nothing.

Lying in bed, remembering, I made myself get up and take her by the shoulders. I made myself apologize and made her listen. "Don't go," I said. "I love you," I said, and with just those three words I saw myself creating a new future for us both.

But of course we know nothing about the future, though we must push into it every day. We are frightened to look at it, and so we spend our lives looking backward, remolding over and over again what we should leave alone, breaking it, changing it, dragging it forward through time.

Lying in bed, I thought: these things are past. They don't have anything to do with you now. I knew it, but I didn't believe it. Why else was I there? Because I imagined we could go back together to some pure and unadulterated time. I thought maybe if I could just get back about 30,000 years before I made all those mistakes . . .

* * *

That day I went down to the Mercado de Ladrones, and I took a ride on a truck out toward Pamplona.

Every year the United States donates large sums for road development in that part of the world, and every year the money is stolen by Dr Mog and his associates, though the streets around the US embassy in San Juan are obsessively repaved every few months. But in the interior the roads are horrible even in the dry season, which this mercifully was—rutted tracks of red mud through the jungle, and it took ten hours to go 200 miles. But before we even got out of the city we passed 16 army checkpoints where soldiers extorted money from passing motorists; I found out later that none of them had been paid for over a year. They took pleasure in intimidating me—fat, dark, sweating men with automatic rifles, and they made insulting comments in Spanish and Arabic as they searched the back of the truck where I was sitting on some lumpy burlap sacks. A green Mercedes-Benz had overturned into a garbage ditch, and the traffic was backed up for half a mile along a street of corrugated iron shacks. A stack of tires burned in a vacant lot, and the smoke from it hurt my eyes and mixed with the exhaust fumes and the polluted air into a hot blend of gases that was scarcely breathable.

A little boy ran in and out between the trucks, and he sold me two pineapples and a piece of sugar cane. He was smiling and chattering in a language I didn't recognize; he charged me a dime, and he flicked the coin into the air and caught it behind his back. It was a hopeful gesture, and soon the truck started to move again, and soon we passed beyond the ring road into a clear-cut waste of shantytowns and landfills, and then into the jungle. I gnawed on my sugar cane and licked the pineapple juice off my fingers, and I was rehearsing all the things that I was going to tell Suzanne, rehearsing her replies—it was like trying to memorize the chess openings in a book. And because my opponent was a strong one, my only advantage, I thought, lay in preparation and surprise.

I went over conversations in my mind until the words started to lose their significance, and then the sun came out. When I looked up, the air was fresh and clean. Yellow birds hung in the trees beside the road, making nests of plaited straw. Occasionally an animal would blunder out the bushes as the truck went past. I sat looking backward, and saw a couple of wild pigs and a big rodent.

We stopped at some villages, and three people joined me in the bed of the truck: two men with jerrycans and a gap-toothed woman, who smiled and held up her own length of sugar cane. Her yellow hair was tied back with a piece of string.

We were coming up out of the plain into the mountains, and toward sunset we passed the gates to the Krieger-Richardson Observatory. I got out, and the truck barreled away. The air was cooler, drier here, and the vegetation had changed. The trees were lower, and they no longer presented an imperme-able wall. I walked through them over the dry grass. A one-lane asphalt road came down out of the hills, and I walked up it with my bag, meeting no one, seeing no one. Suzanne had described the place in one of her letters, and it was interesting to see it now myself for the first and last time—the road climbed sharply for a mile or so until the trees gave out, and I came up over the crest and stood overlooking a wide volcanic bowl. Antennae rose out of it: this was the radio telescope, and beyond it on the summit of Madre de la Nacion rose the dome of the observatory.

Then the road sank down a bit until the telescope was out of sight. There were pine trees here, and a parking lot full of identical white cars, and beyond that a low dormitory among the rhododendron bushes. Light came from the windows, a comforting glow, for I was tired and hungry.

* * *

I came up the concrete steps and knocked on the door. It was locked, but af-ter a minute or so somebody opened it, a teenage girl in a Chicago Bulls sweatshirt. "Excuse me," I said. "I'm looking for Dr Suzanne Denier. Does she live here?"

She stared at me for a while, and then shrugged, and then peered past me at the sky. "She's at work tonight. It's supposed to be clear after nine o'clock."

"But she lives here?"

"She came back from Soria on Wednesday. We've had terrible weather for the past two weeks."

She opened the door and stood aside, and I came into a corridor with brown carpeting. "Who are you?" she said.

"Her husband."

She stood staring at me, measuring me up, and I tried to decipher her ex-pression. Lukewarm. Interested, so perhaps she had heard something. "Do you have a name?" A wise-ass—she was half my age.

"Christopher," I said.

"I'm Joan. Does she know you're coming? We don't get too many personal visitors, so I thought . . . "

"It's a surprise."

She stared at me for a little bit with her head cocked to one side. Finally:

"Well, come in. We're just finishing dinner. Have you eaten?"

"Please," I said, "could I see Suzanne? Where is she?"

I waited in the corridor while Joan went back to check. I looked at the travel posters on the wall: the Taj Mahal. Malibu beach. Krieger-Richardson with a flock of birds passing over the dome. Some health statistics and some graphs. Then another, older, woman came back whom I recognized from a group photograph Suzanne had sent me. "You're Christopher," she said.

Her name was Anise Wilcox. She drove me out to the observatory, a 20-minute ride up along the ridge of the mountain. We spoke little. "The phones are down," she said, and I didn't know whether she was giving me the chance to say that I had tried to call and failed, or whether she was telling me that she had not been able to inform Suzanne that I was here.

"Wait," she said. We stopped in the parking lot in front of the observatory, and she slipped out of the driver's seat and ran up to the door. I sat alone in the twilight listening to the engine cool; I rolled down my window and looked out at the unlit bulk of the dome against the sky. An insect settled on my arm, a tiny delicate moth unlike any I had ever seen.

Then Dr Wilcox was there again, standing by the car. "Come in," she said, and I got out and followed her. She opened the metal door for me. There was a dim light inside next to an elevator, and I turned back and saw her face. She seemed nervous; she wouldn't look me in the eyes. She closed the door and locked it, and then she moved past me to the elevator. It was not until we stood next to each other inside the elevator car that she glanced up and gave me a worried smile.

"Good luck," she said when we reached the third floor.

Inside the observatory all the rooms were cramped and small until I pushed through those final doors and stood under the dome. The air was cold. And it was dark underneath the enormous y-shaped column of the tele-scope; I stood looking up at it, until I heard a movement behind me, off to my right. Suzanne was there at the top of a wide shallow flight of stairs, maybe five steps high. She looked professional in a black turtleneck sweater and black denim overalls, with two pens in her breast pocket. She was carrying a mechanical notebook under one arm.

"Chris," she said, and she came forward to the edge of the top step. Light came from the windows of the observation room. Computer screens glowed there.

I could feel her anger just in that one word. It radiated out from her small body. But I was prepared for it. I have my own way of protecting myself. I had not seen her in ten months, and as I looked at her I thought first of all how plain she was with her pinched face, her scowl, her stubborn jaw. Her skin was sallow in that light, her black hair was unbrushed. A small-boned woman with bad posture, that's what I told myself, and I thought, what am I doing here? Oh, I deserve more than this.

Because she started in immediately: "I can't believe you're here," she said. "I asked you not to come. No, I told you not to. I can't believe you could be so insensitive to my wishes after everything you've done."

"Please," I said, and she stopped, and I found I didn't have anything to say. Much as I had rehearsed this scene, I had not anticipated that she would speak first, that I, not she, would have to react.

"Please," I said. "Just listen to me for a few minutes. I came a long way . . . "

She interrupted me. "Do you think I'm supposed to be impressed by that? What am I supposed to do, fall into your arms now that you're here?"

"No, I certainly didn't expect . . . "

"Then what? Christopher, is it too much to ask that you leave me alone? I have a lot of things to sort out, and I want to do it by myself. I can't believe you're not sensitive to that. I can't believe you think you have the right to barge in here and disrupt my life and my work whenever you feel like it. Don't you have any respect for me at all?"

"Please," I said. "I knew you'd be like this, and I still risked it just to come. Is there any way that you could take a smaller risk and talk to me, instead of just yelling at me and closing me out?"

"Yelling? I'm not yelling. I'm telling you how I feel." But then she was quiet, and I realized she was giving me a chance to speak.

"Suzanne," I said, and I really tried to sound sincere, even though half of me was whispering to the other half that I couldn't win, that I had never won and never could, and that my best tactic was to run away. "You sounded so distant in your letters and I couldn't stand it. I couldn't stand to feel you pull away from me and not do something. I love you. I'm more sorry than I can tell you about what happened, about what I did. I want to make it up to you. I want . . . "

* * *

It sounded weak even to me. She jumped on it: "But what about what I want, Chris? Did you think about that at all? Did you think about that for one

23

minute? Things are different now. How can I trust you when you can't even respect my wishes enough to leave me alone here to think about what I want? What's best for me. I needed time. I told you that."

"It's been ten months. Ten months and thirty thousand years," I said—a line that I'd prepared. She didn't think much of it. I saw her eyebrows come together, her eyes roll upward in an expression of irritation that I'd always hated. "Suzanne," I said, "I know you. I know you could just seal yourself up here for the rest of your life. We had something precious, and it made us both happy for a long time. I can't just give it up."

"But you did give it up. Sometimes I think you forget how this all started. You're right—we were very happy. So how could you do it, Chris? She was my friend."

"No, she wasn't."

"Oh, so it's her fault. I can't believe you. I still can't believe you. How could you hurt me like that? How could you humiliate me so publicly?"

"It wouldn't have been so public if you hadn't told everybody."

"Oh, and I was supposed to just smile and take it? You hurt me, Chris. You have no idea."

"Yes," I said, "I do. I'm sorry."

She turned away for a moment, and stared into the glass of the observation window. I could see the reflection of her face there, and beyond it the flash of the computer screens. "And that's supposed to make it all right? You don't understand. I've got some thinking to do. Chris, I don't want to be the kind of woman who just takes something like this. Who tolerates it. Who just hangs on year after year, hoping her man will change."

You could never be that kind of woman, I thought. But I said nothing. "You don't understand," she said. "I trusted you. I really trusted you. Chris, I'd given you my soul to keep, and you dropped it, and things changed. I changed. I know I'll never trust anyone like that again. What I don't know is, whether we can go on from here."

You never trusted me, I thought. I stared at her, my mind a blank.

"Well," she said finally. "I've got to get to work. I'll tell Anise you can spend the night in my room. I'll be back a little after sunrise, and I'd appreciate it if you were gone. I'll tell Carlos to give you a ride back to San Juan."

I looked up at the big telescope and shook my head. "Aren't you going to give me a tour? You said in your letter you were close to something new."

"Yes." She came down the steps. And then things changed for a little while. Because we knew each other so well, even then we could slip down effort-

24

lessly and immediately into another way of being, a connection that seemed so intimate and strong that I had to keep reminding myself during the next hour that it was all gone, all ruined. She showed me her work, and I took such pleasure in seeing her face light up as she explained it.

She took me all over the observatory, up into the dome, into the camera room. Then back down again into her office, where we sat drinking coffee in the dim light, and she smoked cigarettes and showed me photographs of stars. "We knew the galaxies were moving, because of the red shift. And we assumed that they were spreading apart, because it fit the theory. But of course we didn't know, because we could observe from one point only. But now of course we have two points thirty thousand years apart, and we thought that we could see it."

She sucked the cigarette down to the filter and then ground it out. I sat looking at her face, reminded of how she used to come over to my apartment in the early morning, when she was working on her dissertation. She would wake me up to talk to me, and she would grind her cigarettes out in a teacup that I had, and I would force myself awake, just for the pleasure of looking at the concentration in her face, as she described some theory or some project. "So?"

"What do you think? Our results have been extraordinary. The opposite of what everyone predicted."

"So?"

She smiled. "I don't know if I should tell you. I don't know if you deserve to know."

"It sounds like it's important."

"Sure. But I don't know. Anise would kill me if I told you."

I looked up at the ceiling. Someone had pasted up a cluster of phosphorescent stars. "Okay," she said, "so here it is. We think some galaxies are farther apart now than they are in the 20th century."

For me at least, time had gone backward in that little room. Not because of what she said—I didn't care about it. I sat watching her face.

But I was afraid that she'd stop talking and I'd have to go. She'd bring us back up to the surface again. I said: "And what's your explanation for that?"

She gave a shrug. "It's complicated. Either our observations are mistaken, and we're about to make fools of ourselves. Or else maybe the universe is contracting. Or part of it is. Or else it fluctuates. I have my own theory."

I said nothing, but sat watching her, and the moment stretched on until I smiled and she laughed. "I'll tell you anyway. I think time goes the other direction from the way we imagine. I think that's why the past doesn't affect the present like we thought."

Not like we thought. But it does have some effect. I looked at Suzanne, her beautiful and well-loved face. "So why not forgive me?" I said.

She glanced up at me, a quick, sly look.

"We can make the past into the future," I said.

She smiled, and then frowned, and then: "Sure, that's what I'm afraid of. It's just a way of talking. It's not like when we're born we actually die."

She ground out her cigarette butt. "Seriously," she said. "But maybe time flows in two directions. One of them is the direction of our ordinary experience. Our personal sense of time. But maybe cosmological time flows back the other way. Maybe the conception of the universe happens in the future from our point of view."

I thought about it. "Why do you think we don't meet anybody from beyond our own time?" she said. "From our own future? Certainly the technology would still exist."

It took me a little while to understand her. Then I said: "Perhaps they lost interest."

"Forever? I don't buy it. No—maybe we're talking about two big bangs, one at the end of one kind of time, one at the beginning of the other. One manmade and one not."

I considered this. Falling in love is one. And then breaking apart. I said: "So you're telling me that there's no future and the past is all we have."

* * *

Soon after, Dr Wilcox drove me back to the dormitory and gave me something to eat. She heated up some spaghetti Bolognese in the microwave. She didn't say much, except for one thing which proved to be prophetic: "You must know she won't forgive you. She can't."

She showed me back to Suzanne's room and left me there. It was a small bare cubicle with a window overlooking the parking lot. She had put some curtains up and that was all. There was nothing on the walls. I didn't take off my clothes. I lay down on her narrow, white bed; I lay on my back with my hands clasped under my neck, staring at the ceiling. From time to time I got up and turned on the light. I opened her bureau, and the smell from her shirts made me unhappy. She had a picture of me tucked into a corner of her mirror.

I was smiling. Underneath, on the bureau top, stood a framed photograph of her parents, taken at their 40th anniversary. They were smiling too.

There was a package of my letters in a corner of the drawer, maybe seventy-five or a hundred of them, wrapped in a rubber band.

I had spoken to Carlos and had plotted an itinerary for the rest of my vacation. He told me there were some beautiful beaches on the Mediterranean, which I could reach on a rail link from San Juan. I set the alarm clock for five-thirty and lay down on the bed and listened to it ticking on the bedside table. I imagined time passing over me, forward into an uncertain future, backward into a contented past. Perhaps the ebb and flow of it lulled me, because toward three o'clock I slid beneath the surface of a dream.

I dreamt that I woke up to find Suzanne sitting beside me. "I wanted to show you something before you left," she said. "You know we're close to one of the big reservations here?"

"You told me in your letter."

"Yes. Well, there's a big family of Cro-Magnon that's moved in close by. I wanted to show you."

I dreamt she took me out into the fresh dawn air, and we walked down a path through the woods behind the dormitory. Soon we were in a deciduous forest of aspen trees and mountain laurel, and the breeze pressed through the leaves and made them flicker back and forth. Once out of sight of the buildings, all traces of modernity were lost. We climbed downhill. "Wait till you see them," said Suzanne. "They're so great. They never fight. They're so sweet to each other. It's because they can't feel love. They don't know what it feels like."

A bird flickered through the underbrush, one of the yellow birds I'd seen that morning in the real world. "So you're saying maybe evolution runs the other way."

She frowned. "Maybe we're the ones who are like animals. You know what I mean."

We were standing in an open glade, and the light filtered through the leaves, and the little path ran backward, forward through the brush. Then I bent down and I kissed her, and even in the dream she smelled like cigarettes.

the breakthrough

After getting her certificate, Susan began working as a special education teacher at Drury High School in North Adams. There, in the spring of her third year, she saw a videotape which described an astonishing new therapy. This new technique was called facilitated communication. Because of it children who suffered from severe communication disorders, who had grown up essentially without spoken language, were now being mainstreamed into ordinary high school classes. Dismissed as retarded their whole lives, now they were writing haiku. They were taking history and mathematics.

At Drury there were nine kids in her class. Progress was slow and unsustained with most of them. And the parents were no help. Often she felt like a babysitter rather than a teacher. She had thought about quitting; all year she had been frustrated and depressed. But that summer she spent her own money for a ten-week course in facilitated communication at a clinic near Syracuse.

Susan White was a skeptical person. Alone in her apartment in North Adams, she had watched the videotape several times. She had read books and articles, including one by an autistic man who was now applying to college. It seemed too good to be true, so that when she arrived at the clinic, she was relieved to be disappointed, in a way. None of the children they were working with had achieved those kinds of results.

The most impressive part of the course was the morale of the staff and the enthusiasm of the parents, some of whom had moved from long distances away. Susan spoke to a mother who had moved from the Midwest. "I knew if I just kept working at it I could find a way to reach him. I knew there was someone really in there, and it was like he was hidden by his disability. But I could see him sometimes in little moments."

She was talking about her son, who was learning that summer to spell out what he wanted on his keyboard. "Juice," he would say. "Weres Momy?"

These messages, so simple and unexpected, were enough to make his mother cry.

For Susan that was the difference: these people still had hope. They hadn't given up on their own children. So many of the parents and teachers she dealt with in North Adams, they thought their responsibilities were over if the kids were clean and fed and got their medication. Anything else was too much for them, and they would close their eyes rather than see the obvious, the small flickers of need or loneliness or brilliance. You could understand it. They were sick of being disappointed.

But the premise behind facilitated communication was one of hope, of risk. A child's disability was like a wall, a barrier, and the job of the teacher was not to add to it, but to break it down. Communication disorders like autism were simply that—an obstacle. They had nothing to do with cognition or intelligence or perception.

The boy from the Midwest was named Peter. He was ten years old. He had any number of alarming peculiarities: he could not speak. Around adults or other children he would fidget constantly. He would rock back and forth, and sometimes he would flap his left hand next to his ear. He would distort his face; he wouldn't look at you. When you spoke to him, he would whistle and cry as if to drown you out—these children were so sensitive. Doctors had proved that their perceptions were many times more acute than normal. That their odd behavior came out of an attempt to protect themselves, cushion themselves from a world which even Susan found was a chaotic maze sometimes. Full of crazy signs and stimuli—sometimes it was only when she was alone in her apartment with the door locked that she felt she could make sense of it. In the same way, sometimes when Peter was alone you could see him playing with his blocks, pensively and calmly. Sometimes among the nonsense he would spell out simple words, and then you could see a little boy in him, an ordinary little boy.

The premise of facilitated communication was that a trained therapist could help a child reach that place of calm. And then the words would come out; these children were not stupid. They had ordinary needs. Only the task of speaking was sometimes too difficult, so full of anxieties and failures. Better to communicate through writing, and so they were given simple wooden keyboards, with large squares for each letter and number. There were no moving parts; they could just point to the letter they wanted, and the facilitator would be there to read it. And because so many of the children had problems with their motor control, and because the task of communicating filled so many of them with a trembling anxiety, then the facilitator would be there to calm them. To hold their hands.

Susan was interested in Peter because he reminded her of an autistic boy in her class at Drury. They shared many of the same behaviors: the endless rocking, even the flapping hand. There were differences, too. Jason was already thirteen, although he looked much younger. And while Peter was rarely still, Jason would often have whole hours of calmness; then he would look right through you with his beautiful blue eyes. He had a vocabulary of about thirty words, mostly nouns and numbers, which nevertheless he would whisper very precisely, with beautiful clear diction. The movements of his hands, when he wasn't rocking or shaking or pounding on the furniture, were graceful and firm.

All summer, especially as she watched the progress Peter was making, Susan couldn't stop thinking about Jason. When the course in Syracuse was over, she couldn't wait for school to start. On the first day she asked for permission from her supervisor to try out the new technique; she bought him a keyboard with her own money. She donated her own time. Out of all her students, she felt Jason was one with the most potential. So she chose him to work with. He had none of the physical signs of retardation or brain damage or Down's syndrome; he was a healthy beautiful child with blond hair and clear pale skin. Even when he was rocking back and forth or shaking his head hour after hour, his disabilities almost seemed like an act, like he was faking. In him more than the others you could sense the normal boy inside.

Other children would try and fail even at simple tasks. Jason never attempted anything he couldn't perform; at first he showed no interest in the keyboard. It was a Masonite placard about twelve inches on a side, crosshatched with lines of purple plastic. The letters and numbers and symbols were arranged in rows, and each small square was decorated with a brightly colored image: an apple, a bunny, a cat, etc. That first day Jason flipped the placard over to examine its blank side. Then he discarded it onto the playbench.

But she showed him how to use it, over and over. She held his finger and spelled out words for him: apple, bunny, cat. She attached the keyboard around his neck so that he could get used to it. She tied it with a white ribbon. White was his favorite color.

She would spell out sentences, using his finger. "Hello. How are you? I am fine." Hello was his favorite word.

Once after about a week she found him puzzling over it, staring at the row of numbers. When she approached, he grabbed hold of her finger. Thrusting the keyboard out toward her, he pushed her finger into the row of numbers. But she didn't know what to do, which numbers to pick, and he grew frustrated. His own hands were shaking and he started to cry. Then she took hold of his wrist and made him do the calculations. Soon she had removed her hand, had slid it all the way up his arm until she lightly cupped his elbow, and he was making all the choices himself. "2.2," he spelled. "2.2 X 2.2 = 4.84." Then with evident delight he was picking out primes: 37, 41, 43, etc. Then a bunch of garbage letters.

For about a week they played with numbers. Jason was a child who at three had understood the principle of divisibility, yet at ten still couldn't tie his shoes. And he was endlessly fascinated with primes. "4183," he spelled out. Then a bunch of garbage: AAAXFUP, etc. Then quick as a wink: IS 4183 PRIM? Then, after a moment: N ÷ BY 47.

Jason laughed and laughed. Susan knew nothing about primes. She was astonished by the "is," the first verb he had ever used. She gave up her lunch period for that day and then the rest of the semester. She was happy to do it, because as the weeks went by she could see that Jason was going to make the change that she had dreamed of when she first saw the FC videotape that spring. She was going to be his Annie Sullivan. In two months he was spelling out: SOMTIME IT HURT BECAUSE I M SO ALON LIKE A TREE

"Like a tree?" she asked.

IN A FIELD

Sometimes she would correct his spelling, and once he understood an error he would never repeat it. Or at least not deliberately—sometimes in the quickness of the moment he would still make mistakes. "I" became "you," or more commonly "u," for example. Like many autistics, his sense of his own self was very damaged.

U FEEL SAD

"Me?" Susan asked.

XCUSE ME I

During the moments he was calm, as now, he was the most beautiful boy Susan had ever seen. His face was like a little angel's. His blue eyes looked right through you. I M SAD BKZ THE WEEKND

She cupped his elbow in her hand. "Why?"

I MISS YOU SUSAN WHITE

WHITE IS MY FAVORITE COLOR 2

U2 LIKE THE BAND

I HEART U2
HEART LIKE NY STATE
I HEART U
KZ WE TALK

Susan burst into tears. Jason was agitated too. He pushed the keyboard away, and for a solid hour he was shaking his head and flapping his hand next to his ear. "Hello," he said, over and over. "Hello—what is your name?"

It was hard for Jason to read. His parents were professors at North Adams State, so he had been surrounded by books for his entire life. Enough of it had penetrated for him to use the keyboard. But he had some kind of block there too, maybe some kind of bad association. When Susan gave him books to read, she suspected all he did was look at the pictures. His attention span was still very short.

But he loved it when she read to him. At first she kept it simple, but as time went on she was amazed at his level of comprehension. She read him J. D. Salinger short stories. WHAT S A BANANAFISH? he asked. WHAT IS SQUALOR?

Susan had got the book from Bob Cousins, who was using it in eighth-grade English. "Would you like to take his class?" she asked.

I DONT NO

"Would you like to?"

I WOULD LIKE TO

The class met during seventh period, which was after Susan's day was finished. It was an art class for Jason, but she switched him out of it and volunteered to stay late. Mr. Cousins was enthusiastic, and between them they convinced the head of the department. She was concerned about the other kids, needlessly as it turned out, for they were wonderfully warm and supportive. For years Jason had been something of a celebrity around the school, with his prime numbers and peculiar outbursts.

A couple of weeks later, before Thanksgiving, Susan received a telephone call from Jason's mother, asking if they could meet. Susan had been expecting this. She had received no answer to her letter to the boy's parents earlier in the year, trying to explain facilitated communication and the changes she was making in Jason's curriculum. She had received no answer to another letter, which she had sent when Jason first started taking Mr. Cousins's class. But now everyone had heard of her success; the superintendent had written her a memo, and there had been much excited talk at recent faculty meetings. Teachers who had barely known her name were now stopping her in the halls. So it didn't surprise her that even the most uninvolved mother would eventually recognize what she was doing. Not that she cared about that, but it was nice to have the parents on your side. After all, school was only part of Jason's day.

They made an appointment for Friday at five, but Mrs. Marowitz was late. From her second-floor office window Susan watched a black Volvo pull into the empty parking lot. She watched a small dark woman get out, dressed in boots and a brown shearling coat, as if it were midwinter.

Almost everyone had already gone, and the building was almost empty. Susan had left her door open; she could hear the boots come down the hall. Mrs. Marowitz knocked her knuckles on the door frame and then came in. She didn't wait for a response. She was a pinch-faced woman in her mid-forties, who smelled like cigarettes. She carried a black briefcase, which she dropped next to the door. Then she was stripping off her leather gloves and holding out her hand.

But she hadn't come to offer her congratulations. She got to the point without even sitting down. "Ms. White, can you explain what Jason is doing with this book? He's been bringing it home the past few weeks."

The book was J. D. Salinger's *Nine Stories*. Mrs. Marowitz took it from an inside pocket of her coat and dropped it onto Susan's desk.

"I wrote you a letter. I've been taking Jason to eighth-grade English for his last period."

"Yes, I remember. I thought it was ridiculous even at the time. Ms. White, I hate to disillusion you. It seems absurd to have to explain this to his own teacher, but Jason cannot read."

Carefully, patiently, Susan tried to describe some of the progress they'd been making. "He has some problems with concentration and vocabulary, but then I read to him. He's very smart. He picks things up very quickly. I'm even helping him to write a book report. He'll show you when it's done."

"A book report? You're joking."

"No. Why not? There are some themes of alienation that he can relate to."

Mrs. Marowitz was angry. Her thin lips were trembling. "Listen, I don't know what you're playing at and I don't care. All I know is that you've taken my son out of art class, which was something he could use and he enjoyed. I spoke to my husband, and he said give it a chance. But this is insane."

Carefully, patiently, Susan tried to explain about facilitated communication. Mrs. Marowitz interrupted her. She made a strange, violent gesture with her hands. "All I know is that you've hung that card around his neck, and when he gets home he takes it off and never touches it. You say you're having whole conversations with him—why you? What are you sharing with him that he won't share with his own mother? Or with my husband, who's raised him like his own son?"

Again, Susan tried to explain. Again, Mrs. Marowitz interrupted: "Look, I'm not going to argue with you. I've written to the principal."

Later Susan walked home to her apartment off Ashland Street. From her porch she could see the lights of the college up the hill.

Inside, she turned on the lights and put on the water for some tea. There was a message from her mother on the answering machine. But Susan didn't want to call her. Talking to her mother wasn't likely to cheer her up. "I think it's wonderful how you can spend so much effort on a bunch of children who aren't even yours." She had never forgiven Susan for breaking up with Mark Toureille. "You'll never meet a man like that again. Not around here."

Pasted to the refrigerator door in her tiny kitchen were some photographs of her family. Her father, mother, and little sister, all smiling for the camera. Her father in his orange hunter's shirt and cap. But people only took photographs of the good times. The fights and arguments just disappeared and left no trace.

She made some soup, and then after dinner she called home. Unexpectedly, her father answered the phone. "Hi, princess," he said. She found herself telling him all about the fight she had had with Mrs. Marowitz. It was a relief to talk to him.

But on Monday during their lunchtime session, Jason had some disturbing new things to tell her.

HELLO

"Hello, Jason."

I DONT LIKE THE WEEKEND

"Why?"

FRIDAY NIGHT MY MOTHER H U

NO I MEAN ME

The keyboard square under the letter *h* showed the picture of a heart. Sometimes Jason would touch the *h* and nothing more when he meant "love." Later in the session: MY MOTHER H ME

"Yes, of course she does. Everybody loves you."

NO I MEAN NO

"I don't understand."

SOUND LIKE HART

35

Susan said nothing, and in a little while Jason continued: WITH A HAND

"Where?" asked Susan, but he shook his head, suddenly agitated, and he could no longer make the letters.

"On your butt?" she asked. He shook his head.

"On your face?" He shook his head.

"On your arm?" and he stopped shaking. She rolled up the sleeve of his turtleneck. There was a bruise above his elbow. Nothing big, but definitely a bruise.

In the days that followed, Susan asked him more questions. And she started to make notes of his answers. "Does your mother hurt you often?"

NO SOMETIMES

"What about your father?"

NOT MY FATHER

FATHER GONE

In fact, Jason's name was Adler. "I mean Mr. Marowitz."

PROF

"Yes, whatever. Professor Marowitz. Does he hurt you?"

YES

"With his hand?"

NO

"With a belt?"

NO WITH A COK

"What?"

COK IN U BUT

Phrases like these, once expressed, were enough to send Jason into a spasm of trembling. Often after one of these sessions he would spend an hour rocking and shaking his head. And Susan also was distressed. She didn't know what to do. "Shall I talk to your mother about this?"

NO PLEASE

Then, a little later:

COCK IN MY BUT & MOUT

SHE NOSE

Susan had read books in college which suggested that autism was caused by family trauma. If the child felt unloved or unwanted, he would protect himself by sealing off the world. But this was something more than that. It made Susan want to cry. Jason was so vulnerable, so beautiful. His eyes looked right through you.

Finally she couldn't stand it anymore. She collected her notes and went to talk to Bob Cousins. Then to the guidance counselor. Then to the assistant superintendent. Then to the school nurse, who made a physical examination. Then to a woman named Sheila D'Angelo, who came up from Pittsfield. She was with the Department of Social Services.

"Do you think foster care might be appropriate?" she asked. "Children like Jason are very hard to place."

"I'll take him in."

"Hmm. Let's wait on that."

Sheila D'Angelo was a heavyset woman in her fifties. She sat in Susan's office, looking over the transcripts, twiddling a pencil. From time to time she glanced at Susan over the tops of her glasses. "Of course you know we're talking about a serious offense. You realize that?"

Then: "If the man has other children, we might have to get a court order."

Then, after a little while: "Well, I suppose I'd better take a look." And then they went to find Jason, who was unresponsive. Ever since the school nurse had examined him, he hadn't wanted to talk. He was rocking and trembling, and though Susan managed to get him to sit still long enough to say hello and call out some prime numbers, she could tell that Mrs. D'Angelo was not impressed. The demonstration of facilitated communication would have to wait. In the meantime, Susan showed her the keyboard and explained the technique.

But then, after Mrs. D'Angelo was gone, Jason calmed down. He picked up the keyboard from the workbench and brought it to Susan, where she sat working with another student. He seemed impatient. In the last half hour before he had to get the bus, he and Susan had the following conversation:

HELLO

"Hello."

WHO WAS THAT

"That was the woman I was telling you about. She's going to try and help us so you won't have to go home. So your Mommy won't hurt you."

& NOT FATHER?

"And your stepfather. I want to take you to a place where no one can hurt you anymore."

MAY BE 2 LIVE WITH U

"Well, we'll see."

U WD LIKE THAT

Then: XCSE I MEAN ME

"Yes. I'm glad."

37

Jason shook his head slowly and rhythmically from side to side. He closed his eyes and smiled.

1 TIME I TRIDE TO SCREM BUT COULDNT!

IT WAS IN THE BATHROOM & I TRIED 2

31887 PIECES ON A FLOOR

IT IS A PRIME

Then: WHITE IS LIKE COLOR MIX TOGETHER

ALL COLOR

"Yes," said Susan, touched. Jason opened his blue eyes, but he was still shaking his head. She reached out and put her hand onto his forehead, and he stopped. "Don't you worry about all this," she said. "I'll take care of it."

YES I LOVE U

"Yes."

Then it was time for him to go. From her office window, Susan could see the buses loading in front of the school, and she stood watching Jason as the van pulled up. He was the first in line. The square keyboard hung over the front of his coat.

When she got home, her father was waiting for her in front of the door. "Hi, princess," he said.

He had driven over from Cheshire twelve miles away. He was wearing a sweater and a woolen scarf—not enough for the cold weather. She stood on the sidewalk with her books and papers up against her chest, while he stood on the porch. "Momma told me you weren't going to make it home for Thanksgiving," he said. "Your sister's coming down from Maine. I wanted to see if I could change your mind."

She smiled. It was brisk weather, and his cheeks were flushed. His skin was moist and pink, as if he had just finished some exertion. Sometimes during the winter when Susan was just a child, he would come in from splitting wood or shoveling snow, huffing with his bald forehead red.

He stood aside, and then followed her up the four flights. On the way, Susan said: "It's just that I've been a little depressed for the past week. I was planning on coming, really." Then, when they were inside her apartment, and she was filling the coffee machine: "It's just that Mom is always worse than usual around holidays. Everything she feels bad about, she takes out on the rest of us."

He came up behind her and put his arms around her. "What are you depressed about?"

"Oh, nothing," she said. "Something at work."

Sheila D'Angelo came back on Friday. She took Jason aside and tried to talk to him for a few minutes. Then Susan gave the rest of the class to her assistant and took them back to her office. "I read some things about facilitated communication over the weekend," said Mrs. D'Angelo. "It's just amazing, some of the results."

She had her own ideas about the demonstration she wanted to see. Jason was in a good mood, and the whole thing took about twenty minutes. He and Susan sat at a table side by side, the keyboard between them. Mrs. D'Angelo held up a notebook. On each page she had glued a picture for Jason to identify or a problem for him to solve. Jason was relaxed and sure, though his spelling wasn't always perfect. Susan barely had to touch his elbow. She was afraid the questions were too easy, and he would lose his concentration through sheer boredom. But he was chuckling and smiling.

Then Mrs. D'Angelo asked some questions about the abuse. Jason tried to answer, but after ten minutes or so he started flapping his hand next to his ear. "Hello," he said. "Hello."

"When he gets agitated, it's hard for him to concentrate," explained Susan.

But after Mrs. D'Angelo had left, he said what was bothering him: U TOLD HER

"Yes, I had to."

He shook his head. I TRUST YOU

"I'm sorry. But I thought . . ."

He interrupted her. I DONT WANT TROUBLE 4 THEM

"For who?"

FOR THOSE 2

It was astonishing, she thought, that he still could feel loyalty to them, after they had betrayed him so shamefully. That he could still want to protect them. It made her feel ashamed of her own distance from her family, and so on the Tuesday before Thanksgiving she called her mother to tell her to expect her the next day after school. She would spend the night, for the first time in years.

Mrs. D'Angelo was supposed to have called her on Monday with information about Jason's preliminary hearing, but she didn't. It wasn't until Wednesday morning that Susan managed to get her on the phone. "Ms. White," she said, "I was just posting a letter to you."

"I know these things take time," Susan answered, trying not quite successfully to swallow her annoyance. "But you know things are worse during the holidays. I think it's absolutely imperative that we get Jason out of that house as soon as possible."

"I was writing you a letter. In fact, we had a court date for the middle of next month, but I had to cancel it. I'm sorry."

"What do you mean?"

"It's in the letter. It's just that I'm not sure there is a case."

Susan said nothing, and then after a while Mrs. D'Angelo went on. "Let me say right now that I'd like to believe you. But after the test I made, I asked him more than fifty questions. Asked you. I guess I wasn't being quite honest. But I knew that any lawyer would have to address the problem of influence, so I thought I'd beat them to it."

Then she went on to explain the test with the pictures and the problems. "When I opened the notebook, I showed him one side and you another. You thought you were seeing the same picture, but you weren't. So on the first question I showed you an apple and him a pear, and so on."

She had a way of talking that was so confused, it was intolerable. "What are you trying to say to me?" asked Susan. "Just tell me what you did."

"Well, I'm trying to. All I know is that I asked you both more than fifty questions, and in every case he answered from the wrong side of the page. The page he hadn't seen."

"What are you telling me?" asked Susan.

"I'm telling you he didn't answer a single question, and you answered every one. I knew it when it was going on, and maybe I should have told you last week, only I wanted to talk to a few people here. Ms. White, I'm not doubting your sincerity. But even when I was asking him direct questions after the test was done, he wasn't even looking at the keyboard when he used it."

"So what? It's like touch-typing."

"Well, whatever. All I'm saying is that we don't have a case. As far as the court would be concerned, you're talking to yourself."

Susan was staring at the clock above the door of her office. It was quarter to ten.

"And one more thing," said Mrs. D'Angelo. "I spoke to Mrs. Marowitz. Really, she's very sympathetic. She's already been in touch with your administration; she told me she wanted to take Jason out after the break. She's made arrangements at a private school in Williamstown."

So that was that. After she had hung up, Susan sat looking at the pink receiver, listening to the dial tone. She looked at the photograph of her father and mother on her desk. Then she got up to go to class. And the first chance she got, she took Jason aside. "Hello," she said.

HELLO

He sat with his head to one side, staring through her with his blue eyes. "Who are you?" she asked.

COCK IN YOUR BUTT

"Who are you?" Susan asked again, after a little while.

NEVER LEAVE ALONE

"What do you mean?"

NEVER LEAVE ALONE

He spelled the words out slowly, carefully, and his eyes looked right through her. Later, he left to catch the bus, and neither of them could say goodbye.

a man on crutches

I had been to Los Angeles before and hated it. Whenever I had gone to visit, I had been irritated by the sweat-stained dinginess of the place, its perpetual five-o'clock shadow. I had been irritated by the lack of seasons. But two years ago when I flew out for my father's funeral, I thought something was different as soon as I got off the plane. I rolled down the window in the taxi and the air was cold and sharp. I could see the mountains. I could smell the salt. It was Saturday morning. A woman on Wiltshire Boulevard seemed amazingly good-looking, amazingly well-dressed.

I have a condition which recurs every few years, and you'd think I'd learn to recognize the signs. Instead I'm always taken by surprise. The problem is, the first stage is a pleasant one, so I don't mind. It consists of a feeling of optimism and hope. That morning in the cab, I was in a good mood. I was in a mood to be forgiving, to consider for the first time that my father might have been looking for something when he moved out here. Always I had thought about him running away, pushed instead of pulled. People had always said there was more work for him out here, but when I was a child, "more work" seemed like a bad reason to do anything. A bad reason to leave my mother and the house that he had built. A bad reason to move a continent away and live in a polluted city where the weather never changed. I was ten years old when he left, and I believe I had no conscious resentment. Already by that time he was a stranger. I barely remember him living with us, and it's not because my memory is bad. Later, I didn't miss what I had never known. My mother never spoke of him.

* * *

I checked into my hotel. I planned to spend one night, and then take a bus up the Owens River the next morning. I was too poor to come out just for the

43

ceremony, so I had taken a few days' vacation to go hiking. When I had spoken to my stepmother on the phone, I had found myself asking her whether I could take some of my father's ashes to bury up on Darwin Bench—a place of mystical significance to me, I implied. She seemed delighted, started to cry in fact, which embarrassed me. It's just that having organized my vacation, I thought I had to make it seem as if it were somehow part of the funeral, a cathartic and necessary experience, perhaps. In order to get time off at short notice I told my supervisor the same story, leaving her touched by the impression that my father and I had taken many trips together up into the mountains.

My life is full of such falsehoods, which doesn't make them easier to bear. In my hotel, I laid out my camping gear on the floor of my room. I replaced the bushings on my stove, and then I washed my hands. I took out my funeral clothes from the top compartment of my backpack—a gray wool suit. I put it on, knotted my tie, and stood looking at myself in the mirror on the back of the bathroom door. I looked good in my suit, a fragile version of my father. In it I exhibited the only gift my father ever gave me, though even that had come diluted through my mother. I made faces in front of the mirror and rearranged my hair; always when I had come out to visit my father I had taken trouble with my looks, suspecting in some obscure way that this would offer a reproach to him. That it would make him miss my mother, and miss me. At home I didn't care. This suit was the only suit I owned, which made wearing it a kind of ritual.

I washed my face and washed my hands again. The air in my hotel room had depressed me, but when I stepped out into the street I felt more optimistic, clean in my uniform, mixing effortlessly with Californians on the sidewalk. I found myself in a neighborhood where all the streets were named after eastern colleges; my stepmother had given me directions to the church. It was a ten-minute walk. As I came around the corner of Brown Street, I slowed down. I composed my face.

My stepmother was waiting in a crowd of people. She was named Barbara: younger than my father, a dark-haired woman in her fifties, a writer for a feminist newsletter. In a previous decade she had been a lawyer, and she was still active in environmental and leftist causes, all of which did not keep her from more domestic accomplishments. She was a cook, a quiltmaker. In the crowd on the church steps she stood out, sleek in a dark cape and black leather boots—clothes which, despite their evident expense, nevertheless managed to bring some echo back from 1966, when she had lived on a commune in Colorado. I walked up towards her, ignoring everybody so that I could take my place with her at the top of the hierarchy of bereavement. Tears glittered in her eyes; she reached out black-gloved hands and grasped hold of my thumbs. What was there to say? Not for me some vain condolence; I leaned down towards her, conscious of her smell—was it patchouli oil? Her almost poreless skin.

"Jack," she said. "I'm so happy you're here." She pulled me aside under the portal of the church. I shook my head. And it was lucky that my feelings were beyond words. Otherwise I might have been tempted to admit so much. I had not known, for example, that my father was a Lutheran.

"I'd like you to say something," she said. "There'll be a time when some of the people who were closest to him . . . I spoke to you about it over the phone."

I remembered. I closed my eyes. "You probably brought something," she went on. "But I thought it would be nice if you could read a poem. You know that poem he used to love—'Pied Beauty.' Hopkins always was his favorite poet."

I nodded. Yet I felt cheated, too. The category of "favorite poet" was not one I was aware had existed in my father's mind. Did this mean there might be other poets also, only slightly below Hopkins in his estimation? Who were they? Sappho? John Ashbery? Alexander Pope?

"I'd like that," I said.

"I'm so glad you could come," she said again.

Half an hour later I found myself at the pulpit reading a poem.

Sometimes my voice cracked with emotion—a reflex. Between the stanzas I looked out over the pews. There was a big crowd. My father had produced industrial films. Mostly he had worked as a consultant, and I guess he knew a lot of people. I guess he had a lot of friends. I stared out at them.

Later, I thought about what I saw from that pulpit. It is disjointed in my memory by the stanzas of the poem, and therefore it exists in my mind not as a continuum, but as a series of independent images. I used to examine them, searching for a clue. My father was a prominent man. There had been an obituary in the *Los Angeles Times*. Surely Jean-Jacques would have had a chance to see it, even if he hadn't called my father's office in the days after his death. How could he have kept away? And so I used to examine those images in the church, over and over again as if they were a series of photographs—the faces, the sad bodies, the rows of pews. Surely he is there somewhere. For a while, when I was at my most compulsive, I did remember a figure lurking at the back. Now I don't. Somebody once showed me how, in different editions of a history textbook, the same photograph would appear, but changed somewhat, retouched somewhat, to illustrate some subtle new idea. In a crowd of men, skins would darken, and then grow white again. Hair would grow longer, and then short again. Women would appear, then disappear. Memory is like history. At one time it was imperative for me to see the figure of a man, hiding in the back behind a white column. Handsome in his suit. Sometimes I could even see his crutch. Memory is like history—it absorbs the needs of the present. Now he's vanished.

After the ceremony I went to a reception at my stepmother's house, and I talked to some of my father's friends. Once I was back in the kitchen, looking for more ice, and Barbara was there, fussing with some strawberry tarts. "Jack," she said, "can you do something for me?"

She looked toward the window and then back. "I was at your father's office yesterday, clearing some stuff out. Eddy—that's his partner—says he's got copies of everything and the rest can go. But I feel bad about asking Elaine or someone to throw it all away, without a family member at least looking through it. It's all old files." She looked at me and blinked, but I said nothing.

"I don't have to explain, do I?" she went on. "It tires me out. Your father was a wonderful man. I know it's been hard for you sometimes, but you should understand—he really loved you."

"I know that," I said.

Then she was crying, and I went and put my arms around her. She was staring hard at one of the buttons of my shirt, inches from her eye. She balled up her fist and placed it carefully in the center of my chest. "It's business stuff," she said, after a pause. "The furniture's all rented. Just make sure I didn't miss anything personal. I put everything in a box as you go in."

My father had died suddenly, of a heart attack. My stepmother had been taking a bath, and had heard him crying out. I pictured her naked, wet, shivering, her arms around his glossy head.

In her house there were no photographs of him. I had walked around during the reception, trying to find one. Barbara had had her picture taken with the Berrigan brothers, people like that. But nothing with my father; in his office that evening, I picked a framed photograph out of the box by the door.

He shared space with some lawyer friends in a one-story professional building, not far from his house. I sat down at his desk with the photograph in my hands. It showed Barbara and him together. She was wearing a low-waisted dress. Her braid hung down her back. She turned toward him, smiling.

He, by contrast, looked raffish and unkempt. He stared towards the camera with a puzzled expression on his face. His black hair was uncombed. He wore an Irish sweater and his big chest bulged importantly.

I propped the photograph on his blotter and sat looking at it for a little while. Why was his hair still so black? Perhaps it was one of the things that had united him to Barbara—the fact that both of them had retained their natural hair color long after most people, my mother for example, had turned gray. I remembered searching his medicine cabinet for hair dye when I was about sixteen. I had found nothing.

It was cold in his office. I got up and pulled out a few drawers of his file cabinets, not knowing what to do. Everything was neatly labeled—xeroxes of storyboards, records of old jobs.

Elaine, my father's assistant, had showed me the dumpster in the parking lot when she had dropped me off. I started loading the files into some trash bags, which were already half full. At first I was conscientious, glancing through each folder. It started to get dark outside, and I turned on the light.

I threw out everything from one cabinet, but the bottom drawer was locked. My father had hired Elaine only two weeks before he died; she had given me his keys, but she didn't know what locks they fit. I picked through the ring and then sat down again.

Now I can say I knew it, I knew it, I knew I had found something. And maybe Barbara, testing that drawer, had felt the same thing. Maybe that was why she'd gone away, unable to proceed. Memories of feelings are so colored by the lights thrown back on them; here, now, I can be sure I knew—it was pornography, of course. I searched for the key for almost an hour. The window to the parking lot was completely dark when I found it, hanging from a nail in the closet, high up above the doorframe. I knew as soon as I touched it what it was.

Almost I was afraid of finding something trivial. So at first I leafed impatiently through the magazines, the photographs of naked women in the first part of the drawer—there was nothing, apart from sheer volume, to distinguish them from the ones I kept at home. And the neatness with which they were arranged—each in its hanging folder.

Nor was I shocked, at first, to find pictures of men. The drawer slid out and out. There were short stories in manuscript, creased in thirds, as if they had been sent through the mail. I thumbed through them, looking for the seamy parts—one was full of hard homosexual imagery. It was a story about a father chastising his young son.

I found a manila envelope containing pages and pages of small notations, all in my father's printing. "F.H., 11/2/79, 1pm? #3 only"—the dates went back fifteen years. More photographs in another envelope, snapshots this time. All women, all ages, some naked, most not. I recognized some people from the funeral, also Elaine. She was standing in the woods, a red sweater tied around her waist.

The final two folders in the drawer contained letters from a single correspondent, and what looked liked copies of my father's replies. At first I was excited, and repulsed also to find myself in such company—the first file was labeled "Letters: Jack." There were hundreds of them, and it took me a while to decide that they were not from me.

My fathers' contained no salutation or signature, just a solid block of text, often without paragraphs. The other man sometimes wrote by hand; the first letters were in a childish script, and they were difficult to read. Difficult even to glance at—I leafed forward to the spring of 1982, when he started using a typewriter. He said, "Dear Jerry," which had been my father's nickname. Once: "Dear Father." Once: "Dear Dad." One was signed, "Your loving son." "Your loving son, Jack."

This was a game they'd played, perhaps in place of sex—a make-believe father, a make-believe son. "Dear Dad," one letter read. "I'm happy to have got the chance to see you when you were in town. I'm still excited from your visit, and I don't have so much to say, only that I'm glad you had a chance to see the apartment, and see I was not being so extravagant. I know you will always think I spend my money on expensive things, so I'm glad you could be with me and share my life, if only for one night. Next time you should stay for longer. Dinner was delicious. I haven't had a meal like that since the semester started."

The box by the door included an unopened phone bill; I had seen it as I came in. My stepmother had put it there, intending, I suppose, to pay it later. I retrieved it now and cut it open—pages of long distance calls, many to a single number in Oakland. My father had accepted collect calls from the same phone, sometimes twice a day.

I sat back in my father's chair. And this is the part I don't remember well—I sat there a long time. I'd like to think that I was shocked, disgusted, hurt, but I don't think it's true. Only I was looking at my father's phone, imagining his hand on the receiver, his lips so close to it—how many times? Nothing remained of any words that he had said. There was no mark on the plastic—I don't remember dialing the number, but then I was letting it ring until an answering machine picked up. "This is 964-3187," it said. "If you'd like to leave a message for Jean-Jacques Brauner, please do so after the beep."

I hung up and continued reading. The last folder was labeled, "Letters: Jack (II)." And then, as if an afterthought, "My only son."—the words printed just like that in my father's intolerably precise hand.

"I'm sorry," Jacques wrote in 1987. "I know how angry you are. But I just wish you'd say it instead of brooding. If I was there you could just show me and get it over with, but I'm not, so you'll just have to . . . "

To which my father had answered: "I think you're making a mistake. Eric is your boss; he's the one that you should worry about. Joanne's not in a position to harm you, so her opinion doesn't matter. I know you always want to accommodate everyone, but it's a trait that gets less charming as you age. You may pretend you're trying to be nice, but really, it's a form of insecurity and self-hate. I'm telling you this because I know . . . "

When my father was dying, when he was actually dying in my stepmother's arms, was this the image in his mind? Me with this file of letters, sitting in his chair? Or Barbara? "I'm sorry to hear about Barbara's operation," Jacques wrote in 1989. "It must be very depressing to her. No matter how much you try to convince yourself that these things aren't important, it alters the way you think of yourself, like wrinkles, or losing your hair, though of course much worse. It's funny, it feels like I know her very well, enough to reassure you that I know she'll be all right, and that you're worrying about nothing . . . "

I dialed the Oakland number again. The man's voice was pleasant, his intonation slightly strange, not quite American, perhaps. After the beep I said, "Listen, this is Jack Modine. I don't know how to say this, and maybe you already know, but my father had a heart attack on Thursday morning. I just wanted to tell you, and to ask you please not to send any more letters, because I don't want them forwarded to my stepmother. As I say, it was very sudden, and he wasn't in any pain."

I paused for a moment—it seemed so strange. I also have a tendency to accommodate, not that my father had ever remarked on it. "Don't worry about anything," I said. "I'm telling you because I guess you cared about him. If you want to know more, I'll be home after the fifteenth. My number is . . . " I said, and I gave him the number of my apartment in Meridan.

I called him again a few weeks later and then a few times after that. I never got the answering machine again, and I never said anything either. I would just listen to him go, "Hello? Hello?" and then he would hang up. After a while he disconnected his phone. But I can remember at least one time, when I was at the height of my craziness, I suppose—I dialed his number just to listen to the recorded message from the phone company.

I look back on that from a life which is, if not happy, at least regular, at least full of a routine. And it contains, I feel sure, some of the ingredients of happiness. Now I am able to isolate them—friends. Sex. Work. I have hopes that some day I will learn to mix them in correct proportions. But I was desperate then, and part of the reason was that everything I had discovered about my father seemed unreal so quickly. I threw it all into the dumpster. The unknown, beating heart of my father's life—I threw it in the garbage. I didn't even read most of the letters. Late that same night I got up from the bed in my hotel and got dressed. I had some idea of finding the bus station and waiting there until morning, but instead I walked around the streets of Santa Monica, trying to retrace the way back to my father's office. I wanted to look over his letters again. I wanted to go through them and read over where he mentioned me—I remembered once I went out to visit him and Barbara. He came down into the kitchen at three o'clock in the morning to find me watching TV, and he took me to an all-night hamburger stand somewhere. "The best egg creams in California," he said. Surely, I thought, he would have told Jacques about that. I remembered the date, or at least the year.

I didn't find the office again. The vial of ashes Barbara gave me—I threw it away too. By the time I got back to Meridan that phone number in Oakland was the only thing left, and when I found out it had been disconnected, I felt as if some essential link had been destroyed. A link to urgent knowledge—now it seems obvious. Now it seems easy to say where my trouble really started. In the absence of facts, in the absence of anything to hold on to, I began to imagine a whole world.

And the moving spirit of that world was Jean-Jacques Brauner. From the beginning, of course, I had been thinking about him, trying to make a picture of him in my mind. Or rather, not trying—the picture came by itself, and I found myself looking at it, hour after hour. It was so clear, I began to think it must be founded on something, some snapshot in my father's file that I couldn't quite remember. It took me a long time to realize that the model for the picture was myself. I am five-eleven. Jean-Jacques was six feet. I am handsome. Jean-Jacques was beautiful. Men and women turned to look at him when he walked past.

The foreign name, the hint of foreignness in the voice on the tape, I thought, must be an affectation, the residue from a privileged childhood spent abroad—he didn't really need the money that my father had been send-ing him. Where had he gone to college? Some expensive school, Berkeley, perhaps. No doubt he had graduated near the top of his class. No doubt he had won prizes, cash prizes which gave him the time and the prestige to pick and choose among employers. Whereas I had gone to the University of Con-necticut and my mother had paid. A second-rate B.A. with third rate grades—it was hard for me to find anything. I had a job in a health club for six dollars an hour.

This sounds carping and resentful, but in fact I did not envy his success. He was too far away. In the morning I would watch the Weather channel, and it never rained in Oakland. The temperature was always fifty seven degrees. I had never been there, but in my mind's eye I pictured it, conveniently located atop the San Andreas Fault, midway between Yosemite National Park and the stupefying beauty of Big Sur. The capital of a new and perfect California, where fathers loved their sons and chastised them lovingly. Where college graduates found interesting, high-paying jobs. How could I begrudge Jacques anything? He was my counterpart, my double in that uncorrupted world.

And yet there must have been some conduit between that world and this, because from time to time I would catch sight of him. Not at first. At first all I noticed was a tension in the air, a sudden electricity. At certain moments in the street in Meridan, during my lunch hour perhaps, I would feel a new small sensitivity. I would know Jean-Jacques was thinking about me, that our thoughts were colliding like cold and hot fronts over Kansas. Colliding but not mixing—frustrated, later, by our lack of communication, I began to imag-ine that he was leaving me clues. Arrangements of sticks, of trash, junk mail, graffiti on the street, all seemed like messages in a language I could not de-code.

But I'm going too fast. These delusions came gradually. And always there was part of me that was still rational. I remember talking to Servando, who was an aerobics instructor at the health club where I worked before I was let go. I told him a suspicion I had that my father was still alive, that he had faked his death, faked his cremation, fooled his wife and all his creditors, and was living in the Bay Area. It was just a theory. I had not come to any definite con-clusion, and I was weighing the evidence with Servando, and listening to him carefully when he said it was unlikely, that it probably wasn't true. I believed him. I was reassured. But then I got to thinking about it later in the week, and it occurred to me that maybe Servando wasn't necessarily disinterested, that maybe he had received a letter from Jean-Jacques, or maybe some message in one of the arrangements of objects that I was finding so difficult to interpret. It drove me crazy, the idea that everything around me was so pregnant with information that might change my life, and yet I couldn't understand any of it.

That summer I decided to take the LSAT's. I had been fired from my job after an argument with the desk manager. I think I was probably in the wrong. Maybe I even told her that—in any case, she didn't hold a grudge. She arranged for me to receive six months' unemployment. At the same time I got a letter from my father's lawyer, saying that I had been left a legacy of $15,000. The lawyer's name was Mr. Ordauer; he also said that my father's estate would defray the expense of any further education—it was a nice letter, and I liked the language, the formal phrases. It made me want to follow in Mr. Ordauer's footsteps. I knew being a lawyer was a good job, perhaps a better job than anything Jean-Jacques had yet achieved. I called Mr. Ordauer on the phone. "Listen," I said, "was there another legacy? Did my father leave anything to a man named Brauner, in Oakland?" Mr. Oraduer had a pleasant voice. "No," he said without hesitating. "He left no money to his business associates."

How wonderful a gift, I thought, to be able to lie so effortlessly! So I signed up to take the LSAT's at the University of Connecticut, and I bought some training books. And when I was studying them I realized that this was definitely what I was intended to do with my life—I knew every answer to every question in the sample tests without any problem at all. Those questions about the couples square-dancing, and who's next to whom. I just knew it; I could see them spinning around, coming to rest.

As I say, I had never wished Jean-Jacques any harm. But I could tell now that he was worried, anxious, jealous of me. Jealous of my closeness with my father, who would be sending me to law-school—I guess he decided he had to come back East and do something, because it was about that time, the third week in July, that I first saw him. As I say, I had some idea that he had been at my father's funeral, but I couldn't be sure. He was lurking behind a pillar. I hadn't seen his face. The first time I saw it, I was walking down Orange Street in New Haven, and there was a beautiful dark-haired man in front of me. His right leg was bandaged, and he was swinging himself along on crutches. He turned back to look at me.

I had gone to New Haven to visit an old friend. He had seemed concerned and upset that I was sleeping so badly; the conversation was disagreeable, and so I left. I was walking back to where I'd parked my car when I saw this man, and even then I didn't think much about it. I just noticed his beauty, his dark eyebrows and his dark eyes. His fat soft mouth. But it wasn't until I saw the same man in Meridan, looking at me from across the street, that I knew who it was. Almost I went up to him. Almost I confronted him. He smiled at me and made a minute gesture with his hand. I thought, I won't play into his game. It's not just out of chance that he allowed me to see him. He wants something from me.

I turned around and walked away from him. But I could feel his eyes. And I could feel his presence around me, the next day and the next. During the weeks before the test, I was tormented by a series of absurd accidents. Once, an egg fell on the sidewalk just in front of me. Once, a dog barked all night, just when I was finally able to rest. I'm not saying that even at the time I held him responsible for these events. I can't picture him limping along the roof-tops, an egg in his hand. I can't picture him dragging a dog to sit outside my room, inciting it to bark. It's just that I could feel myself deflected and dis-tracted by bad luck, just when it was most important for me to concentrate. To rest, to gather my resources, but always, every day there was something. My landlord raised my rent. I twisted my foot, stepping off the curb in front of my apartment. I sat down, holding my leg, tears in my eyes, and I could feel that sudden tension in the air. And though I couldn't see him anywhere in the street, especially not through eyes blurred by tears, I could feel his presence. Not that I blamed him—it had been my own stupidity, my own clumsiness. But in a way that made it worse—he was using my own worst flaws against me. He was making it impossible for me to hate anyone but myself.

But still, I refused to let myself be deflected. I studied the training books over and over. I memorized the responses. I could feel the tension growing all around me; on the morning of the test, I was very nervous. I got into my car. And I had had trouble driving for a few days—there was something wrong with my spatial perception, and I was always afraid that I was getting too close to things. Streets I had driven down a thousand times seemed narrow, and I was concerned that I might scrape the paint off cars parked along the curb. So I drove slowly, carefully, anxious when cars approached me in the opposite direction. Anxious when people passed me, or honked at me from behind.

That morning I had dressed in my suit. I was taking time with everything. I had given myself fifty minutes for the drive, but when I looked at my watch, I saw I had to hurry. I was out in the country by that time, driving past a golf course. It was separated from the highway by a guard-rail and a steep embankment. There was a strip where you could pull over. And when I looked at my watch, I had to take my eyes off the road for a moment—I admit it. It's not as if he ran in front of the car; he was just standing with his crutches in the breakdown lane when I hit him.

I pulled over as quickly as I could and then just waited for a while. I left the car running, because I was still in a hurry. More than ever, in fact. An hour later I would blame myself by thinking that even in this matter of life and death I could be cursory and careless, just like the other cars that were rushing past me without stopping. But when I got out and looked at the bumper, there was no mark. I walked back down the strip, trying to find him, and I couldn't. Yet I had seen him clearly, standing with his crutches. His dark hair, dark eyes. I had felt the shudder in the car as he slid off the front bumper.

But I didn't know what to do. I was already late. And it was possible that I had been mistaken. As I thought about it more, standing in the hot morning by the side of the road, it seemed more likely—what would he have been doing here? How had he gotten here? How could he have known that I would come this way? It was absurd. I went back to my car and drove to the test site without stopping. I was prepared—I had my pencils and my clock. I went in and we sat in rows, and I listened impatiently to the instructions. We were in the basement of Monteith Hall, and it was well lit down there. They passed out the test booklets, and then we started. The first section was analogies—it was harder than the sample I had practiced with, and I could feel myself making a few errors. But that did nothing to shake my confidence. It would have been silly to expect to perform perfectly, especially after such a disturbing incident in the car. But I felt confident that I was able to distinguish subtle shades of meaning, even though it was hot in Monteith Hall that morning. I finished the section exactly on time.

But after a while I found it harder to concentrate, because I was thinking about Jean-Jacques. What if he was still there by the side of the road, and I hadn't seen him for some reason? Maybe I had dragged him underneath my car. Or maybe he had rolled down the embankment, or been thrown over the guard-rail. I had been going almost forty miles an hour.

This was in the middle of the quantitative section. Ordinarily, it would have been so easy for me, except I couldn't concentrate. It was all pie-charts and parabolas—basic stuff, but I was wondering if I could be arrested for leaving the scene of an accident. I wondered whether I'd been seen. So that when they told us to stop, I wasn't finished. And that was my best section—the next one was analytical, and the second question was about some traffic accident. I couldn't believe it. I just stared at the question.

After ten minutes, I closed my booklet. I left the pencils but I took the clock and walked out, back to my car. There was no mark on it anywhere, but even so I got in and drove back to the golf course. I thought maybe he had rolled down into some bushes near the road, or maybe he had been injured, and had managed to drag himself away into the trees. There was a copse of trees near the ninth green; I parked my car near the guard-rail and climbed down the embankment. I thought maybe I would find his crutch. I poked a stick into a bush, looking for his crutches, and then I walked across the green and through the copse. I sat down on a bench on the other side, and I watched some people set up their tees. A man in a red shirt and beige pants hit a long, straight ball over the water hazard.

As I sat there, it occurred to me that Jean-Jacques had tricked me. And maybe he hadn't even been there, maybe he had never left California, but even so he had tricked me, and robbed me again. It occurred to me that he had stolen my life from me as he had stolen my father's love. That he had stolen my life, that he was living it and enjoying it, while I was sitting on this bench. I was sitting alone on the white bench, watching the man in the beige pants trudge down the hill. It was a hot, bright morning.

After a while, I got up to follow him. And I thought, it's something just to be able to get up and walk. It's something just to climb up an embankment and sit in the front seat of your car. I sat there with my hands gripping the steering wheel. I closed my eyes, and for a blissful moment I couldn't remember why I was so upset. I saw myself sitting in my father's office in Santa Monica. The fluorescent lighting overhead. The dark window and the parking lot. But this time it was different. This time a single hour had been excised from my memory, cleansing what had gone before, cleansing for a blissful moment what came afterward. Suddenly I couldn't remember whether the file cabinet had five drawers or only four. Or else the bottom drawer was locked, and I tried, and tried, and failed to pull it open.

Simultaneously, perhaps in order to replace that excised hour, I remembered something new. I slid forward on the car seat. I pulled my wallet out of my back pocket and retrieved from it a letter, written years before and never sent. I unfolded it carefully, for it was worn along the creases. "Dear Dad," it said. And then in part: "I hate you. I hate you for every bad choice I ever made."

People talk so carelessly about how life gets better, about time and patience, about bravery and strength. Be brave, they say, be strong. People connect the two. But in the real world they are opposites. They never go together. Strong people are like tank commanders driving through a field of bones. No courage is involved. Courage is the virtue of the weak.

After a while, I buckled on my seat belt. I turned on the ignition and drove home. I went indoors and lay down on my bed. All that time when I was growing up, before my father moved to California—there was no reason to remember what he did, or what he didn't do. Only later, in my mother's kitchen. Once she said: "He did the best he could. He just wasn't cut out for it. He didn't have the instinct to protect." Once she said, with no lightness whatever in her tone: "You used to bring out the worst in him."

Shortly after his death, Barbara had sent me a package containing a roll of super-8 film. They were home movies taken at my mother's house. I didn't have access to a projector; all I could do was hold them to the light. Now I took the roll from my bedside table and untaped the end. I sat up on my bed and held a strip of film up to the window. It showed a man about my age, sitting cross-legged in the grass, holding up a baby.

I pulled six or eight feet of film down between my thumbs. The image didn't seem to change.

get a grip

Here's how I found out: I was in a bar called Dave's on East 14th Street. It wasn't my usual place. I had been dating a woman in Stuyvesant Town. One night after I left, I still wasn't eager to go home. So on my way I stopped in.

I used to spend a lot of time in bars, though I don't smoke or drink. But I like the second hand stuff. And the conversations you could have with strangers—you could tell them anything. "Ottawa is a fine city," you could say. "My brother lives in Ottawa," I could say, though in fact I'm an only child. But people nod their heads.

This kind of storytelling used to drive my ex-wife crazy. "It's so pointless. It's not like you're pretending you're an astronaut or a circus clown. That I could see. But a Canadian?"

"It's a subtle thrill," I conceded.

"Why not tell the truth?" Barbara would say. "That you're a successful lawyer with a beautiful wife you don't deserve. Is that so terrible?"

Not terrible so much as difficult to believe. It sounded pretty thin, even before I found out. And of course none of it turned out to be true at all.

Anyway, that night I was listening to someone else. Someone was claiming he had seen Reggie Jackson's last game on TV. I nodded, but all the time I was looking past him toward a corner of the bar, where a man was sitting at a table by himself. He was smoking cigarettes and drinking, and I recognized him.

But I didn't know from where. I stared at him for a few minutes. What was different—had he shaved his beard? Then suddenly I realized he was in the wrong country. It was Boris Bezugly. It truly was.

I took my club soda over to join him. We had parted on such good terms. "Friends, friends!" he had shouted drunkenly on the platform of Petersburg Station, saliva dripping from his lips. Now he was drunk again. He sat picking at the wax of the red candle. When he looked up at me, I saw nothing in his face, just bleared eyes and a provisional smile.

57

We had met two years before, when a partner in the firm was scouting the possibility of a branch office in Moscow. Even in Russia he was the drunkest man I ever met. When we were introduced, he had passed out and fallen on his back as we were still shaking hands. Maybe it was his drunkenness that kept him from recognizing me now, I thought. After all, it had taken me a moment.

But we were in New York. Surely running into me was not as strange as running into him. And why hadn't he told me he was coming?

"Sdravsvuytse," I said, grinning. "Can I buy you a drink?"

What passed over his face was an expression of such horror and rage, it made me put up my hand. But then his face went blank and he turned away from me, huddling around his candle and his drink.

He had lost weight, and his black beard was gone. In Russia he had worn a hilarious mismatch of plaid clothes, surmounted by an old fur cap. Now he wore a tweed suit, a denim shirt open at the neck. The cap was gone.

"Boris," I said.

In Russia his English had been absurd. I used to tell him he sounded like a hit man in a Cold War novel, and he had laughed aloud. Now he spoke quickly and softly in a mid-Atlantic accent: "I think you're making a mistake."

And I would have thought so too, except for the strange expression I had seen. So I persevered. I pulled out one of the chairs and sat down—"What are you doing?" he cried. "My God, if they find us here. If they see us here."

These words gave me what I thought was a glimmer of understanding. In Moscow, in the kitchen of his tiny apartment, Boris once had put away enough vodka to let him pass through drunkenness into another stage, a kind of clarity and grim sobriety. Then he had told me what his life was like under the Communists—the lies which no one had believed. The interrogations. When he was a student in the sixties after Brezhnev first came in, he had spent two years in protective custody.

Now maybe he was remembering those times. "My friend," I said, "it's all right. You're in America."

These words seemed to fill him with another gust of fury. He tried to get up, and I could see he was very drunk. "I don't know you, I've never met you," he muttered, grinding out his cigarette butt. But then the cocktail waitress was there.

"I'll take a club soda," I said. "And my friend will have a Smirnoff's."

"No," he snarled, "that was the problem with that job. Get me a bourbon," he told the waitress. Then to me: "I hate vodka."

Which surprised me more than anything he'd said so far. In Moscow he had recited poetry about vodka. "Yeah," he told me now, smiling in spite of himself. "Tastes change."

Apparently he had reassured himself that no one was watching us. But he waited until the waitress had come and gone before he spoke again. "Boris," I said, and he interrupted me.

"Don't call me that. It was just a job, a two-week job. I barely remember it."

"What are you talking about?"

He smiled. "You don't know, do you? You really don't know. Get a grip," he said. "It's like candy from a baby."

I saw such a mix of passions in his face. Envy, frustration, anger, fear. And then a kind of malignant grin that was so far from my perception of his character that I stared at him, fascinated.

"You never went to Russia," he said. "You've never met a single Russian. You were in a theme park they built outside Helsinki, surrounded by people like me. They were paying us to guzzle vodka and wear false beards and act like clowns. 'Sdravsvuytse,' my ass!"

He was crazy. "My poor friend," I said. "Who was paying you? The KGB?"

He knocked his heavy-bottomed glass against the table, spilling bourbon on the polyurethaned wood. "Not the KGB," he hissed. "The KGB never existed. None of it existed. None of this." He waved his hand around the room.

He was in the middle of a paranoid breakdown of some sort. I could see that. And yet the moment I heard him, I felt instinctively that what he said was true.

"They never would have taken you to Russia," he went on. "Not to the real Russia." As he spoke I brought back my own memories—the grime, the cold, the sullen old babushkas with rags around their heads. The concrete apartment blocks. The horrible food.

He put down his empty glass. "Thanks for the drink. And now I'm definitely getting out of here before somebody sees us. Because this is definitely against the rules."

Then he was gone, and I walked home. And maybe I wouldn't have thought much about it, only the next day I was walking up Fifth Avenue on my lunch hour, and I passed the offices for Aeroflot. I went in and sat down with the people who were waiting to be helped. We were in a row of armchairs next to the window.

This is ridiculous, I thought. And I was about to get up and go, when I found myself staring at a travel poster. One of the agents was talking on the phone, and there was a framed poster of Red Square above her desk. And was that Boris Bezugly in the middle of a group of smiling Russians in front of St. Basil's? The beard, the hat, the absurd plaid?

The Aeroflot agent was a dark-haired, heavy-chested woman, dressed in black pumps, beige tights, and a black mini-skirt. A parody of a Russian vamp. And what was that language she was speaking on the phone? The more I listened, the more improbable it sounded.

I asked the woman sitting next to me. She frowned. "Russian, of course," she said. How could she be so sure? Made-up gobbledygook, but of course once you let yourself start thinking like that, the whole world starts to fall apart. Not immediately, but gradually. I took the woman from Stuyvesant Town to a musical on Broadway. Critics had pretended to like it, though it was obviously bad. Audience members had applauded, laughed—who were they trying to fool?

At work sometimes I found it hard to concentrate. I was representing the plaintiff in a civil suit. Yet no actual client could have been so petty, so vindictive. In my office I sat staring at the man, watching his lips move, waiting for him to give himself away.

And of course I spent more of my time at Dave's. I would go there every evening after work, and in time I was drinking more than just club sodas. But it was weeks before I saw Boris again. He came in out of a freezing rain and made his way directly toward me, where I was sitting at a table by myself.

He sat down without asking and leaned forward, rubbing his hands over the tiny candle flame. "Listen," he said, "I'm in trouble," and he looked it. He needed a shave. His eyes were bloodshot. He wasn't wearing a coat.

"Listen, I can't do it any more. All that lying and pretending. I've screwed up two more jobs and now they're on to me. I can't go home. Please, can you give me some money? I've got to get away."

"I'll pay you fifty dollars for some information," I said. I took the bills from my pocket, but he interrupted me.

"No, I mean your watch or something. I can't use that bogus currency." He pulled some coins out of the pocket of his pants, big, shiny, aluminum coins like Mardi Gras doubloons. In fact as I looked closely, I saw that's what they were. The purple one in his palm was stamped with the head of Pete Fountain playing the clarinet.

"I don't even have enough here for a drink," he said.

"I'll get you one." I raised my hand for the waitress. But then I saw her at the corner of the bar, talking with the bartender. As I watched, she pointed over at us.

"Oh my God," said my Russian friend. His voice was grim and strange. "Give me the watch."

I stripped it off, though it was an expensive Seiko. "Thanks," he said, looking at the face, the sweep of the second hand. "And in return I'll answer one minute's worth of questions. Go."

"Who are you?" I asked.

But he shrugged irritably. "No, it's not important. My name is Nathan—so what? What about you?"

"I know about myself," I said uncertainly.

"Do you? Paul Park, Esq. Yale, 1981. But what makes you think you were smart enough to go to the real Yale? Do you think they let just anybody in?"

Actually, I had always kind of wondered about that. So his words gave me a painful kind of pleasure. Then he went on: "Twenty seconds. What about your marriage? What was that all about?"

"I'm divorced."

"Of course you are. The woman who was playing your wife landed another job. It was never supposed to be more than a two year contract with an option, which she chose not to renew. Last I heard, she was doing Medea, Blanche Dubois, and Lady Macbeth for some repertory company up in Canada."

Again, this sounded so hideously plausible that I said nothing.

"Forty seconds."

"Fifty seconds."

"Wait," I said, but he was gone out the door. He left only his Pete Fountain doubloon, which I slid into my pocket.

Then in a little while the police were there. A man in a white raincoat sat opposite me, asking me questions. "Did he say where he was going? Did he give you anything?"

"No," I said. "No. Nothing."

But then when I was watching TV later that night, I saw that Nathan Rose, a performance artist wanted in connection with several outstanding warrants, had been arrested. There was a photograph, and a brief description of his accomplishments. Nathan Rose had been a promising young man, recipient of several grants from the National Endowment for the Arts. The newscaster's voice was sad and apologetic, and she seemed to look out of the television directly at me. She made no mention of the crime he'd been accused of.

What was it—impersonating a Russian?

That night was the beginning of a quick decline for me, because success in life depends on not asking too many questions. The patterns of illusion that made up the modern world require a kind of faith, a suspension of disbelief. The revenge on skeptics is quick and sure, and I soon found myself hustled out of what I'd thought was my real world as rudely as I might have been thrown out of a magic show, if I had stood up in the audience and explained the tricks while the performance was in progress.

But of course at that time I could only guess at the real truth. I conceived the idea that the government had hired an enormous troupe of actors, administered and paid for by the NEA, to create and sustain an illusion of reality for certain people. At first I played with the idea that I might be the only one, but no. That was too grandiose, too desperate a fantasy. So much money, so much effort, just to make a fool out of a single citizen. The Republicans never would have stood for it. Providing jobs for actors just wasn't that important, even in New York.

I lost my job, my friends, and my apartment. I refused to work long hours for play money. And no one could tolerate me. People I knew, I kept trying to catch them in small lies and inconsistencies. I would ask them questions. "If this is just a job for you, why aren't you nicer to me? Surely we'd enjoy it more. How can we turn this into a comedy? A farce? A musical?"

By the middle of December I was living by the train tracks, inside the tunnel under Riverside Park. Maybe it wasn't necessary for me to have gone that far down all at once. But at a certain moment, I thought I'd try to penetrate down below the level of deception. Because I imagined that the illusions were falser and more elaborate the higher up you went, which is why so many rich people are crazy. Wherever they go, part of their brain is mumbling to the other part, "Surely the actual Plaza Hotel isn't such a dump. Surely an authentic Mercedes corners better than this. Surely a genuine production of Hamlet isn't quite so dull. Surely the real Alps are higher and more picturesque."

But that night in my tarpaulin tent next to the train tracks, wrapped in my blankets, it was hard for me to think that the real Riverside Park was even darker, even colder, even more miserable. I was dressed in a dinner jacket I had kept from my apartment. I was glutted with hors-d'oeuvres, drunk on chablis, because New York provides many opportunities to a man in black tie, especially around Christmas time. I had attended office parties and openings all the way from midtown, pretending all the way. I had been an architect, an actor, a designer, a literary agent. In each place as I grew drunker, the lies I told grew more outrageous, yet people still smiled and nodded. Why not? They were being paid good Mardi Gras doubloons to pretend to believe me.

In my tent, I slid my hand down into my pocket and clasped my hand around my own Pete Fountain coin, perhaps, I thought, the only genuine thing I'd ever owned. I lay back against a pile of cinders. The temperature was below freezing. Drunk and despairing, I let the cold come into me, let it calm me until I wasn't sure if I could move even if I'd wanted to. My hands and legs were stiff. I looked up the tunnel into the dark and imagined how the world was changing outside, how in the morning I would climb out through the grate into a new world of heat and light and honesty.

As the hours passed, the walls of the tunnel seemed to close around me. But yes, there was some light down toward the tunnel's mouth, too bright, too soft for dawn. Yes, it seemed to fill the hole, to chase away the darkness, and it was as if I had left my body and was drifting toward it, suspended over the tracks. There was heat too, beyond my fingertips, and as I drifted down the tunnel I felt it penetrate my body and my soul. I imagined faces in the tunnel with me, people standing along the rails, smiling and murmuring. As I passed them I reached out, especially to the ones I recognized: my mother, my grandparents, my childhood friends, and even Barbara, my ex-wife. Yes, I thought, this is the truth.

It couldn't last forever. I was sprawled over the tracks, and the light was coming toward me. I listened to the muffled voices and the creak of the wheels, and the light was all around me. It was so bright, I had to close my eyes. As I did so, I heard somebody say, "That's it, I guess. That's a wrap."

When I sat up, I was in a crowd of people and machines. The big lamp had gone out, replaced by a yellow fluorescent line along the middle of the vault.

By its light I could see much that had been hidden from me. For one thing, the entire tunnel was only about twenty-five yards long. I could see the brick ends of it now, cunningly painted to look like train tracks disappearing in both directions.

In front of me there was a lamp rigged to a platform, which ran on wheels along the rails. Now that the lamp was out, I could see the movie camera beneath it, the cameraman stripping off his gloves and his coat; they had turned off the refrigeration machines. There was a whole line of them along the wall, and I guess they had been making quite a racket, because now I could hear all kinds of talking from the crew as they finished up.

I threw aside my blanket and sat rubbing my hands. Nobody was paying any attention to me. But then I saw my mother coming toward me through a crowd of technicians, and she squatted down. "Congratulations," she said. "That was great."

"Mother," I stammered, "is it really you?" I admit I was surprised to see her, because she had passed away in the spring of 1978.

She was wearing a silk shirt, blue jeans, and cowboy boots. She was smiling. "Yeah, that's great. I tell you, these last few weeks you've made me proud I ever got to work with you. Proud you're my son, so to speak. The paranoia, the anger, the disgust. It was all so real."

"Mother," I said, "I can't believe it. You look so young."

She winked. "Yeah, sure. You've probably never seen me without makeup. But let's not get carried away. Somewhere along the line you must have guessed. That was the whole point of this game."

She stood up. And now others were helping me to my feet. I recognized a few old faces, and then Barbara was there. "Your suit's a mess," she said.

I was stunned, overwhelmed to see her. Her freckled nose. Her crooked smile. She reached up to touch my damp bow-tie. When I'd known her, her breath had always been a little sour, a symptom of chronic gastric distress. Now she was standing close to me, and I caught a whiff of the mints she used—the same old brand. At least that was for real, I thought.

Her little head was close to my lapel. Packed with brains. I'd always said that was the reason she so easily outwitted me. The space inside her skull was so small that her thoughts never had more than an inch or so to travel, to make connections. Her ideas moved faster, like molecules in a gas when it's condensed.

And at the moment when I smelt her breath, I felt a little surge of hope. Even if there was no place for me in her old life, maybe now there might be some new way for us to be together in this new world. Cleverer than me, maybe she had already had the same idea, because I felt her arms around me, her head against my cheek as I bent down. "I'm sorry I was so mean," she whispered. "But I had to. It was the script. Sometimes it broke my heart, the things I had to do to you. I'm not normally so promiscuous."

Mother and the rest had disappeared, and we were surrounded by technicians packing up equipment. "I just wanted to tell you right away," she said. "Before anybody else talks to you. Sex and betrayal are the only things that keep the yuppie games alive. The only reason anybody wants to play. So I had to. That thing where you caught me with your boss's wife—I actually protested to the writers. I cried for days when we were finished."

Then she took my hand and led me outside. It was early morning. We walked through a park that seemed all of a sudden only twenty-five yards wide, and it was rapidly disappearing as people rolled up the astroturf and wheeled away the papier-mache balustrades.

The night before, I had come down to the park the way I always did, along West 98th Street. Now as we approached Riverside Drive, I could see as if from a slightly different angle the painted plywood facades of the buildings, all just a few inches thick. On 98th street itself there was a huge crew striking the set, so instead of going back that way, Barbara led me north, uptown, and soon we were lost among streets I didn't recognize, although I'd lived on the Upper West Side my whole life.

"Where are we?" I asked faintly.

"Toronto. They always use it for the New York shoots. The real New York is so expensive. It's like American actors—no one can afford them any more. We use Canadians for everything."

"So what was this?" I asked. "A movie or a game?"

"Both. It's interactive TV. A few hired professionals like me and your mom, and then tons of paying customers. They do most of the minor characters, the extras and what not. Then the whole thing is broadcast live, with your thoughts picked up on an internal mike as a kind of voice-over. That's what made the show—you were so innocent, so clueless. The show started when you were fifteen, which meant it took you twenty-two years to figure out what was going on. It's a new record. And in the end we had to give you massive hints. "

"When I was fifteen?"

"Sure. All the rest was just recovered memory syndrome. Who wants to make a show about a kid? I mean except for all the shows within the show. Beaver Cleaver and so forth."

"Beaver Cleaver?"

"No expense was spared," said Barbara. "It's the information superhighway. But you have to understand—this was a huge deal."

She was right. By the time we hit Yonge Street a crowd had gathered. Old ladies, teenagers, men, women, all wanting to shake my hand and get my autograph. I was a celebrity, like O. J. Simpson or Woody Allen, except of course I really existed. I was a real person, and not just a collection of computer-generated film clips.

"Mr. Park," somebody shouted. "When did you know for sure?"

"Show us the doubloon!" demanded another, and when I took it from my pocket, everyone laughed and clapped.

An old man grasped my hand. I recognized him as the super of the building next to mine. "I just wanted to say you've given my wife and me such pleasure over the years. Most of the shows should be banned from the airwaves, if it was up to me. But you never even raised your voice. No violence at all. Not that you weren't tempted," he said, giving Barbara a severe look.

Then the limo arrived, small and sleek. Inside I could hear a small hum, as if from a computer. No one was driving. We pulled out slowly into the wide street, and then we were heading downtown. "So what was the show's name?" I asked.

"It was called GET A GRIP," said Barbara. And when she saw my face, she grinned. "Oh come on, don't take it like that. Sure, you were kind of a wimp, but the guy was right. It was a wholesome show. Every day we found new ways to humiliate you, but you just soldiered on. Most of the time you didn't even notice. I mean sure, you were a total moron, but that was all right. It was your dignity that people loved."

We drove on through the unfamiliar streets. "I guess it didn't keep me from being canceled," I said.

"Well, to tell the truth it was all a little dated. And you needed a good female lead. That fat tart in Stuyvesant Town just wasn't doing it. People seemed to find your life less interesting as soon as I bailed out."

"I guess I felt the same way."

Barbara patted my hand. "But you were still popular among retirees. You have no idea how bad most of the competition is. Like the guy said, they gave over most of the twentieth century to war games. Vietnam, KKK, Holocaust, Cold War, Hiroshima. Those are all the American shows. Kids love them, even the minorities. But I can't stand them."

"Hiroshima?" I asked.

She smiled. "Meanwhile, we thought it was a stroke of genius to work all that into the background of GET A GRIP. To show what life in America might have been like if it had all really happened. Of course we had to change the footage and the point of view—reshoot a lot of it. Most of those shows are ridiculously patriotic."

"Ingenious," I murmured.

"But that's how we got into trouble. ABC claimed it was copyright infringement, and the American ambassador protested. But GET A GRIP was a satire, for God's sake. Even the US courts ruled in our favor."

After a little while I said, "So what did really happen?"

"Well, that's what I'm telling you. The Americans were furious for years. So ABC finally made a hostile bid for Ottawa Communication, which produced your show. The deal went through last week, and GET A GRIP was canceled. But there had been rumors for months, which was why the writers brought back all that Russian stuff last fall. They wanted to take the show to its own end."

"No. I mean, what really happened? In the world."

She squeezed my arm. "Don't worry. You'll soon catch up. Besides, we're here."

We pulled up in front of a hotel. "You'll love it," she said. "Czar Nicholas III stayed here last time he was in town."

So I got out and followed her up the steps. In through the revolving doors. The lobby was all ormolu and velvet and gilt mantelpieces. The elevator ran in a cage up through the middle of the spiral staircase. "What am I doing now?" I asked as we got in.

"God damn it, Pogo, don't be such a dope." I hated when she called me "Pogo." It was a nickname left over from my earliest childhood, and she only used it to annoy me. But as I rode up in the elevator, it occurred to me that maybe no one had ever really called me that. Maybe all those painful memories had been induced when I was fifteen. Maybe they had all been covered in a flashback, when GET A GRIP first went on the air.

My eyes filled with tears. "What's the matter now?" said Barbara. "Honest to God, you'd think you were being boiled over a slow fire. It's the best hotel in town. I thought you might want to rest for a few hours, take a shower, change your clothes before the reception at the President's house tonight. The Russian ambassador will be there—I tell you you're a star. A symbol of Canadian pride. Come on, is that so terrible?"

Then when we were alone together in the jewel-box room, she said, "Besides, I've missed you."

But I wasn't listening. I was looking at my face in the mirror above the dresser. The same curly hair and gullible eyes, as if nothing had happened. "My whole life has been a parody," I said, watching my lips move. But then I had to smile, because it was exactly what I might have said back in America, back during the salad days of GET A GRIP.

Barbara was behind me. In the mirror I saw her undo the first few buttons of her blouse, and then slip it off her shoulders. "Let me make it okay for you," she said. Then it was like a dream come true, because she was leading me to the bed and pulling off my clothes. I had thought about this moment so many times since we split up, directing us as if we were the actors in a scene. In my mind, sometimes she was harsh and fast, sometimes passive and accommodating. Sometimes it took hours, and sometimes it was over right away. But none of my fantasizing prepared me for this moment, which was not sublime so much as strange. During two years of marriage, I thought I had got to know her well. But I had never done anything of the things she required of me in that hotel room; I had never heard of anybody doing them. But, "Things are different here," she whispered. "Let me teach you how to make it in the real world," she said, before I lost consciousness.

Then I came to, and I was lying on the bed. Barbara was in the shower. I could hear the water running. I sat naked on the side of the bed, staring at the television. It was in a lacquer cabinet on top of a marble table, and the remote was on the floor near my foot. There were hundreds of buttons on it.

Then suddenly I was seized with a new suspicion, and I flicked it on. I flicked through several channels, seeing nothing but football games. But there I was on channel 599xtc, butt-naked, staring at myself. Behind me the hotel room, the ripped sheets and soggy pillows. And on the bottom corner of the screen, a blinking panel which said:

PRESS ANY KEY TO CONTINUE

Then Barbara was there, toweling her neck, looking over my shoulder. "Okay, so it's not quite over yet," she said. "There are still some things you ought to know."

untitled 4

It had been years since I had written a publishable story. But there were some sketches I'd abandoned at various times, and so in desperation I chose two of them—no, no, it's not by telling lies that I will recover what is mine. Perhaps there's something about prison that makes us devious and paranoid. No again—it's not prison that's to blame, though I can feel myself tempted to explain my emptiness, the way my smallest thoughts turn to violence, by describing my life now. So let me put that to rest by admitting that I'm not badly treated. I have special privileges. The warden keeps a battered copy of *Thirteen Steps* behind his desk. My first day here, he asked me to sign it. He says it changed his life, years ago.

After our most recent revolution, I was reminded that the new vice-chairman's son admired a certain volume of short stories, which I had once attacked in print. Literature and literary opinions are suddenly important in my small country, not for their own sake. I spend most of my days in the library, where I've been given a study carrel and a word processor. Or I work longhand in the reading room, a high, empty space with tall windows and long tables. The fact is, prison can be liberating, and the fact is also that whatever sickness was afflicting me before I was arrested has continued here. Ideas are as scarce as lizard's teeth for me, which was why I took the teaching job in the first place, why I chose to hide myself in the rhetoric of discontent, why I refused to defend myself in court. At the time I was living by myself in one small room, smaller than my cell here in this place.

Now electronic mail comes to me from all over the world, and conventional letters too. A turnkey delivers them to my carrel, or my table, or wherever I am sitting. She does not tamper with them. One day I received an envelope with a disk inside, and a letter: Dear Mr. Bland, I know you will be surprised to hear from me. Sometimes the defense of liberty requires unfair choices. More than anyone, I am sorry about how things turned out. Believe me, when I was assigned to your case, I thought it would be hard to feign an interest in your subject. My supervisor was obliged to remind me several times, in the words of our greatest statesmen, that we all have stories to tell. Still I continued to deny that part of myself. Now my political advancement has been rapid, and I have you to thank. The months I spent in your class meant a lot to me. I'll admit that my first few assignments were prepared by others, so as not to alert your suspicions. But after that I insisted on doing my own work. I hope you noticed the improvement! I always valued your comments, and I tried to thank you in the tone of my report. Even routine bureaucratic tasks can become point-of-view exercises! Things could have worked out a lot worse. I mention this so that you won't think it forward of me to ask you to take a look at the enclosed texts, my final project, which you never had the chance to read before your class was interrupted. I know you have time on your hands. Etc., etc., sincerely L. Raevsky. PS—I recently picked up a copy of *Thirteen Steps*. What an amazing book that is! You must be very proud.

No one testified against me at my trial, but the indictment quoted things I'd said, not things I had written. In my mind I had already identified the informer, a beautiful girl in my ten o'clock seminar. She had golden hair and a developed figure. When I was lecturing on advanced trends in modern literature, I always felt I was speaking to her alone, because she paid such close attention. But now I found I'd done her and her tight sweaters an injustice. Even so, I never would have suspected Raevsky, the salt of the earth, I'd thought— steady, solid, unremarkable, with a background in automobile repair and a wife and child at home. He used to come to class in a necktie. I had always been drawn toward my less talented students, the ones from untraditional backgrounds, as I had been myself.

When I accepted a job at the University of P.R.B., I was in such despair. It was a sad joke to think I had been able to help anyone, even a stool pigeon. I had taken to drinking before I went to class. Then I would listen to myself making the most provocative statements—it was only a matter of time before I drew attention to myself. Once I had told my students to write a description of a party meeting, using actual quotations from various officials as they were reported in the newspaper. Then I had asked them, without changing anything but the point of view, to imagine the same words in the mouths of retarded persons and obsessive compulsives. The meeting had involved metaphors of government and the new uses of fiction, I remember.

Or once I had tried to make the argument that plot itself was an outmoded concept, and that we had to work to liberate our characters from the tyranny of our own will, which so often reflects bigotry, or bad judgment, or even sadism. Nor was it the answer to expose our stories to the whims of readers, as has been attempted in various experiments with "hypertext". That was merely to exchange an authoritarian model with a "democratic" one, with its illusion of consensual control. Instead I looked forward to a new kind of writing, where our characters could achieve their destiny, and torment us and terrorize us in their turn.

An obvious legal strategy would have been to claim that I had meant this literally, not, as it was taken, as political satire. But when I heard my words read back to me in court, I was ashamed. It seemed transparent what I was actually admitting, that I had lost faith in myself. In the end it was impossible for the judge to imagine that the author of such a carefully plotted piece as *Thirteen Steps*—you know the rest. Sometimes it is hard to understand what people say about one's work.

But when I pressed Raevsky's disk into the wooden slot, I saw that he at least in his small, tone-deaf way, had tried to take me at my word. On the disk were two short stories, each about three thousand words long.

The first consisted of a plot without characters. As I have said, Raevsky was a professional mechanic, specializing in transmission repair. Reading with this in mind, I could not but imagine a driverless car. And so then I found his second story must suggest an old-fashioned van with no wheels, parked by the curb, the passengers inexplicably still inside.

I had given Raevsky high marks he had not deserved. Now I imagined a certain masturbatory pleasure in editing his work. As I had once told my class, successful stories often start at the conjunction of two unrelated ideas. I thought if I could force down the accelerator, if I could smash the empty car into the motionless but crowded van, something might happen. At least it would be possible to describe the accident.

Raevsky's documents were called Untitled 1, and Untitled 2. After I combined the files, there was indeed a wreck. Bodies were thrown clear. But one of the tricks of the professional writer is the ability to reanimate the dead. So I was thumping on their chests, running wires from the car batteries into the muscle tissue—you can see this metaphor is not under my control. You can guess the problems I've been having. In fact there was no levity in the way I set about to punish Raevsky's characters and mock his situations—not that I wasn't justified. How dare he send me his ridiculous scribblings? Each story was worse than the other. The first was about a bed. Or it was a description of an empty room in what appeared to be an old hotel. There are traces of blood on the counterpane, which have not yet soaked into the mattress. The pillow is still warm. There is a revolver on the bedside table. The window has been shattered, and pieces of glass lie on the fire escape outside. A letter on the floor begins, "Dear friend: This is so difficult for me . . . " but then the rest of the text is crumpled and obscured. A smell of gardenia perfume lingers in the air. A tiny porcelain dog lies in pieces on the hearth.

It is, in fact, a melodrama with no actors. Are we to assume that Character A, having received a disappointing letter, has come to confront Character B, perhaps at the scene of another guilty rendezvous? Carrying the letter and the porcelain dog, perhaps a memento from happier times, A paces back and forth, while B sits on the bed, terrified, the counterpane drawn up. Then, still unsatisfied, A seizes his or her revolver, and . . . but if so, what has become of these people? Have they exited via the broken window? Or are we, as readers, waiting for the sound of a flushing toilet? We cannot see how many shots, if any, have been fired from the revolver, but perhaps we are talking about a suicide or an attempted suicide, and the victim has just staggered from the room into the hall, where his or her blood is mixing with the pattern on the long carpet.

This mania for fiction writing which has gripped my country is a recent phenomenon. It comes from the top down. Now even some of the trade unions are holding mandatory seminars in characterization and tone. It is because the party chairman, since the attack on his life, now speaks only in metaphors. It is possible he was more seriously hurt than was reported. At first his public statements took the form of fables and parables, which it was still just barely possible to translate into legislation. But now every day his writings have become more complicated and indirect. Has policy suffered? It is hard to say. Luckily we are at peace. But what is clear is that people like myself are experiencing new anxieties. In the current situation, I have become well-known in political circles. There were waiting lists for all my classes by the time I was arrested. At the same time, the pressure to publish has become even more uncomfortable. Already the secretary of the association has given me a deadline for a new submission to the national magazine. He has written me a letter, a description of what has happened to others—household names once, but forgotten now. I cannot but imagine a hollow square of readers dressed in black. They shake their skinny fists and shout while my nominations are trampled underfoot.

My prison sentence is not a long one, and it is necessary for me to consider what might happen if I were to be set free. The secretary is reconsidering my stipend, which so far has not been affected by my legal status. He has enclosed new government guidelines, based on the evolving characteristics of the chairman's work, which specifically prohibit the use of any autobiographical material, or indeed anything in the first person. But as I sit day by day at my long oak table, or in my cell, or staring at the letters on the screen of my processor, all that occurs to me are stories from my childhood, as well as various pornographic images which are equally forbidden. Often these involve the girl with golden hair and extraordinary breasts, whom I had been obliged to chastise in my mind, during the days when I thought it was she who had denounced me. Now of course she has been rehabilitated, which has not affected her state of chronic undress.

I admit I was surprised to see that she was also a character in Raevsky's second story, which took the form of a symposium in the home of a national hero, the author of several famous works of fiction. At his cramped table are seated various students and politicians, all unnamed, but identified by various physical characteristics. Raevsky is one. Another is the girl. There is the chief of the municipal police, whom I remember from the time when he was an ordinary hotel watchman. And in the darkness at the end of the table, overcome by rich food and ennui, sprawls the obese, sleeping figure of the party chairman.

The national hero is a powerful and commanding figure, with a mane of gray hair and nicotine-stained hands. Burst blood vessels on his nose testify to private vices, but in spite of these he is self-confident and virile. He does not lecture his students, but allows them to talk, though from time to time he will interject some trenchant words. His voice is not shrill. It is pleasingly low. Though all her conversation is about philosophical and political topics, it is clear that the golden-haired girl is infatuated with him, and he responds in a paternal, kindly way.

Nothing happens in this story, as I've said. A spaniel wanders in and out of the room. Food is eaten. Cigarettes are smoked. Mineral water is consumed. Platitudes and bromides are exchanged. And there is one small detail which I scarcely noticed until I began to combine this story with the first. At a certain moment, the character I had identified as Raevsky, after recounting an anecdote involving his infant son, reaches under the table to touch the girl's knee. Annoyed, she slaps his hand.

But she does not seem mortified or surprised. Perhaps if the national hero had not been present, she would have responded differently.

* * *

In this context, much of the Raevsky character's dialogue acquires a new, suggestive tone. Was it jealousy, I wondered, that turned the real Raevsky into a police informant? On my processor I began to write a series of sketches, moving the characters from Untitled 2 back through the hotel room, which now I recognized from a monogram on a stained towel thrown carelessly across the bottom of the bed. As soon as I saw it, all the other details now suddenly came back to me: the cracked ceiling, the floral wallpaper, the elegant pre-war furniture. This building, the old Plaza Athenee hotel, still stands near Martyr's Gate, though of course it has been requisitioned for government purposes.

Now I can almost hear the sound of the old piano in the lobby, where on Thursday afternoons I used to wait, breathless with anxiety and guilt, for the sight of my secret friend. She was an editorial assistant in the office of Ullman Freres. She was an acquaintance of my former wife.

These memories, coming on me suddenly as I sit in my study carrel, affect the tone of several of my sketches, especially those involving the girl with golden hair. In the first one I finished, she lay on the bed with the national hero, while the party chairman slumped asleep in one of the armchairs. (He persisted in this pose through several sketches, and he always managed to sleep through even the fiercest action. Nor did he wake up on the few occasions when the revolver was actually fired.) To continue—Raevsky storms in with the letter in his hand, which in all versions now completes a text which my friend the editorial assistant wrote to me years before, and which I still remember word for word. Raevsky confronts his faithless lover, while the national hero suffers a nose-bleed, to which he is prone. Raevsky marches to the window and throws it open, revealing the chief of police crouched on the fire escape, dressed in a double-breasted trench coat and slouch hat. It has been raining, and he is very damp. He climbs into the room, but is astonished and nonplused to see the party chairman in such circumstances. The porcelain dog, which was balanced on the window sash, falls to the ground.

But sometimes the guilty couple is asleep, worn out from their endeavors. The blood on the counterpane comes from the passion of their embrace. Raevsky enters without knocking, and he spends a long time surveying the scene, calmly walking back and forth, touching with the tips of his fingers various objects in the room—the porcelain dog, the gun. He kicks the crumpled letter with his foot. Neither the party chairman nor the chief of police makes an appearance, though they are mentioned in brief, impressionistic flashbacks.

In some versions, these scenes of mine acquire a certain poignancy. But there are others, I'm ashamed to say, in which the girl with golden hair is forced to disrobe, and she is shamefully assaulted by Raevsky, the party chairman, the chief of police, even the spaniel on one disgusting occasion. Her cries are heard by the national hero, who bursts in with a revolver. He shoots, to no avail. Sometimes the bullet shatters the window . . .

One very short scene involves the dogs confronting one another, one porcelain, one real. And in one, the party chairman lies sleeping in his armchair with the spaniel curled up on the hearth rug. The twitching of the chairman's right hand, the dog's left foot, reveal their dreams. The blood, the smell of gardenias, are unexplained.

Perhaps, I thought as I was working, Raevsky had given me a new way to write about the past, a way to write about myself and still maintain the new guidelines. Perhaps, I thought, I could even publish some of these sketches, especially the ones in which the golden-haired girl did not appear. Perhaps I could find a new approach to autobiographical material, in which characters from my past and even I myself are carefully, even lovingly described, and then put into artificial situations. Perhaps also one could imagine a new kind of pornography, appropriate to the guidelines, in which one describes only transitions between scenes of terrible excess.

And I was wondering also if, in his benighted way, Raevsky was giving me these tools deliberately, as an expression of remorse. Certainly it had been years since I had worked on anything so feverishly as on these sketches. I was just attempting one in which the chief of police finds himself in what he first interprets to be a compromising position with the party chairman, when an icon on my processor screen started to flash. It was the stork with the baby in its beak, a signal that I had received electronic mail.

The processor is of an old design, a screen ten centimeters square, forming one end of a long rosewood box. I speak letters and punctuation marks one by one into a small tube, and watch them appear hesitantly on the screen. There is no modem or keyboard, as I have seen on various newer models. A single wire connects the box to a hole in the linoleum floor.

"Open," I said, and I heard something rattle in the tin drawer, which hangs down from the bottom of the box. I unhooked the clasp, and the drawer sagged open, revealing some pieces of paper, folded together many times into what was almost a cube. Opening it gingerly, still I couldn't help tearing it along the folds. Finally I was able to separate it into three pages of lavender note paper. I did not recognize the handwriting, which was in purple ink.

The letter was written in English, which I read only badly. Here is my translation: Mr. Bland, some of the things you have written are so terrible, I can't even understand them. I have appeared in over a hundred stories, some by authors even more celebrated than yourself. Until recently I was not even required to take off my shoes. Knowing your reputation, I explained very carefully to Mr. Raevsky what I would and wouldn't do, etc., etc., Miss. M. E. H., Society of Fictive Artists . . .

The icon flashed again, and again I unhooked the tin drawer. This time there was a shorter note, also in English, written in soft pencil on the back of a laundry receipt: I've been rubbing the damned pine in too many damned stories lately, so let me tell you I was promised a speaking role.

Rubbing the pine? I have no idea what this means. One of the turnkeys brings me a dictionary of idioms in the English and American languages. As it turns out, the phrase is an allusion to a certain game. "Held in reserve," would be an adequate translation.

A third time the icon flashes, and something clatters in the drawer. This time it sags down by itself to reveal a hardened pellet of dog feces—no, I put my head down on my desk and weep. An artist like myself is not insensitive to criticism. Better than anyone else, I know when my efforts at characterization, based as they are on former students and people I have scarcely met, are unconvincing and unoriginal. Yes, it's true: I have borrowed characters, in some cases, from other people's work. Better than anyone else, I know these sketches of mine have not attained the standard of realism which I established for the first time in *Thirteen Steps* and then maintained in several later works. It is not necessary for me to receive these complaints, here, now. But how wonderful it would be to find in my tin box a word from an actual human being, not these trained animals and hired hacks. At that moment I would have given anything for a word from the golden-haired girl, or even the miserable Raevsky! Critics had praised my earlier work by saying that it had duplicated ordinary experience so precisely as to render it superfluous. There was no reason, for example, to attend another dinner party after reading my description. Couples interested in maintaining a social schedule might read the same passages to each other every Friday and Saturday night, and stay at home. There was no reason for them to have affairs, get divorced, or sit drinking coffee and smoking cigarettes on rainy afternoons.

What I would have given at that moment for a word from my old friend, the editorial assistant at Ullman Freres! Or rather, that's the way I still thought of her, though in fact she had married again, had children, grown older, risen (I had heard) to a high position in the party hierarchy. Still I remembered the smell of her perfume. What was it called? And then a cold feeling came over me as I tried to imagine the scent of gardenias, which of course do not grow in my country. All this time in my sketches I had been mentioning this smell, mixed sometimes with that of gunpowder. But as is so often the case in second-rate fiction, these are just words. Now a bell in my processor signals a new message, and the tin drawer opens. The dog feces are gone. Instead there is a blue apothecary's bottle in the bottom of the drawer. There is no reason to open it, because at that moment my small carrel (indeed, I imagine, the entire prison library) is overwhelmed by a heavy, pungent, acrid smell. The hand-written label on the bottle reads: GARDENIA/CORDITE.

"If you want the truth," I spell out letter by letter, punctuation mark by punctuation mark in to my tube, "let me tell you I'll die first."

The party chairman was found slumped over at his desk, a gun in his right hand, a copy of *Thirteen Steps* on the ink blotter in front of him. In fact (it was claimed in an official editorial) this book had been responsible for many suicides, as readers came to wonder what could possibly happen to them, that had not been more vividly and accurately described in print.

The party chairman did not die, of course. He shot himself through the roof of his mouth and still managed to miss his brain. In a sense, he has recovered fully. Nevertheless it is a cause for national concern, how much he still might be affected by these complicated modern texts. When it was discovered that the author of the book had sent it to the chairman as a birthday gift, the government requested a charge of attempted murder. But the letter which accompanied the book, which reminded the chairman of unfortunate events and begged for his intervention with the national editorial board, was of course suppressed. As a result, a judge discarded the indictment. Assassination cannot be an accidental process. As usual, the court's decision satisfied no one.

Less ambiguous was a case still unsolved after many years, in which a jealous husband was shot to death on the fire escape outside his wife's hotel room. An obvious suspect in the murder had been an important national figure, the woman's correspondent, who had not been brought to trial. Many people at the time assumed he had been protected by powerful forces. The question now was whether that protection would persist, after the attempt (as it was called) on the chairman's life.

This was the case that still bothered me. Now, sitting with the smell of gardenias and cordite all around me, further details came back. I began to speak into the tube. But now the bronze letters on my screen did not follow anything I said. Instead, slowly, they spelled out a memorandum addressed to me from the secretary of the national association: We insist that the date we gave you for a new submission must remain firm, if your annuity is to be continued. We have heard you are working on something new, a credible account of certain terrible events. We would be interested in publishing this project and no other.

It is obvious that they have becomes impatient with me, impatient with the sketches I have written so far. They want to restrict my choice of characters to the people I knew best: myself, my friend, her husband. The date the secretary refers to is today, which gives me one more hour: ample time, especially since I have not written anything since that April afternoon ten years before, when I had stood in the hallway of the old Plaza Athenee, off Schubert Square. Various aspects of my life had come to an end that day, but nothing new had started. Until I received the summons from the university, I had spent ten years in my little room, scarcely going out except to shop for cigarettes, whisky, and breakfast cereal. For ten years the only fiction I had written was in the form of desperate letters to the association and to certain national figures, imploring them not to terminate my stipend but indeed rather to increase it, for the sake of my past work. I had written to the chairman himself, praising him yet threatening to reveal certain details of our shared history. I had enclosed my book. I had meant no harm. But after the chairman's accident, the authorities had pried me from my room like a conch out of its shell. Agoraphobic, semi-retired, I nevertheless was forced to give lectures to classes of forty or a hundred students, some of whom would interrupt me with applause, especially if I chanced to say something "revolutionary," or specific to current events. Nor was I able to discover who had hired me, or for what purpose. It was easy to imagine that the government might want to strip away my tiny shelter and expose me. On the other hand, the "opposition" now considered me a hero, especially after the text of my letter to the chairman was revealed. Based on it, someone had requested an investigation.

This is what I said in my lectures: the only way for authors to surrender their authority is to tell the "truth"—that is, to set their work in that strange, foggy landscape, in which both character and author are equally blind. If the party chairman was the "author" of the nation, as he had recently claimed, this was the landscape in which he was most readily confronted. Now I must admit that these words had been scripted for me, though by which political interest was unclear.

I imagine that after ten years of falsehood, no evidence remains. Without some kind of confession, the chairman's name cannot be cleared, nor can I be punished for the harm I did to him. But if I give them what they want, perhaps they will be grateful and not keep me here. They will renew my stipend. No doubt they are only interested in destroying my reputation. After all, we are talking about something which will appear in a fiction magazine.

But how unfair this is! The woman in the case was given a political appointment, though I hear now she has fallen out of favor. The hotel guard was made a police captain. Only I, who suffered most, was given nothing. Every day I was forced to live with the humiliation, the memory of that long walk down the hall with the porcelain dog (a gift from her, which I meant to throw down at her feet, or else lay down carefully on the bedside table) clutched to my breast, together with the crumpled letter.

And now I must admit that I am glad they are only interested in a false confession, a fictional account. I will consent to nothing that makes me sound ridiculous, or makes me play the part that I was actually obliged to play. Some things are worse than being thought of as a murderer.

Now, tired out from my imagining, I begin to spell out in third person my final sketch. There are certain details I must make clear. The porcelain dog now falls from the window sill. The text of the letter on the floor remains obscure. I cannot explain why I should possess a gun or why I should have brought a gun to a romantic encounter, but a skillful writer knows what to leave out. I make much of my confusion, my desire to protect as, woken from a guilty sleep, we see a dark shape at the window. We hear cries of anger, a hammering on the glass. It is all over in a minute.

As I write, the image of the golden-haired girl, which has been so real to me, now floats from the bed and disappears. Lying in her place is the elegant, frail figure of my friend the editorial assistant, now a high official. She is dressed in a white camisole. She reaches out her hand to touch my face, and it is as if no time has passed. I find I can no longer see in my mind's eye the picture of her sitting up in bed, the counterpane around her naked shoulders. She is screaming, but I can't hear her. I have burst in with the hotel guard, but I can't see him, nor the unmistakable and already quite fat young bureaucrat who stands facing the broken window with the revolver in his hand. All that lingers is the smell of cordite and his foul cologne.

tachycardia

I retired from the Corps of Engineers when I was 65. During the afternoons I'd play golf at Colonial or City Park. I'd have lunch with friends, or dinner and a couple of drinks. Then I'd go home to my house on General Pershing Street and turn on the lights. I kept that place as clean as a hotel. After Mary Elizabeth passed away, I took down most of the photographs, cleaned out most of the things.

It says in the Bible that death can come at any time, so you might as well not fret about it. I was on the seventeenth tee at City Park. I sat down on the grass, because I was dizzy and my pulse went to 250. That day I was paired with Bobby Squires, who's a doctor I've known for years. He drove me downtown to his office at University Hospital—the old Hotel Dieu on Tulane Avenue. I hadn't been there since Geoffrey was born. In half an hour I was on a table in the emergency room, and the technician was putting in a drip.

Bobby explained the whole thing as I lay there with a needle in my arm. There is an amino acid called Adenosin that stops the heart. After eight seconds they switch to saline and start it up again. Usually that takes care of the problem, which is called tachycardia. But my heart was still roaring even after the procedure, so they decided to try it a second time. I couldn't breathe because of the pressure in my chest, and I passed out.

How can I describe what I was feeling? Your heart stops, and everything is still.

My wife once read a book that says you hang suspended in the air above your body. I thought that was ridiculous, even at the time. I was sitting in the dirt, rubbing my knees and the backs of my hands, and then my chest and thighs.

It can be painful to grow old by yourself. If you outlive the members of your own family, you've lived too long. Now my heart was quiet, and I didn't breathe. I sat until my eyes were accustomed to the darkness. Smells came to me—mold, concrete, a trace of urine. The dirt under my hands was clotted with spider web, and it seemed to me that I could hear the whining of a mosquito.

Now I could see the limits of that place, a concrete box about ten feet square. The ceiling was low, and I didn't want to stand. Instead I crawled forward on my hands and knees. There was a gray light that got stronger as I crawled toward it, though it remained indistinct and didn't throw off any kind of shadow. It wasn't until I reached the opening that I understood why. The concrete passage to the outside air was narrow, and it turned back on itself in two ninety-degree angles. Squatting on my haunches, looking back toward where I had been sitting, I saw deep, horizontal slits in the wall above my head, blocked, I imagined, with vegetation or debris. I could see now where I was, a concrete pill box or bunker, with walls many feet thick. And though I understood the principle of the entrance, I was not prepared, as I turned the corners, for the brightness of the outside air. As I crawled out into the open, the brightness was like a punch in the nose, and my eyes were watering.

As I had had to get used to the darkness, now I got used to the light, which took a longer time. I collapsed onto my knees and forearms and put my head down. I could see that I was wearing my golfing clothes, and my hat was on my head. My shorts and polo shirt had seemed appropriate to a fall day in New Orleans. Abruptly, now, I felt like a fool.

There were huge, shaggy trees all around me, with roots like the fins of a rocket. There wasn't much undergrowth, and the ground was dry. Through the tree trunks I could see the ocean. Except for the entrance, the pill box behind me was obscured with moss and hanging vines, masses of purple flowers.

I've spent a good amount of time in the swamps of Southeastern Louisiana. We had a camp near Slidell. But this was not like that. The smells were different. And the bugs as they lighted on my skin—I didn't recognize them. They didn't cause me any trouble. My golfing shoes were full of ants that didn't bite.

I got up and staggered to the shore. Leaning on a tree, its bark as smooth as skin, I shaded my eyes and looked out toward the sun on the water, which was like a mirror. There was a mud cliff that was subsiding into a swamp, and then the open sea beyond. There was no wind.

As we get older, it gets easier to summon dreams and images from the past. After a moment, I thought I'd figured out where I was. My father's older brother had been a captain in the Marines. He'd had a stroke after he retired, and when I was a teenager I used to go visit him in a nursing home in St. Bernard Parish. It was a depressing place, but he'd taken a shine to me, and I'd sit by his bed and listen to him complain about "that faggot, Douglas MacArthur," as he called him. He'd tell me stories about New Guinea. I knew about the Japanese defenses, the mangrove swamp where my uncle's unit had been pinned down. "It was a day in hell," he said.

All that was long ago. The place was empty now. After a few minutes I turned away from the shore and followed a path through the bushes.

When my son Geoffrey was a little boy, on weekends I used to take him down to Audubon Park. Right by the zoo there is a stand of oak trees, and we used to play a game. He would toddle off into the undergrowth, and I would count for a minute and come after him. Usually I'd find him hiding about twenty feet away in some obvious place, or else standing in plain sight. But one day he disappeared, and after a few minutes of searching I was yelling as hard as I could. I assumed he really was hiding from me, even after I told him the game was over. But what had happened was this: He had fallen into a hole where someone had buried some illegal trash. He was up to his waist in the debris. And though I had passed within a few feet of him, he had been too frightened to cry out.

What is it that brings certain memories suddenly to mind? My son. Maybe the image of his face is never far away from me. That day my threats had not consoled him. Terrified, I yanked him out, and his leg caught on a piece of metal. He had to get a tetanus shot.

Why do certain images come to us, whole and complete, as if out of the air? Is there always a reason? Maybe this was my train of thought: There were some sounds from jungle animals I couldn't see. Maybe there were some monkeys crying on the other side of the fence, which separates the park from the zoo. Now, as I took the path away from the shore, I thought about the animals my uncle had told me about, the ones he had seen in the camp near Buna in New Guinea, or else heard crying in the darkness. Why are they so frightening, the dangers we cannot see? In my son's face, even up to the last days, I could not guess what he would do.

Though I could hear the noises, I myself could make no sound. When I stumbled at the bottom of a small ravine, I opened my mouth and no sound came.

I had fallen to my hands and knees, and hurt myself, which surprised me. There were big stones and a small trickle of water. I barked my shins and scraped my palms. I found myself staring down at an imprint in the mud, a foot mark that was filling up with water—an animal, a dog I thought, though it was bigger than any dog's foot mark I'd seen. I felt no fear, even when I looked up. I was not capable of movement. I tried to speak, but there was a pain in my chest. My hat was gone, and I lay on my back at the bottom of the ditch.

And when my eyes had cleared, I saw that I was looking up at a human face, a black man. I have always been a prejudiced person, but I was happy to see these fellows—there were several of them. The sunlight was behind their heads. It slanted through the tall trees. They were primitive people who wore shells around their necks, and they squatted over me. Then I felt them help me to my feet, and they were pushing me through the long leaves, and I could feel the pain in my chest. Then they laid me down and left me, and I turned onto my side, and I could see Geoffrey, my son.

He was about twenty feet away. He was standing inside a bamboo cage, dug into the slope so that only the top third of it rose above the surface of the ground. I lay in a kind of a dell that had been cut into the raw earth. I lay on wood chips, and near me was a campfire.

I rose to my knees and tried to speak, but no sound came out.

"Geoffrey," I tried to say. He wasn't looking at me. He was staring through the bars of his cage, his arms as thin as the sticks of bamboo, as they had been toward the end. Surely he'd been mistreated. The fire was smoking. On a stump near the fire lay an army helmet covered with netting and leaves.

Who had done this to him? What enemy had attacked us? I tried to speak but could not. Geoffrey stared listlessly away.

There was a pain in my chest. Still I managed to crawl forward and reach out my hand. "Geoff," I tried to say. But then there were some explosions that shook the ground, and I dropped down into the dirt. When I opened them again, I was lying on my back on the table in the emergency room, the needle in my arm. My heart was beating at a normal rate.

"Jesus," said Bobby Squires, "I thought we'd lost you. You were gone for over two minutes. They had to use the paddles."

"I need more time," I said, which he misunderstood.

This was after they had brought me upstairs to his office to recuperate. I was in a wheelchair, though I felt fine. Bobby was going over my prognosis, and telling me to quit drinking and the little cigars I smoke. I'd heard it all before. I take medication for high blood pressure and high cholesterol, and he was telling me about that. He wanted to keep me overnight in the hospital for observation and tests, but I said no. I wanted to get home.

Later I sat on the back porch of the house on General Pershing Street, drinking an Old-Fashioned. My wife used to make them for me, but she'd left the recipe, and to tell the truth, they tasted better now.

This was the house we'd moved to when Geoffrey was about six. He'd gone to school around the corner. Looking out over the back yard, I could picture him playing in the dirt between the chain-link fence and the gardenias.

Everything had been fine for a long time. I was working hard to put food on the table. I'd have to go up to Baton Rouge.

So then he went away to Grinnell College, which is not what I'd wanted for him. He had excelled in high school, and I guess he expected to excel there too. This was in the late sixties. He had what you might call a nervous breakdown, although I never called it that. But it was enough for his deferment, and after that he came home to live. I admit I was unsympathetic. He was my only child. I wanted what was best. Looking back, knowing myself, it's hard to image what I'd do differently. Nowadays, of course, you can cure any of those mental problems with a few pills.

A few days after this experience with my heart, I went out to the camp north of Slidell in the Honey Island Swamp. I hadn't been there for almost thirty years, since Geoffrey's death. It had been an important place to him and me. Now, after my experience in the hospital, for the first time I understood why the pictures in my mind had been so vivid as my uncle told his stories about New Guinea. There was a stretch of shore near the cabin—I could see it now. For a long time it had been hidden from me by some trick of the mind. Instead of cypress, I had put in mangrove trees. I had made a steeper slope above the beach. And of course I had put in a whole ocean, the Solomon Sea, I guess, instead of the wide, brackish waters of the river.

But the shape of the land was the same. Only the scale had changed. Perhaps when my uncle described the place to me, he had allowed the image of that shore to supplement his memory—he also knew the place well. Whatever the reason, as I came in over the old road, I thought about what I would find. I parked the Caddy at the turnaround, then got out and leaned against the hood for a while. It was evening time, after a clear, dry day. There were some lights at the neighbors' house, where Mrs. Douglas lived year-round.

Some cousins of mine still used the camp on weekends. I walked down the dirt path and then onto the bridge. The cabin was built on stilts over the water, a one-room, tin-roofed shack with a deck on three sides. There'd been some new work on the place, and it had been painted green, though not recently.

There was a padlock on the door. I couldn't see anything through the windows, just some boxy shadows, though the table was the same. No one knew I was coming. Most of that part of the family, I hadn't spoken to in years.

The water was low. I lit a Dutch Masters to keep the bugs away, and sat out on the deck, dangling my feet, looking back toward shore. There was a new boathouse in the trees. After a while, I unwrapped a pint of bourbon, which I had mixed in the bottle with some of that Old-Fashioned syrup. I wasn't taking any of my medications, but even so, the doctors had warned me how it could be years before I had another episode of tachycardia. I could die first, which didn't interest me.

The water lay black and flat to Honey Island. It sucked at the pilings. I finished the cigar, then walked across the bridge, around past the new boathouse, down the slope onto the strand. It was an odd feeling—a place I knew well, except I hadn't been there in over twenty-five years. Weeks together in my childhood, long weekends with Geoffrey or alone, then nothing.

The shape of the shore was just as I remembered it. The creak of the dry mud underfoot. I walked toward the fallen cypress where they had found the body. It had washed among the cypress knees, under some bushes that overhung the water. No current to speak of—a dry, November night like this one. He had been drinking, they said. Mary Elizabeth was with me, and when we were driving back to the city from Slidell, suddenly we hit a squall over the lake. The streetlights and the raindrops on the windshield made a pattern on my wife's face.

I have had good luck in several aspects of my life. The worst things are not failures, but what can't be helped. My wife was religious at one time, which was no consolation, even though her priest was a reasonable man. The teachings of the church are clear. It is a sign of God's love to be able to help others. We would have done anything.

Geoffrey had gone up to the cabin for the weekend to think things over, after I blew up at him and told him he couldn't live with us anymore. He had to get out on his own. The police said his death was accidental, which I didn't believe and neither did Mary Elizabeth—that's what ate her up. Now I stood on the same shore where he had stood. Next time, I thought, I would not be unprepared or empty-handed. I would do my duty as a father and a husband.

But of course I had a long time to wait. It wasn't until June that I experienced my second episode of tachycardia. I had been drinking some, and my blood pressure was high. "You look terrible," said Bobby Squires. It was the first time I had seen him in months.

"Just a little more time," I said.

When he finally understood what I was asking, he shook his head. "Are you crazy? We're not going through that again."

He didn't have a choice. I passed out in his office, and when I woke up I was lying in the darkness on a concrete floor. There was a smell of varnish in the air, and I knew where I was.

There was a pirogue on saw horses, a line of brilliant light under the door. As before, everything was still. I lay on my stomach for a moment. But I had no time to waste. I was afraid the boathouse was padlocked on the outside. Then I put my hand against the door and it swung open.

The light was so sudden, it brought tears to my eyes. The grade was steep, and I pitched downhill onto the strand. The sun was bright on the water. It was the middle of the day.

I was afraid to raise my eyes and look. The water was a few inches beyond the toes of my loafers. I studied the tassels of my loafers until I couldn't bear it any longer, and then I looked up. He was there, half-submerged under a cage of branches among the cypress knees. At first I thought he was just floating on the current, but then I saw him move his hand. I saw his head come up, his bony neck and long wet hair.

"Geoff," I said, and I could hear my voice. I felt in my pocket for my wife's pruning shears, which I had brought with me, along with several other tools. As I got close, I could see Geoffrey was caught. Something had him by the leg. I waded into the water and saw that his pant leg was caught on a submerged log, and he was yanking at it occasionally, trying to free himself. There was no urgency to any of his movements. Most of his torso was above water. He was lying in among the roots of a submerged tree.

He had on one of those colored shirts I used to hate. It's funny how you forget. Was this really how it had happened? He had just flopped around like a fish until he died? It was pitiful. The tide never ran more than a few inches here. Sure he was drunk, but that was no excuse. I saw his bony face with his cheek next to the water, his lank brown hair. He had been a strong boy, an athlete at Jesuit, but as he lost weight those last two years, his mother's weakness had come out in his face, her fine bones. His skin was paler than mine, dusted with red freckles. He'd gotten too much sun. It was a hot day.

He was pretty well caught. There was a hole in his jeans, and the cloth had twisted itself around a jutting stub of branch. The water was dirty and full of weeds. I worked at the wet denim with the garden shears until it gave way. All the time, Geoffrey was looking at me stupidly.

Like his mother, he was myopic, and his glasses had come off. It took him a while to figure out who I was. Then he was angry, and he tried to pull away. "Shut up," I said, as I was dragging him out of the water. "Enough of this crap. I'm taking you home."

He hadn't shaved. He smelled of whiskey and the swamp. I pulled him up by the collar of his shirt. He was twenty-three years old, and like a child. "Your mother will be worried stiff," I said.

"Leave me alone."

I wasn't having any of that. I pulled him toward the cabin. "Let me go. I can take care of myself," he said, which was ridiculous. I didn't have to answer. I didn't have to be his friend. But I wanted to get him away from that place where he had died. I kept in my mind the beach from my uncle's story, the camp deserted only for a moment. The camouflaged helmet on the stump.

Geoff was filthy and he stank. "Come on," I said. "Let's get cleaned up. You must be thirsty," I said—he was very frail. I put my hand around his upper arm and led him up the slope. There was an empty bottle in the mud.

"Where are my glasses?" he said, and I picked them up. But I wouldn't let go of his arm until I had brought him up the slope past where the boat house had been, and over the bridge to the cabin. It was the same weathered gray that I remembered, and the deck was broken in along one side. The screen door was ripped, and behind it the door stood open. There was Geoffrey's old rucksack on the bed, and clothes strewn around, and dirty dishes in the sink. "Let's clean you up and get you into some dry things," I said.

All that had happened between us, I know it was my fault. Mary Elizabeth used to tell me I had worked too hard when he was young. She didn't say so at the time. This much is true—the problems we had, I didn't see them coming. Now I poured out some water from one of the ten-gallon jerry cans into a pot in the metal sink. He wiped his face with a dishcloth while I looked at the calendar for 1973. It was from a car dealership off Chef Menteur. Beside the stove pipe, thumb-tacked to the wall, was a grocery list in my handwriting.

Geoffrey was quiet, and I turned my back to let him peel off his shirt. "You are a son of a bitch," he said, finally.

I glanced at him, then looked into his eyes. Clean-shaven, with a haircut and some meat on his bones, he would have been a fine boy. Although my heart was quiet, still I had an ache in my chest. The truth was, the whole time he was a kid we'd gotten along fine. There hadn't been a lot of talking, which was just as well. You can never figure things out just by talking. We'd gone to Pelican games on Saturday afternoons and never said a word. Later I'd taught him how to catch a fish, how to drive a car.

I hoped some day he'd remember some of those things. It didn't matter now, and there was no reason for me to get angry. In the back of my mind I knew we were in danger. There was no time for him to speak before I smelled the fire.

Someone had lit the deck on fire, torched the bridge. I tried to go out, but the heat was intense. It was unnatural the way the whole thing went up. The deck surrounded the house on three sides, and I stepped between the bed and the table to the window at the back, which looked straight down over the water. I broke the screen out of the frame and called out to Geoffrey, who was rummaging through the rucksack on the bed. The fire was bursting through the planks over the sink. The calendar curled up, dropped off the wall. And Geoffrey wasn't moving. He had his rucksack in his hand, and he was looking toward the open door, which was full of the roaring flame. I grabbed his wrist. The heat was intolerable, and I couldn't be gentle. I climbed over the sill and bundled him down into the water, which was about five feet below the sill and about five feet deep.

He wasn't resisting me. He followed me down and then I pulled him into deeper water, because I was afraid some of the beams of the house would fall. Then we paddled a little way downstream where we could touch the bottom as it rose onto a shoal of mud, thirty feet from the bank. The heat was on our faces as we squatted down to watch the burning house, and also of the woods behind it catching fire, and the fire moving up and down the shore along the dry ground. There was fire on the other side of the river, too, and the sky darkened. Clouds came in, and a stiff wind, and it was dark except for the fire along the bank. There was all manner of scrub trees, but the treetops were dark and the tree trunks silhouetted by the flames, because the fire seemed to burn only low along the ground. So it got dark. The beams of the cabin collapsed into the water in a gust of sparks. The water was cold. I put my arm around Geoffrey's shoulder, and was surprised to find him heavier and more solid. He held onto my arm, and I could feel him being pulled away, as if there were something in the water that was holding onto him. I didn't have the garden shears any more, but I had my sheath knife attached to my belt, and I pulled it out and hacked at the water while Geoffrey clung to my neck. All this time the wind was coming up, and there were waves on the river. The clouds were ripped to pieces overhead. I took hold of Geoffrey around the waist and brought him over the shoals onto the bank. The mud sucked at my shoes. The rain came toward us over the water, and it covered the fire and put it out, and we had to take shelter in the trees. Around us was the crash of breaking branches. I put my forearm over my eyes and then took Geoffrey by the hand. He followed like a boy, and I led him up the slope and through the smoking woods to my old Caddy—not the hunk of junk I own now. This one was solid as a tank, which was a good thing. I pushed a fallen branch off the roof, opened the door, and Geoff slid across the seat, and we were safe. The keys were in the ignition. The Caddy started up.

Then we were driving through the dark, and after a while the rain stopped and the wind quieted down. Geoff snuggled up against my side, and then he lay with his head on my knee. He didn't say anything, and after an hour or so we came into the lights of the city. He was lying on his back with his head on my knee, looking up through the windshield and the light was on his face. I drove right downtown. I parked the car on Tulane in a no standing zone, then carried Geoff into the Hotel Dieu, and then upstairs. I had him against my shoulder, and I was supporting his head. I knew the way. There were double doors to the maternity ward, and I went into the big room, and there was Mary Elizabeth looking as pretty as I'd ever seen her, though she was tired, and her head was against the pillows. But her face was glowing. I put Geoff into her arms, and he curled up contentedly. He hadn't cried the whole way. He was a good boy.

But I was a mess, and I didn't belong in that place. Mary Elizabeth scarcely glanced at me. Geoff had curled up under the covers, and there were some nurses giving me rotten looks—black women—as I say, I've never had much use for those people, though I've known a few. I didn't see a reason to stay, so I went upstairs to Bobby Squires's office. I didn't have to wait long to see him, just a few minutes, which was just as well. I had a pain like an elephant on my chest. "Christ Jesus," said Bobby—he was pretty shaken up. But after a few minutes I felt fine again.

Afterwards I walked down to the Quarter, which was the first time I had been there in years. But it was a beautiful evening. I walked down Canal Street and across Royal, and found a little outdoor place near Jackson Square, where I could drink a cup of coffee and smoke a cigar. There were some bands playing for the tourists in back of the cathedral. I sat there for forty-five minutes or so, listening to the music and watching the people walk by. There was an Oriental girl with hair clear down to her behind. And I just sat there and sat there, and in my whole life I never felt so good.

christmas in jaisalmer

"For a quarter, any idiot in America can ring a bell in my house," Marcia's father once said. John always avoided calling, even when things were good. But Christmas morning he goes down from the fort to the post office telephones in Kanti Path to see if she got in okay, to say hello. By the time he gets a line it's after ten o'clock at night in the US. The phone rings several times.

"Hello," says Marcia's mother. But there is something wrong with the connection. "Hello," she says, "who is this please?" John can hear perfectly. She, nothing at all. He yells into the phone for a few seconds until the Sikh in the next booth looks towards him, smiling, and puts his finger in his ear.

John listens to Marcia's mother turn away into the kitchen. There's a kind of a window above the sink. It lets into the dining room, and he listens to her put her hand upon the sill. "It's him again," she says. "Nothing," she says, in answer to a question. "Although it sounds . . . "

He listens to Marcia's father put down his book and get up from the couch. John hears his footsteps, then his voice: "Listen, please stop calling us, whoever you are. It's Christmas Eve." They live in New York City, near Columbia.

Then Marcia picks up the extension in her room. "Mom," she says, "is that long-distance?" John hangs up the phone and spends another half an hour not getting through, not getting through.

Then he walks out into the hard glare. The wind is full of dust. Several rickshaw wallahs swoop toward him, ringing their bells; he puts on sunglasses, then turns back toward the old town. Crossing the road, he feels weakened momentarily by a swell of pure sensation—the diesel fumes and the soft tarmac, the traffic noise, the smell of garbage, smoke, incense, urine. A movie billboard shimmers in the heat.

He buys an orange from a sidewalk vendor and feeds the peel to a cow. Near the bus stop he picks up a saddhu, who comes with him a few blocks, not smiling, not talking.

The saddhu is a middle-aged man in yellow robes, carrying the metal trident of Lord Shiva. His hair is long and wild, his brow is marked with charcoal. At the temple in the Mall he stops by the elephant-headed statue, and raises his hand in farewell.

In December, Jaisalmer is full of pilgrims. There is a lake in the desert four miles out, with bathing ghats and a big Shiva temple. But in the old town there are many smaller shrines. On that morning John stops by certain places on the way back to his hotel. The Swastika Cafe. The Mona Lisa. Marcia and he had sat there at that table by the curb. Back in the city after an absence of two weeks, he visits each one in turn.

He walks up the causeway to the fort. He pauses by the sandstone gates. Was it here? A tout had come, desperate to bring them to his brother's sculpture studio. Rejected, he had turned abusive. "What are you doing in my country?" he asked—words which made Marcia cry, here by the iron door. "I feel like they all want a piece of me," she said. Later: "I can't tell what they mean."

John walks through, and up into the narrow streets of thousand-year-old houses inside the fort. Each street with its pie-dog who can smell a foreigner a hundred yards away; he passes through successive zones of barking. Ramesh is waiting for him at the corner.

"Marowitz," he says, "that Dutch fellow is gone. You can take your old room back."

John had arrived the previous night from Jodhpur. It was the last leg of a three-day trip from Delhi, where he had put Marcia on the plane. Ramesh had not been at the station, nor at the hotel. Now he comes forward with his hands outstretched. "Marowitz," he says. "My heart is glad."

He calls John by his last name, a habit he's adapted from novels about English public schools. "And your wife," he says. "Did she get off?"

Ramesh looks elegant in a white shirt and pressed pants. "Where did you go last night?" asks John.

Ramesh shivers ostentatiously and rubs his arms. "My uncle died a year ago. I was at the ghats for the anniversary. Bathing, you see—an ancient custom. I believe I caught a chill."

They walk together up the street. At nine o'clock it is already hot. John's t-shirt is sticking to his chest as they come to the stone porch of the hotel, as they climb up to the room where he spent the night.

Already the houseboy has cleaned it out. He is on the third-floor landing with the whiskbroom in his hand, touching his forehead until Ramesh shoos him away. Ramesh stands in the middle of the floor as John loads his backpack. Then they climb up to the roof, up to "the penthouse," as Ramesh calls it—a stone chamber with two rope beds.

John goes in. Ramesh stands on the roof under the clotheslines and watches him through the open door. John puts his pack against the wall. He sits down on the left-hand bed, where he and Marcia had made love so many times.

"You are comfortable here?" asks Ramesh. "You are our only client now. Therefore our number one priority."

Not so often, really. Some days it had seemed too hot, too difficult. Some days when the sweat had beaded on her skin and in her hair, and he had been content to look at her. Wastefully, foolishly, criminally content, unable to predict the obvious.

"It's fine," he says.

"I think you could be staying at the Laxmi Niwas. I think you would prefer some running water or a w/c."

"They don't have the view." Sitting forward with his elbows on his knees, John bows his head and runs his fingers back through his hair. Ramesh moves to the edge of the roof and looks out over the desert.

The Palace Hotel has been open less than a year. Peacocks are carved on its exterior, but inside it is dark and dusty: unimproved, unfurnished, unpainted sandstone rooms around a square well. It is built into the wall of the fort, which itself is on a hill above the city. You can see for thirty miles from the roof, all the way across to Pakistan.

"It was my uncle's house," says Ramesh. "My father did not want to leave it empty. It was not my idea—I was in school. What can I do? We have no capital, you see."

This subject—the lack of capital—feeds often at the surface of Ramesh's conversation. It comes up momentarily and then sinks down: now Ramesh points toward the horizon. "Will we go to the tombs today?"

"I'd like to, yes."

From the rooftop, they are a line of nineteen boxes on a dry red hill.

In the afternoon, Ramesh and John leave their rented bicycles and walk across the hard salt pan. Ramesh, who was in his last year at Benares Hindu University before his father pulled him out to manage the hotel, is knowledgeable. "This is the tomb of Udai Singh IV, who was poisoned by Aurangzeb," he says. Four marble columns support the marble roof. Inside, sand has accumulated in the corners. There is nothing else except two feet side by side, carved into the center of the floor.

It is the seventh tomb in the line. They sit down on the porch, in the shade. Ramesh is smiling. He is holding a school satchel in his lap. He says, "In Benares, often in the morning I was praying to Lord Shiva. But sometimes also to Lord Jesus Christ—I like this fellow too. Tell me Marowitz—December 25th, is it a national holiday for you?"

John sits back against one of the columns. "It's Christmas."

"Yes. I told this to my mother. She and my smallest sister made this food for us. Holiday food, you see—halvah. Also burfi and rasgullahs for our festival of lights."

He takes from the satchel a damp paper bag. And then he lays out on the step an assortment of small cakes wrapped in newspaper. John takes one. It is incredibly sweet, incredibly sticky. The rosewater runs down John's arm.

He offers one to Ramesh, who smiles and wrinkles up his nose.

Ramesh sits with his legs crossed, his fingers clasped around his knee.

He seems anxious, until John has eaten at least two cakes from each pile.

"In India," he says, "for Divali we sing songs."

This is a favorite game with him. During the past month, John and Marcia have taught him cowboy songs, folk songs, workers' songs. He is tone deaf, but his memory is good.

John sings "Silent Night." He fakes most of the words. Ramesh leans back against the step and nods his head. When John is finished, Ramesh sits with his eyes closed for a few seconds. Then he claps his hands.

"Bravo, Marowitz," he says.

They are looking towards the city, surmounted by the golden fort where the brahmins live. "All calm, all bright," he says. And then: "Is Mrs. Marowitz with your family today?"

"No." And then: "She's not my wife."

Ramesh smiles. "She is your mistress," he says after a pause. He knows about mistresses. At school he was reading D. H. Lawrence.

"No. She's just a friend." John is thirsty. He tries to wipe his hands off with a piece of newspaper. They are sticky with the sugar juice.

"Ah, Marowitz, you and I are friends. But a woman, it is not like this. My fiancee . . . "

He frowns, purses his lips. "Although friendship is important," he says. "Do you know why I brought you here, to this tomb in particular? I was here last night, after my bath."

He laughs. "Oh, I was cold. But hot in here," he says, his fist over his heart.

"I saw her."

John is surprised. Ramesh has told him many times how careful he must be. The wedding is two months away. Still, were he even to exchange a letter with the girl, his father might demand a bigger dowry than her family could pay.

"But what about the old man?" John asks.

"Yes, the greedy bugger. I decided it was worth the risk. We are modern people—it is right for us to talk. To be friends. I have this photograph I showed you. It was not enough. Ah, Marowitz, you see how you inspired me. I had my brother-in-law speak to her sister."

"Were you alone?"

"Who?"

"The two of you. Last night."

"Of course not. We are not like you and this woman. We are conversing only. We are sitting side by side, right here." He rubs the step with his delicate long hand.

He gestures for John to take another cake. "Why do you hide these things from me?" he says. "Good friends can trust each other. They do not have these secrets. Why did you not tell me what this woman was to you, this Marcia? Hah," he says, cocking his head. "Perhaps because you do not know yourself. To you these things mean nothing."

John wipes his fingers on his jeans.

"Why do you hide these secrets from me? Last night my father asked me your profession and I couldn't say."

"I told you. I work in a bookstore."

"This cannot be true," says Ramesh. "You are a man of wealth. You are a man of education. You have your degree. I was thinking we could be in partnership."

John shrugs. He looks down at his feet.

"The Palace Hotel requires renovation. But it can be a fine establishment."

"Things are different in America," says John, not looking up. But he can feel a pressure on his face as Ramesh looks at him. It is strong at first, then less, then nothing.

"So we can agree to disagree. Marowitz," says Ramesh, "we cannot quarrel. I forbid it." He jumps to his feet. "Come," he says, "I have a Christmas present. For you and for me too. Come. It is a surprise."

He looks at his watch. Suddenly he's in a hurry, packing up the remains of the sweets, and then he's off down the steps. It's half a mile back to where they left the bikes, and though the sun is now subsiding, John has a hard time keeping up. There is a sugar crust over the inside of his mouth.

At the road, Ramesh takes off, pedaling hard. John follows more slowly. By the time he reaches the Atlas rental stand in Ashok Marg, Ramesh has disappeared, though the bike is there. John pays for them both, and then climbs up the causeway. Ramesh is waiting at the gate. "Come quick," he says. Then he's off down the narrow alleys, dodging the cows. The Palace Hotel is to the right; he goes left.

"Wait," says John, laughing, out of breath. "Isn't this her street? You're not supposed to be here."

Ramesh turns back to him, laughing too. He takes him by the elbow. "Yes, of course," he says. "It is forbidden. But you are a tourist, you see, in my hotel. I must conduct you where you wish to go. I have no choice in this." He indicates the wall which hangs above them. "This part was renovated in the 16th century."

The houses, their sandstone fronts ornately carved, lean out over the street, blocking the sun. Now Ramesh walks slowly, stopping often to point out some detail. But he turns his face away from the last house. He moves past it through a small stone gate, which leads them to a bastion in the fort's curtain wall. There, a cannon points over the desert.

John walks out to the bastion's lip and looks down over the sheer wall. There is a village of untouchables. A boy leads a donkey by a rope.

The sun is low now in the sky, only a few inches from the hills. It is sinking in a layer of dust, above a line of camels in the distance. Behind John, the yellow walls of the fort seem to glow, as if they themselves were a source of heat, of light.

John and Ramesh stand side by side. Ramesh's eyes are fixed upon the sun. And it is only through a difference in his breathing that John understands something has changed.

After a few minutes, John turns his head. At the top of a thirty-foot wall above them stands a girl. She is dressed in red, with a red shawl over her face. She too is staring at the sun. She does not look down. At a certain moment, she strips the shawl away.

self portrait, with melanoma, final draft

I was able to retire when I was forty-five, thanks to the development of several new applications. People asked me whether I'd be bored. But for me working had always been a means to an end, something to give me the time and freedom to achieve certain values that had always been more important than any job. I'm talking about the world of art and ideas, which is in some ways the only "real" world. I have always understood where my chief talents lie. It was my creative thinking that got me in on the ground floor of certain developments in software—ideas that literally came to me in the middle of the night. My idea of heaven was always to sit in my office and dream. Instead it was the rat race I found tiring, the commute, the competition, the infighting. There was nothing about my job at Macrosystems that I was ever likely to miss.

Since college I have enjoyed painting watercolors for my own relaxation. Over the course of several years I had finished a series of seascapes at Point Reyes, and once I prevailed upon senior management to allow me to have a show in the conference room. I sold nearly every piece, but even so, I wasn't satisfied with technical mastery. I was looking for something else. Often I imagined there was something inside of me trying to break out, something that would enable me to express myself and also to attempt some universal themes. I'm talking about how a person can overcome an illness and a difficult childhood and yet still manage to make a contribution and achieve success, even in today's economy. This is an important lesson for people who are just starting out.

Of course it was the particulars that would make my story unique. Themes have to be approached indirectly. So I sat down and started thinking about the crisis periods in my life. This was in the house in Palo Alto, the summer after Jean and I split up. At night I managed to maintain a social schedule, but during the day I was mostly alone. I am a disciplined person, and I quickly established a routine that was comfortable to me: up at six, three mile run, etc. And though I was sometimes discouraged by the difficulty of this new work, still in a way I was happy just to try and fail, to participate in something so challenging, even when I was suffering from "writer's block." Because in fact it is almost impossible to do justice to the complexity of real life, to imagine things—a conversation, say, or a telephone call—not necessarily from my own point of view. I have always been blessed with a strong memory, but I soon found that this was only one of the skills that goes into recapturing the past. There is also, paradoxically, the ability to invent. Finally, as in business, you have to be able to distance yourself, separate yourself, make yourself cold even to subjects you care passionately about.

I can't pretend this was all I did, every day. I like to meet new people and spend time outdoors. But during that first summer I persevered, and by the end of it had managed to produce a half a dozen stories. I thought two were better than the rest. One was about the Macrosystems buyout, which had happened the previous winter, just when my wife and I were realizing our marriage was over. The other was about a summer long before when I had been sleeping with two women at the same time.

One night a week I took a writing class at the Stanford extension school. Later, sometimes I took the teacher out to dinner. She was the first person who suggested I send my stories out for publication, though to tell the truth, I wasn't satisfied with them. They seemed too "flat," too obvious. But maybe my standards were higher than any potential reader's, because I better than anyone understood how complicated the original events had been. Amy said it was a trap to think your stories were never finished, never good enough, and you ought to begin sending out your work as soon as possible as a matter of routine. She gave me some names and addresses, and on my own I ordered subscriptions to some of the leading periodicals, including *Plowshares* and *Story Magazine*.

It was the editor of *The Arkansas Review* that sent me my first personal rejection, which Amy assured me was some kind of milestone. I mean instead of just a form letter. By now the class was over, though Amy and I were still seeing one another. She was a beautiful young woman just out of graduate school. Her skin was very pale, and she freckled easily in the sun. Sometimes we would drive over to Half-Moon Bay.

Part of the letter read:

> ... I'm not sure what kind of game you're playing; I'm just sure I don't like it. Is this some kind of experiment in metafiction? Writers sometimes produce stories that amplify and comment on other stories (though usually they choose an author better known, not to mention more firmly deceased, than this one): *Grendel* and *Mary Reilly* are two obvious examples. But I've never heard of anyone who would bother to submit a flimsy paraphrase of someone else's work to the same place that published the (vastly better) original. [...] So Mr. Dandridge (or whatever your name is), if you are trying to make some sort of obscure and humorless fun at our expense ...

I didn't show this letter to Amy. Instead I went to the library and looked up the back issues of *The Arkansas Review*. And sure enough, in Volume 18, Issue #2, I found that a man named Jaime Goldberg had already written about the Macrosystems buyout in a story called "Soft", published that spring.

And the editor was right. This was the better story, because it was more complete. I had written mine in the first person. But this was a third person narrative, much richer and denser, and involving several minor characters. By contrast, mine read like a sketch. For example, here is a paragraph from the first pages of "Soft":

> The house was an old one by Palo Alto standards. It was built in the thirties in the Spanish style: white stucco and a red tile roof, and a long wooden gallery overlooking the garden. The neighborhood was pretty, and convenient to the campus, where once she had imagined she might find a fulfilling job. Now, tonight, between the third vodka tonic and the fourth, she was able to remember these things, before self-hatred gave way utterly to rage. She was able to remember how her first sight of the house had filled her with a sense of joy, of love for Roger and an instinct for her own potential. It was only later, standing alone in the night under the whisper of the fan, her silver rings digging into the gallery rail, that she imagined that the house had eaten and digested her, or at other moments only slightly less fanciful, that the yellow, thick, encrusted plaster walls formed a stifling and protective cocoon.

Here is the corresponding section in my own story:

> That year I was finally able to buy a new home with a balcony, which was a detail I'd always wanted.

I had been surprised when my wife decided to leave Palo Alto and take an apartment in Berkeley. I'd always assumed I'd lose the house. Could I have invented all her feelings from the expression on her face when I'd offered to move out? I had tried hard to imagine how she felt sometimes when we were having our problems, or I'd had to work late. But I'm not sure what kind of insight would have led me to suspect a drinking problem now. Nor had she once expressed an interest in any job of any kind.

Later, after I was able to distance myself, I decided I didn't like Mr. Goldberg's use of commas. The whole thing seemed a little overwrought and sentimentalized—in fact it's hard for me to recapture what I felt. But I'll say this—I was furious. I supposed that a lot of the ins and outs of the buyout had been covered in the industry press and was a matter of public record. I knew there'd been an article in *Wired*. But I could only assume that Mr. Goldberg had been in touch with my ex-wife and some of my ex-associates, had soaked himself in their side of the story, and had produced a work with themes very different from the ones I had envisaged—I don't know. Amy says I think too much about control. "Just let it come out by itself without trying to push." I tell her that's what my proctologist says, too.

Worst of all, Mr. Goldberg had used my wife's and my real names. I imagined talking to a lawyer, when something else happened to make me pause.

"Soft" ends with Jean moving out of the Palo Alto house after Roger has confessed to some extra-marital affairs. But it is told in retrospect from the vantage point of maybe a year later when the divorce is coming through. Jean writes Roger a letter, which says in part:

> . . . so now I hear you've been going around with some anorexic blond number about half your age, an MFA yet. It's hard to imagine she knows what she's talking about. Isn't that what writing is, being a good judge of character? I swear I don't know how you do it. I suppose all that money doesn't hurt, but that's not really it. I can't believe there's still more to you than meets the eye. And I don't know why this still hurts me, but it does. It always will. Because I know with you it's always going to be the same old crap forever . . .

I had scarcely heard from my ex-wife since we split up. But the odd thing is, I did get a letter very like this only a few days later, while I was wondering if I should get in touch with her myself. The letter wasn't exactly the same, of course, not as well-written, but close enough. Yet "Soft" had been published months before, probably written months before that.

Amy Koslowski had gone to the writing program at Stanford, one of the most prestigious in the country. She was a highly competent young woman. She was a natural blonde, but she used henna on her hair, which gave it an unreal, reddish tint. No, the money didn't hurt, but then it never does. I could tell she was genuinely fond of me. We played racquetball, went for walks along the beach. And she certainly gave me lots of free advice about my writing. Of course I wondered sometimes if she really knew me. She had read my stories, but not Goldberg's. And as it says on the second page of "Soft":

> . . . He had the kind of sunny, bone-headed good looks that many women find reassuring. To Jean, coming away from such a long depression, he seemed too good to be true—tall, athletic, a powerful and relentless lover, yet someone who couldn't help but admire a woman like her, because of all the qualities he lacked. [. . .] But she soon came to realize that he was like a blind man who has learned to compensate, that he had a combination of deviousness, mendacity, and narcissism that allowed him to function at the highest level without any brains at all.

This was closer than anything I had written, but it still missed the point. There's a great advantage in being underestimated, as I'd learned at Macrosystems.

The Arkansas Review was published from Fayetteville. I was intrigued by the editor's use of the phrase, "more firmly deceased." It made me think he knew Jaime Goldberg personally. So I called directory assistance for the numbers of everyone with that name in northwestern Arkansas. It wasn't a long list. I soon found the man I wanted. He answered after a few rings.

I didn't give my real name. I told him I had admired his story in *The Arkansas Review*. At first he pretended not to know what I was talking about. But when I persisted, he laughed and said the only reason "Soft" was ever printed was as an act of charity. The editor was trying to help him with his medical bills, owed him a favor before he actually died—he was very forthcoming. In fifteen minutes I knew a great deal about him. Like most writers, he loved to talk about his work: "I was trying to do something a little different. But I'm not sure how it came out. To tell the truth, the subject got away from me."

By "subject," he meant the theme. "The character was too likable," he said during our second conversation a few days later. "I was trying to express something about the sheer hypocrisy of people, how they can ruin the lives of everyone around them and not notice. You know, stealing other people's ideas and then not even realizing when he was basically fired. But there was something innocent about him, about the way he took his compensation in stock options for those years when Macrosystems was worth nothing. In some ways he deserved to end up with all that money."

"I found that poignant," I said.

"You're kidding. Christ, even I wouldn't go that far. But like I said, something else was coming out without my knowing."

"You seem to know the software industry," I said.

He laughed. "I don't know shit about the software industry. And you know it shows: I couldn't come up with even one technical detail. I don't even have e-mail. But I just can't stop thinking about this schmuck, I don't know why. I'm telling you, I dream about him."

"You must have done a lot of research . . . "

"What research? I made it up."

"Well, but you know Macrosystems is a real company. There really was a situation with an employee named Roger Dandridge . . . "

"Christ, you're kidding. Luckily no one reads *The Arkansas Review*. Luckily I'm dying. What did you say your name was?"

I repeated the name I had first given him, which was that of the protagonist in my story. "Well, that's very nice," he said. "Will you excuse me? I have to take some pills and then throw up."

I spoke to him several times over the phone. Goldberg had cancer. "Everybody thought it was AIDS, but don't you have to have sex for that? No, the stupid thing is, I never even smoked. With me, everything is second-hand."

"I'm sorry," I said.

"No really, thanks for talking to me. I've been very isolated. And please, don't aspirate so much when you say my name. My mother called me 'Hymie' until last year. I was always a baby to her. That umbilical cord? It was made of iron. We were like two people on a chain gang."

"Where's your mother now?"

"Dead, and it's a good thing too. This would have killed her. Ha, ha, ha."

In fact the flattest characters in fiction are more complicated than people in real life. Hymie Goldberg was a bizarre kind of cliche, as if he'd been formed out of other people's prejudices. When I thought about him, it was hard not to imagine him short, bald, and ugly, with a big nose and soft, childlike hands. I imagined a small apartment filled with cheap antiques and bric-a-brac and dying house plants. I imagined a lampshade with a beaded fringe.

He was an out-patient at Washington Regional hospital in Fayetteville. Since he had no insurance, Medicaid was paying his bills, which didn't allow for much in the way of home care. I imagined being able to change that. I imagined sending him a check so he could hire a private nurse.

"Why are you doing this?" he'd say. "What did you say your name was?"

In fact it wouldn't be that much money. I was amused by the idea of a fictional character coming to life to comfort his creator. Or if you put it another way, a real person being able to comfort a fictional creation. "It's because I admire your work," I'd tell him.

All this time I had been seeing Amy Koslowski. With her help, my writing had improved. Look at the following paragraph:

> She stood naked by the window in the long afternoon light. I could see where her skin was roughened by the time we'd spent outside, even though she'd worn sun block. But she hated hats and wouldn't wear them, and as a result her cheeks now seemed to be covered with white dust, under which her burnt cheeks shone. That was in contrast to the rest of her body, which was a ghostly pink, all spattered with freckles and moles. She had worn bicycle shorts that left her knees uncovered, and there too the skin was burned and chapped upon the knees themselves, while behind them the soft skin was streaked with drops of water from her shower. How beautiful she was, her small breasts and flat stomach. She rubbed her short red hair with a towel, yet even in these simple movements she seemed tired and stiff. When she turned toward him and held out her hand, there was something careworn in the gesture, something guarded and self-protecting in the curl of her arm, though in another way she seemed to be revealing something too, a pregnancy, perhaps an illness.

There you see. The point of view has almost disappeared. Distance is the key. It's what you have to learn.

I remember the day when she was reading a story on my bed. She was lying on her stomach, dressed only in a pair of blue striped boxer shorts. I sat down beside her and put my hand on the small of her back. She said, "I was looking forward to the time when you'd stop writing about yourself."

"And you."

She shook her head. "You've written about my body. You've never written about me."

"Hey—we write what we know." I slipped my fingers under the waistband of her shorts.

"I don't like this part," she said. "He sounds like such a cliché."

She indicated a paragraph with her thumbnail. The protagonist is sitting in his small apartment, surrounded by 19th century photographs, gilt-edged mirrors, and Victorian bric-a-brac.

"There's such a thing as going against type," she said.

"It's just the way I see him."

"That's a surprise. But you know it's such a clunky device, to have him look into a mirror."

"Physical descriptions are difficult in first person," I said.

"Tell me about it."

"This guy is the only Jewish faggot in the Ozarks," I said. "You don't think he's aware of playing a role?"

I slid my fingers into the crack of her thin ass. Later I revised the story according to her specifications. Hymie became Jaime again, and I took out much of his distinctive way of talking. But still she wasn't satisfied. One morning, dressed in a gray t-shirt and nothing else, she sat sprawled in a leather armchair, letting the pages drift one by one onto the floor.

She made a face. "It's still too static—something needs to happen. Someone ought to go and visit. Not just phone calls, but something personal. You know, bring him some soup or something. Not this boring fool—what's his name? Didn't you use that in your first story? You know, the one about the buyout."

"Yes."

She frowned. "So what are you trying to tell me here?"

"I don't know. Maybe I don't ruin everything I touch."

"Hmm," she said, "now there's a worthy theme."

Then, after she'd read a little more: "You say this is Fayetteville, but it could be anywhere. There's not a single detail. Or one: 'Washington Regional Hospital . . .'"

I shrugged. "It's a college town."

I suppose the narrative could be classified as fantasy. A writer is thinking about someone who might not be real. Or else a writer is inventing a character based on interactions with a real person, and at a certain point the character comes to life in a way a real person cannot. There are chunks of a new story embedded in the text, a story within a story that becomes the story itself. The moment of transition is made slippery, because of the use of painkilling narcotics. Here it is:

> When I felt stronger I sat up, and sat looking at my reflection in the mirror for a long time. Then I put my hand out and put it on the surface of the glass, hiding my face. Looking down, I saw the paper on my bedside table, the paragraph I'd been working on before my last attack of nausea. What was he like, the man I was describing? I pictured him shaving for some reason, or maybe having shaved—staring at me as if into a mirror, caressing his slippery jaw. There is a towel around his neck. He's in his early forties. His eyes are deep-set and his jaw is

strong, but his face is dominated by his high, sharp-bladed nose, and
the wide, waxy slope of his bald head. He has a small moustache which
he is trimming now with what look like surgical scissors . . .

I take up my pen now to continue, but there is a knock at the front door. I
have left it unlocked for weeks now, to save me having to answer it. Whoever
it is seems to know this and pushes the door open. I hear the rustling of a coat,
and then footsteps down the long passage. The sound hesitates at the bottom
of the staircase, and for a moment I imagine a stranger, someone who doesn't
know I have moved out of my bedroom into my study on the first floor. For a
moment I imagine I don't recognize the steps. Having just raised my eyes
from the description of my protagonist, for a moment I imagine that it might
be he. But it is only Amy, my student, who has paused for a moment to negotiate her burden through the passageway into the living room. I've given her
my unlisted number and asked her to call first, but she never does. Now I see
her through the double doors, carrying soup in a round Tupperware container. And now I am reminded what I should be writing instead of these stories I will never finish: her recommendation to the Stanford graduate program while there's still time, and I can still remember her work. Would she be
this solicitous if she knew I hadn't done it yet? Would she smile hesitantly and
then pause with that expression of uncertainty? No, of course she loves me,
and they all love me. It's just that she can't get used to how much I've
changed, my beautiful hair all gone, my face so wasted that it seems all nose
and eyes. "I've brought the mail," she says, peering at it nearsightedly and
then telling me what I've already half-guessed, that the important-looking
letter on the top is for Hyman Goldberg who lives down the street, and who
routinely gets my mail while I get his.

Amy sits down beside me on the side of the bed, exhibiting the brave desire to be close to me that I am used to now in other people; if I were well, she'd
never sit so close. And she starts talking about this and that, the soup and the
mail still in her hands. She's a charming girl, really, slightly chubby, very shy,
with wire-rimmed glasses and soft shoulder-length brown hair, streaked
with pale gold now in the morning light, which slants down out of the high
windows. She's looking out into the garden and seems distracted by the sight
of goldfinches around the bird feeder; "What a beautiful house this is! You
must love it. Is Alexander going to live here?" she says, meaning my son. But
then she stops short, embarrassed.

"I don't suppose he will," I say.

She peeks at me sideways while I examine the backs of her hands. Her skin is covered with red freckles. It is so pale that it seems thin to me, stretched too tight over her sharp finger bones, and for a moment I imagine it to be entirely transparent, and I'm looking down as if through a tight plastic membrane, Saran wrap, perhaps. It keeps in place the green blood vessels and the red proliferating ones. It keeps in place the mottled sinews, the pink bones.

Now she tries to make up for what she said before, which I imagine she imagines showed a lapse of faith. "I mean until you're feeling better . . . "

"I'll feel better once I'm dead," I almost say, but stop because she has tears in her eyes. Very carefully, she puts the letters down on the quilt next to her leg on the side away from me. She puts the soup down too. Then she takes some bunched-up kleenex from the sleeve of her cardigan. For a young woman, it seems oddly old-ladyish to keep it there.

In fact as I look at her, as I think about that gesture, memories of her work come back to me: artful stories she submitted during the fall semester. They are stories about herself: her problems with sex, her ambitions for the future, her fear of pain. In one, her mother tries to comfort her during a childhood illness by bringing her a series of inappropriate gifts. In another, she is mistakenly locked out of her parents' house, and spends the night alone in the woods when she is nine years old. In a third, her father takes her duck hunting, and she watches the ducks come crashing down out of the sky. At the time I tried to tell her how you could sometimes bring things closer to yourself by bringing them farther away. I'm not so certain of that now.

"I just wish I could do something for you," she says. "I wish I could do something just once. I feel my life has just started and already it has gone so wrong."

Again, this is quite typical. People's emotions come to the surface around me. It is a recent phenomenon: my sickness brings up something to the surface. Then they find it easier to talk about themselves, and so do I.

I'm not feeling very well, and I ask her to help me get my feet up and lean back against the pillows. Now I can look at her more easily, as we are no longer sitting side by side. I ask about her boyfriend, a computer science major named Robert or Roger or something like that, but she gives a quick, dismissive gesture. Things are going badly, I guess. Robert or Roger has always been quite rude to me, whenever I have seen him around campus.

So then we talk about her work, which is easier. I am interested in the story she's submitted in her application to Stanford, because in a sense it's about me. For the purposes of making fiction, she has taken my illness and put it onto herself. I, in the story, am quite well, a robust, attractively professorial figure who sometimes visits her in hospital. I am touched by how much she has bothered to learn about radiation and chemotherapy, though in the story her cancer is of a different type from mine. The scenes in Washington Regional—a depressingly run-down facility—are vivid and well-drawn. She's captured perfectly the boredom and embarrassment of the disease, the impossibility of really talking about it, the way the mind tries to invent other topics, other futures for ourselves, even when there are none.

I am less convinced by the future she's come up with, an extended fantasy which threatens to over-balance the real story. In it the narrator is already a successful fiction-writer living in California. She's having a sort of quizzical affair with her student, a middle-aged tycoon and would-be watercolorist. She has grandiose ideas about the power of fiction, its ability to redeem human beings, change the world. "Isn't this fellow too much of a cliché?" I ask.

"Isn't he a little crude? Don't you think it might be better if . . . ?" I ask, but she's not listening.

"Maybe you should try one final draft," I say, as if to myself.

"Just one more should do it." But I don't think she's listening. She's looking out the window at the goldfinches. What's the good of talking? No, illusion always takes on its own life.

"It's just I'm so afraid," she tells me, and I reach out to pat her hand, not knowing what to say.

This is how her story ends, if I'm remembering correctly.

Editor's note: Amy Koslowski died in Fayetteville in the spring of 2001 after a long illness. She was a senior at the University of Arkansas. This story first appeared in *The Arkansas Review*.

if lions could speak:
imagining the alien

(Author's Note: This text was first presented at the Max Planck Institute in Berlin, during an investigation of human origins at the 2001 Summer Academy.)

Many have written on this subject to confess failure; who am I to claim success? The objections line up like policemen: Alien intelligence does not, in fact, exist. So when we try to describe it, our thoughts do not connect to any object except ourselves. The words we put into an alien mouth, the feeling into an alien heart, the tools into alien hands, what can they be but imitations of our words, feelings, tools? Even if we could conceive of something different, how would we communicate it so human beings could understand? And if human beings don't read our work, how can we expect mass sales?

You cannot think of something outside human thought. On the other hand, the concept of alien intelligence is what animates a great deal of science fiction, and the elusive goal of describing it is something almost every writer tries. Often you can see the way the story bends back in frustration, turning toward the human once again. The alien intelligence becomes part of the landscape, something to be experienced or overcome, something to show us aspects of ourselves. In the range of science fiction literature, certain broad groupings suggest themselves, which nevertheless have this aspect in common.

For example, you have the They Come Here story, in which a technologically superior species arrives on Earth. Ordinarily, this species is aggressive. Often, not to put too fine a point on it, they are a race of homicidal maniacs. Initially at a disadvantage, humans eventually prevail because of some emotional quality, some aspect of "humanness" that the invader cannot match. Self-congratulation ensues.

Alternately, you have the We Go There story, in which we hold technological superiority over some simple, inoffensive race. Often we split into two camps—those who advocate violence and those who don't, and the narrator of the story is in this second camp. Paradoxically, the more he knows about the alien, the more he is able to affirm his own most "human" instincts, which eventually prevail. Self-examination ensues. In both these types of story, though—there and here—whatever growth takes place is human growth. The alien learns nothing.

Those are two large groupings. Here are two more:

Sometimes when a writer conceives of an alien species, she will extrapolate what human beings would be like if they shared the alien's morphology. The writer asks herself: What would it be like to have two heads? Or six sets of opposing genitalia? Or a life span of a thousand years? Sometimes this morphology has been arrived at conscientiously, by which I mean the writer has paid pseudo-scientific attention to the conditions that produce these adaptations. And sometimes the morphology has been selected at random, or for dramatic effect.

Alternately, the writer will imagine a human being with one psychic or emotional quality exaggerated, or added, or removed. That is, the aliens will be quite like humans but for their enormous physical cowardice, say, or diffidence, or sudden rages. Or else they will be just like you and me except for their telepathic abilities, or the fact they have no soul. Aliens of this type are often physically similar to human beings, but for one trivial difference. They might, for example, have pointed ears.

These two groupings—the extrapolation from bizarre morphology and the almost-human—we will refer to with some oversimplification as the American model. Again, to oversimplify: American science fiction tends to be plot-driven, and aliens of the type we have described fit neatly into conventional plot situations. That is, the alienness of the alien can take its place among the many aspects of the story, without threatening to overwhelm it or make the plot irrelevant.

Let's call the second category the European model, thought the more I think of it, the more foolish these distinctions seem. Never mind—we will be disciplined and persevere: In the European model, the strangeness of the alien and our inability to understand it becomes the center of the story. If the writer doesn't mind this happening, great things are possible: the sentient ocean in *Solaris*, for example, or JH Rosny's crystal cylinders, illuminated with flashes of light. Inescapably, though, these things are viewed from the outside, as impenetrably exotic. Lack of communication becomes the theme of the story, and all other plot elements and resolutions fall away. And though you've avoided the problems of anthropomorphism, its sentimentality and intrinsic falseness, you are no closer to describing or communicating alien intelligence. You're just sloughing off the work onto your readers. In fact . . .

* * *

At this point I could feel anger stirring up within me at the thought of these lazy European writers. I looked up from the draft on my computer and saw Laura standing by the hall doorway. It was late, and I was at my desk. She had been watching television—I had been aware of it from time to time: laughter, applause—and now here she was, standing in a white nightgown. She had come to disturb me, which was a relief.

All day I had been suffering from an irregular heartbeat, brought on, I thought, by the stress of abstract thinking, which is not natural to me. I had not told Laura about my symptoms, because of her hypochondria. Still, it was a relief to have her near me. If worst came to worst, she could drive me to the hospital. But how pathetic it would have been to suffer a heart attack at my desk, while my wife sat oblivious in a downstairs room!

She said nothing at first, but just hung and flickered in the doorway while I pretended to work. I didn't look up. I couldn't meet her eyes. She and I had had an argument that day. I was going to Berlin and she resented it, resented the fact that I had made my plans without her, without indulging in the fiction that she might have wanted to come too. But for a year her illness had been getting worse, and for the last six months she'd cancelled out of everything without warning at the last minute: even a visit to a friend's house or, most recently, a trip to the movies. Irritated, I had made a single set of airline reservations, which had wounded her. It was as if I had no faith in her, which I didn't. And of course, she dreaded spending a week by herself.

Now I felt guilty for ignoring her as she stood there. And I ignored her because I felt guilty about the airline tickets; psychosomatic or not, her symptoms were real. It was true. I should have pretended to have a little more faith.

"Are you coming to bed?" she asked, and I tried to figure out what she meant. Did she mean she wanted me to come? Ordinarily I would have thought so, but there was something in her tone to suggest she might have been attracted to the idea of lying sleepless under the sheets while I worked in another room. Maybe she could come and hover over me at two in the morning or at four, each time more distracted and disoriented, each time grimacing in the harsh electric light.

While I sorted this out, she disappeared into the bathroom. I sat back in my chair. But my train of thought had come derailed, and besides, feelings of hopelessness were now threatening to overwhelm my argument. How could we talk about this subject in a world where other human beings are such a mystery, where we have such trouble understanding ourselves? To write about our own feelings ten minutes ago is an enormous imaginative leap.

As if released by this impulse of negativity, new thoughts occurred to me. I had been avoiding them, because my plan for my paper was an optimistic one: to begin with protestations of impossibility, while at the same time suggesting or even showing how alien consciousness could plausibly be rendered. But my optimism depended on not remembering, on looking squarely to the future. Years ago I had written a novel, for which I'd had high hopes.

Most of my books are not started with any ideas in mind. But this one had an idea, a plot, which I wrote out at the beginning. I was to write the definitive story of alien intelligence, and my plan was this: During the course of the book, the viewpoint character was to undergo a transformation from human to alien, and was to bring the reader with her into a progressively different consciousness.

On another planet, long colonized by human beings, a member of a native race has been turned into a human woman, through gene splicing, plastic surgery, and most importantly through psychotropic medication, which she takes daily. This medication closes down certain areas of brain function, and smoothes out what remains into the normal spectrum of human mental activity. This woman is in the social elite of her own race, whose unmedicated members are terrifying and incomprehensible to her, as they are to us.

But at the beginning of the novel, this young woman's supply of medication is cut off. By the end of it she is a different kind of creature, who thinks in a different way. Because she is the viewpoint character, the reader is able to witness this transformation from the inside, and to adjust to it. My idea was that anyone who picked up the book and tried to read the last chapter, say, without reading the rest, would find it literally incomprehensible. A new vocabulary of words, feelings, and concepts would have gradually been introduced.

The published text fell short of these ambitions.

Now I found myself listening to the sound of Laura cleaning her teeth. This was an elaborate process, lasting ten minutes and requiring specialized

IF LIONS COULD SPEAK

equipment. The sound of it exasperated me—strange gurglings. When I had first met her, she had brushed her teeth like anybody else. In every respect she'd been a normal person.

Soon she stood barefoot outside the threshold once more, leaning against the doorframe while I looked up and smiled. "How's it going?" she asked.

I shrugged. "I wonder if I should talk about *Coelestis.*"

"I loved that book."

Startled, I looked up. What did she mean by this? She stood shivering in the doorway, her hands clasped around her elbows, though I didn't find it cold. "It didn't get to what I wanted," I said.

"What do you mean?"

"No conceptual breakthrough."

She laughed. "You're lucky that's not why people read."

Irritated, I said nothing, and she went on: "Stories aren't the place for conceptual breakthroughs. People read to feel things, and that's different from understanding them. Maybe it's the opposite. If people cared about understanding things, they'd read academic papers for fun."

"Well, an academic paper is what I'm writing," I said. "I'm trying to say stuff people don't already know."

"And how's it going?"

I did not dignify this question with a response.

Laura came into the room. She pushed some of my papers aside and curled up on the bed behind me. Her feet were long and thin as she drew them up. "I can't believe you're going to Germany in the middle of the summer," she said. "That's when it's so beautiful here."

I swiveled my chair around to stare at her. There were some pieces of notepaper beside her, which she was brushing off the pillow. She picked one up. "'If lions could speak,'" she read, "'we wouldn't be able to understand them.'"

"When in doubt, quote Wittgenstein," I sighed.

The trouble with Laura, and the central problem in our relationship, was that she was much more intelligent than I. "Or the opposite of Wittgenstein," she immediately countered. "Anything that can't be said, you must express obliquely—that's what I'm telling you."

Laura suffered from insomnia, among other complaints. Exhausted during the day, past midnight she was taken by a hectic energy. Under the bedside light her cheeks were flushed, her fingers restless. She had a habit of playing with a curl of hair under her ear. Her eyes, as she looked at me, were focused and intense. I imagined if she'd sat down at that moment to write "If Lions Could Speak", she'd have been finished in about twenty minutes.

For most of her life, her critical skills had been directed outward. She'd helped me understand the world, myself, even my work. But in the past year I had watched her turn these analytical weapons against herself, resulting in terrible damage, I thought, though she would not have said so.

Independent and skeptical by nature, now she had acquired a psychotherapist, an acupuncturist, a masseur, a support group, and an herbalist. It was as if she were a temperamental racing car, requiring a team of specialists to keep her on the road.

Unemployed now, she had lost interest in her surroundings. And I too, since I'd come to rely on her, felt sometimes I was wandering in a fog of social currents, liable to hurt myself on objects that loomed suddenly. So it was with an apprehensive sort of relief that I now listened to her reach out tentatively into the world of ideas, where she had once played happily. "You know fiction is an indirect art form. It's not good for talking about politics, or theory, or conceptual ideas of any kind. Or else it pretends to talk about those things since none of its real subjects can be communicated plainly—I mean sensation and emotion. It's like a magic trick. You show something in your hands, and you try to make it beautiful. But the power of what you're doing comes from something else—I swear to God, you know this! Why are you patronizing me? Don't patronize me." And she burst suddenly into tears.

It is at moments of shared pleasure or pain that we feel closest to other people. But when someone is seized by an emotion that we cannot share, then it is easy to feel alienated. I sat in my chair, rocking slowly back and forth, studying the tears on Laura's cheeks, her brimming eyes. At such moments I was aware of my own body—the feel of the chair under my sweating palms.

Most people are familiar with how, after a few simple repetitions, an ordinary word like "helmet," say, or "nice," can lose all meaning. The words Laura spoke now seemed like that to me. Baffled, I stared at her mouth, which was beautiful and full, with beautiful big teeth.

"Sometimes I don't think you are a real human being. I talk about sensations and feelings—I mean, are there any feelings here at all? Why don't you say something? Please say something. You seem so far away from me right now."

Studying her, trying to understand her, my work was compounded by a further disadvantage, which will not take the acute reader by surprise. Laura was right—there's nothing human about me. I am a hollow man, a circular façade. You might say even the concept of "Paul Park" is an erroneous one, a role I am less and less competent to play. Heart pounding, I sat immobile in my chair, as if her words had reduced me to catatonia. Perhaps they had—it wouldn't have been the first time.

When I say "hollow man," I mean it literally. At certain moments I am like a captive inside myself, my humanity frozen and constrained in a small space. Impotent, I watch while all the functions of my body are carried out by others. I watch them creeping up and down my synapses, moving my lips and tongue and hands. When they turn away from those tasks and fall to arguing among themselves, I can do nothing.

"I just wish I could feel some sympathy," Laura said. "Just some human warmth. I know you're tired out by all my issues—well, so am I. Do you think it gives me pleasure to go over these same things over and over? I wake up in the middle of the night and I'm suffocating. That's why it hurt me so much for you to announce you're going away without me. Because I'm afraid you might never come back. And if you really did leave me forever, that's just what you'd say. Just straight out cold like that: 'I'm going by myself.' There'd be nothing to discuss."

What was she talking about? At such times I feel inside of me a cacophony of voices, which started when I wrote *Coelestis*, years ago. "Nice book," they said. "Bad book." During the hours I spent breaking my head against the problem of alien intelligence, it was as if I'd opened myself to tiny emanations from above. In time they came to live in me, more and more because I'd welcomed them in. I'd given them small, cute names. Because they were, or so I thought, the product of my own imagination, I did not anticipate that they would combine or conspire against me, and keep me prisoner while they went on to make a havoc of my life. No wonder Laura just got sicker and sicker, more and more neurotic. I was unable to protect her.

One of these presences was from a planet I call Lepton. In our search for extra-terrestrial intelligence, we crave contact with something large, about the same size as ourselves. But these creatures that move through me are very small. One of them, I say—her name is Moonbeam—now comes flickering through the wind chamber of my lungs, where a convocation is taking place. She moves up to the speaker's chair, which adjusts to her. A tiny crystal vial hangs suspended, and a mote of light flickers inside it like a firefly.

Now there is silence in the crowded hall, as the delegates take their seats. All attention is on the mote of light; Moonbeam is an important presence in the chamber, and commands respect. An image appears in each tiny consciousness, and in mine as well. As if on a dais behind the gleaming vial, an enormous figure now takes shape, and I recognize myself.

The delegates spend a good deal of time discussing such images. My problems and thought processes are a compelling source of interest for them. Each has a different way of describing me, of which Moonbeam's is the best, I think. The figure is in a cage, and he moves slowly because of the manacles on his hands and feet. He is asleep. He is often asleep.

As this image suggests itself—I presume to all of us—thoughts come too. I imagine "thoughts" are a constant in this bunch, perhaps the only one. I call the figure the "Proteus monster," because the remarkable thing about it is not its actual morphology, which is embarrassingly naked. Rather it's the way the figure changes: constantly, imperceptibly. Or not imperceptibly—it's like staring at the minute hand on a clock. Sometimes the figure has hair all over its body, which then gradually recedes and is absorbed. Or sometimes it is massive and fat, and then the flesh will drain away. Sometimes the face is heavy and fierce, sometimes epicene and soft. Sometimes claws grow in, or scales, and the figure seems at first glance to be a lizard or a bear. Yet always I can recognize myself.

Now I see the creature's chin grow soft, as if the bones were melting underneath. I see its chest slowly inflate. But now Moonbeam pulls my thoughts away, and now I'm looking at the other object on the dais, a small computer or machine, a cube maybe three feet on a side. It is beeping. Lights flash.

From Moonbeam I get the impression something is wrong. I myself have no mechanical instinct. But the clicking sound is weaker and the lights are dimmer than usual—I see that now. Others see it too. One of the delegates—I call him Sharpie—stands on his chair, waving his claws.

Moonbeam is effective because she doesn't tell you what to think. The sense of urgency comes from within. As if projected on a screen on the top of the hall, I can see Laura through my eyes, and I watch her pretty mouth. There is a spot above her lip. I hear her voice reverberating through the empty space inside of me, and all is still. Nerve ganglia flop and writhe uselessly in the shadows. I cannot move my arms.

"Is it too much to ask, to expect some humanity from you? Just some words, some comfort. How long has it been since you've kissed me, or taken me in your arms? I swear I think you're like a robot sometimes. Either there's just nothing going on, or else you're just watching me—recording data to use against me later—talk to me! Say something! We rattle around this house together, and sometimes we spend the whole day without saying anything to

IF LIONS COULD SPEAK

each other, and it feels as if I'm starving. It feels as if I'm starving to death."

I blink. Below me in the convocation hall, there is pandemonium, and I see why. Six panels of multicolored lights run across the top of the cube, and now two of them are dark. The rest glow weakly. In his cage the prisoner appears to be inflating like a balloon. The flesh over his wrists and ankles swells around the iron manacles.

Sharpie is waving his antennae. His claws make a rasping, chitinous squeak, and I can hear his high, almost imperceptible scream. "Kill!" he says. "You kill!" and more like that. I admire him because he is predictable. I feel my fingers jerk and spasm on the arms of my chair, as if they had a mind of their own. Laura is a pretty woman, especially her arms and neck, which are delicate and white. She wants me to touch her, I think. I'll touch her.

Many of the delegates come from races that have transcended mere technology, but Sharpie has not. He loves gadgets. Gadgets float around him, tiny machines consisting of a few molecules—self-protective devices, I imagine. They move around his legs and claws as he gesticulates. He's like a little crayfish in some ways.

Moonbeam soothes him, showing him pictures I can't see. But he resents it. Now suddenly a swarm of little machine bugs are darting toward the crystal vial. But when they get too close they pop and explode, zapped by some current in the air. Others form like eggs among the folds of Sharpie's tail.

In times past, late at night as I lay awake next to Laura, listening to her snore, Moonbeam would take me on a tour of the hall, introducing the delegates as they spoke. I would look at a small creature as it climbed up to the speaker's chair. Information would suggest itself, which was Moonbeam's work. And as I learned things, the creature would seem to swell and grow, and I would notice its details. "There, you see. No eyes, no mouth—it's all smells with him. Those are rows of transmitters and receptors underneath his wings. When you talk, see them open and shut like tiny barnacles. They change the words to smells, so he can understand. Don't fart—he'll think you've lost your mind."

No, this voice is not Moonbeam, though it often accompanies her. I call the voice Dorothy. She speaks in an accent that is vaguely Continental—French, perhaps. She has none of Moonbeam's cool objectivity; she is always making fun. She'll buzz and twitter in my ear: "That guy is an idiot. Don't pay any attention." But I never catch a glimpse of her. She is one of several presences that seem to have no physical manifestation. Still, it is odd she speaks such colloquial English. It is she who suggests names for all these creatures.

Now Moonbeam has given up the chair. Someone else now materializes, a small, human figure that Dorothy refers to as The Drone.

"Oh, Christ," she says. "This is all we need."

The Drone's mouth is toothless, soft: "I . . . it should be evident, obvious, pa . . . pa . . . patent, o . . . o . . . pen, com . . . compre . . . comprehen . . . sible . . . "

The interpreters sit in a circle above the floor. Whenever there is a vocal transmission, they start to jabber and gesticulate. But as the Drone speaks they are silent, waiting. " . . . That we are approaching, co . . . coming up to, or initiating a cri . . . a crisis or ca . . . catastrophe, a disaster. I a . . . aver or mean or sig . . . sig . . . signify in the life or existence of our host, our vi . . . victim, our friend, our su . . . su . . . subject, who has been so . . . so . . . kind . . . receptive . . . dying . . . dead . . . "

In back of him, the prisoner has come awake. The flesh has bulged over his manacles, and he is bleeding from his hands and feet. "Oh," he says, "I hurt." As always I am embarrassed by him, his words, his obvious sincerity. Tears fall from his eyes. He himself is a simple fellow and feels no embarrassment. Sometimes I have seen him masturbate, provoking both silence and applause.

His arms and shoulders seem mountainous, but he cannot break his chains. Blood drips from his fingers. Tusks are growing from his mouth, and he is chewing at his wrists, scratching at his feet. The computer blinks beside him, and above, the screen lurches to life.

Weak hearts run in my family, and my heart is racing now. There is an ominous thumping in the soft walls of the convocation hall, though the noise of my breath is now subsiding. "All right, all right, I take your point," Laura says. "I know you well enough to know when you're feeling wounded. Part of it's my fault, I know. I can't help coming after you when you're like this, because it hurts me. But then I know you get into this passive-aggressive spiral—it's been the death of us, can you see that?"

"Kill, kill," Sharpie admonishes, and again I feel a tremor in my fingers. The little mechanical bugs swarm out and seize hold of the Drone, dragging him backward from the chair as he kicks and waves his arms. I can see Moonbeam flickering, hoping to take control of the ascending chaos: Among the curving rows of seats, delegates discuss the seriousness of the situation and the risk to themselves. Others, more vociferous, begin to fight. The open space in front of the speaker's chair is full of struggling, small bodies. I recognize The Meadow Muffin and The Snake, or rather Dorothy brings them to my attention. The Snake exists in one dimension only, which makes him easy to dodge. He and his adversary fight viciously without touching at any point.

"And the retards have kept their seats," continues Dorothy, imitating a sports announcer. She is referring to the lower circle, which is reserved for delegates under time constraints. Some appear and disappear at intervals. Some are slow as stones: All biological existence is like a minute to them. Others live like fruit flies, or even faster. Several experience time backwards— they know how this story ends, but grope vaguely toward its starting premises. One comes from a planet without any time at all, because the gravity is so strong.

Mr. Magoo, as Dorothy calls him, is a pudgy little fellow from a world without cause and effect, which in these proceedings has given him an air of continued bafflement. But now for the first time he is smiling and nodding: This is a bad sign. Watching him, I can appreciate how serious my situation is. The sound of my heart crashes and swells, and the soft floor shudders under us. "Uh, oh," says Dorothy, as a spinning circle, a whirlpool of colored wind takes form in the middle of the chamber. All the delegates stop mid-word, mid-fisticuff. There is a roaring sound. The whirlpool of wind or smoke or cloud turns a succession of subtle hues: ash rose, black lavender, while a strange perfume comes to us. And there are lights flashing in the center of the spiral, and all the delegates are still. They cannot move, except for Sharpie, who climbs down out of his chair. He holds wrenches and screwdrivers in his many hands.

Above the whirlpool we hear Laura's voice. "All right," she says, "just sit there. And if you really want to hurt me, you can just close your eyes—yes, like that. Just like that. Why don't you fall asleep while I tell you something I've never told anyone except my therapist, which I didn't even remember until she brought it out of me—do you think people are the way they are for no reason? Just a chaos of desires and thoughts? Yes, you do think that, I know you do, because it is impossible for you to look inside yourself. Something just closes down inside of you—I pity you. I really do. I pity you because you'll never get better, as I am getting better. You'll never go forward. You'll never change. But I know things have happened to me that have made me what I am—causes and effects, over and over. But if you know what's happening, then you can change. So let me tell you now what brought me to this place, where I am living with a man who's so closed off, he actually closes his eyes when I am talking to him, closes his eyes and grimaces with pain, because of what I'm saying to him. It doesn't matter. Let me tell you—"

Laura's voice now gradually subsides, and I can't hear it anymore. All I can hear is the roaring wind and the shuddering in the walls. And my eyes are not closed. I am watching the barred cage on the dais, where the animal or man is now gigantic. He is weeping from the pain of the iron bands. Tears flow down his hairy cheeks. But at the same time he is in a rage, and he snorts and drools and gnashes his tusks together, and seizes hold of the bars and rocks his body back and forth until the cage rocks with him. There is an ominous crashing as the cage tips and falls back, and at the same time the chains break, and the manacles break apart. The colored whirlpool turns in the center of the room, and no one moves except for Sharpie, who has clambered up onto the dais. Now he comes forward to the flashing cube, and he breaks the top open with his screwdrivers, and he reaches his claws into the cavity, and I can see the wires come apart. The lights go out, and in the cage the giant grasps at his left side, and staggers, and falls. As he falls, already he's begun to shrink and soften. Dead, he will resemble pasty, hairless me.

Now there is pandemonium as the hollow man collapses and caves in. The roof collapses. There is darkness in the hall. There are lights and flashes as the delegates scatter for the exits. My throat is jammed with them so that I cannot breathe. Even in this catastrophe, some take leave of me before they flicker away. "Oh, me go, me go, me go—nice time," they say. "Sweet house of joyfulness. Sweet place of life." But some are trapped and crushed. The shuddering in the walls goes still.

One escapes, buzzing like a tiny bee, too small to hear. She works through the forest of my nose. "Nice time," she says, and flies out past the computer screen, where the text of "If Lions Could Speak" glows reproachfully, never to be completed. Laura can't see, doesn't see. She is worried now, finally, and she's amazed when the window breaks: a little hole, a fracture in the glass like a bullet hole. Then that little bee is up through the dark night, fighting air and gravity as thick as mud, a minute fleck of light rising and gathering speed, gathering mass as well, bulking up on hydrogen for the long journey. Then she's up into the brighter way, past the atmosphere where the long spaces begin. Looking back, she can see the world spread out, but not a blue sphere in its nest of clouds—nothing like that. Instead she sees it in a different way, uncloaked by the self-referential illusions of humankind, the vain projections and imaginings. She sees a vast, flat plain, covered with a layer of viscous jelly many miles thick—no, actually, she doesn't see that. She sees a vast inverted bowl, its surface troubled with waterspouts—not that either. She sees a blinding tablet, on which are recorded certain numerical constants—not a chance of that. She sees not one world but many billions, each closed and locked and silent—no. She sees an astonishing paradise of lakes and mountains and warm winds, where gigantic men and women fornicate in the long grass—no, I for one don't believe she sees anything like that. Surely here we've reached the limit of this story, the boundary that even death can't penetrate, unless it can. There is a skin of mirrors on the outside of the world, and our little friend is pressing up against it, making a bulge in it, pressing on valiantly, eager to come home.

That's where this story ends, or else should end. It cannot end with even the tiniest rip in that mirrored skin, and it will not end with that small creature flickering through. But surely on the other side her passage will be quick. Perhaps at every multiple of light-speed she will stop again and wait for our imaginations to catch her. Perhaps in the far future she will come safely down. And there will be a strange, discolored forest, with pale leaves falling on the pale hills—it won't be strange to her. Under the trees there will be tawny, roaring beasts covered with fur. They will open their mouths: "Break us of eyes here. Eggs break and eggs don't break. Help is a forgiving noise for all that sloshing in the bitter pool. Birds come around then come around, and if you step there will be stairs. If you touch there will be things. Luck of all lucky ones," they'll say, and we will almost understand.

the lost sepulcher
of huascar capac

When I was six my eyes started to fail, for reasons no one could understand.
Now tonight in this dark hole, now that I'm a man, I can appreciate how hard
this was for everyone. I can appreciate my father's sadness, how it ate at him
and wasted him and finally killed him. Doctors and neighbors also found
themselves affected: I was the only child of a dead mother, and my father was
already old. At a certain moment in their lives, men and women find a skill for
recognizing stories; when I was six I was too young. Too young to be sensitive
to their idea of tragedy, though sometimes I was frightened. There was no
need. The three years of my blindness now appear to me like other years,
though at the time there was no reason to suppose I would recover.

I don't mean that I was too young to remember. I can remember every day.
I can remember almost every word of almost every conversation with my father, and can recite them backwards and forwards. That year when I was six, I
was building my first memory palace. I was laying out the plans for a whole
city. My father showed me how.

In my city there is a street near the Hemicircle of Deformities, perhaps a
half a mile away. It is lined with big stone buildings, Central Records 1952,
1953, and so on. In all that quarter of the city, it is perhaps the dullest street.
The buildings are so grand, so dull. Each is laid out around twelve square
courtyards, one courtyard for each month, three rows of four. I was six in
1951, and that building is identical to the rest, only most of the 30 rooms and
antechambers (less or more) which surround each courtyard are locked; it is
only from about September on that I can enter where I please, and take whatever I want out of the wooden cabinets that line each wall. In September, my
eyesight was already very bad, and my father was in a frenzy of labor, helping
me with the construction. This city, and especially this section of the city, was

his gift, a place to wander and play among the bright mnemonic images as the world got dark.

Central Records 1945 through 1950 are doorless, windowless hulks—any objects or piece of paper that I possess from those years are copies of inaccessible originals, and they are all filed elsewhere. But in 1951, 52, and 53, the cabinets are filled with blueprints, and mimeographs, and sketches in my father's minute handwriting. They are what remain of conversations that lasted sometimes ten or twelve hours each day. At the time, the detail was bewildering to me—this section of the city is his gift; also his legacy, for around the Central Records buildings are some of the strangest sights in the whole city. It is the part that we built first, and it consists of the contents of my father's own memory city, which he was transferring then to me.

A palace in an adjoining alley, for example, is built around a sloping spiral almost forty stories tall. The spiral is lined with images, and during the years when I used to climb it, looking from one statue to another just to test myself, or else just wandering or exploring, I would remember how they were first installed, during three desperate evenings in the first week of March when I was seven years old. They are my father's reconstruction of the causes and processes of the First World War—you enter underneath a marble pediment, inscribed with the dates of the conflict. Immediately to the left, at the beginning of the spiral, stands my father's monument to Gavrilo Princip. The young man sits on the stone floor, his shoulder pressed against a grate. He holds a bloody napkin to his lips, and in his other hand he still grasps his revolver. Beside him, an untasted plate of sorbet, and 23 roses in a glass vase.

Although I couldn't see it at the time of the first installation, the young man is beautiful. In this way my father demonstrated his own anarchist sympathies—the memorial to Princip's victims, under the pediment on the right-hand side, is less impressive. The archduke and his wife are intensely fat. They are sprawled in the back seat of their car, covered with blood; the bullet has shattered the windscreen, shattered also the archduke's spectacles.

This is the major image, but it is surrounded by twelve small grotesques, each one a mnemonic clue. For example, a black dwarf in a beret, naked from the waist down, carrying a book entitled "6,281,914 Spanish Eggs."—an image meaningless to you, but for me it contains the location and the date of the assault. A toad upon a velvet couch gives me the victims' names.

This palace contains thousands of such figures. Every six months or so, as I moved up the spiral corridor, I would pass von Schlieffen and von Kluck, Samsonov, the Kaiser, Lloyd George, von Moltke, and assorted Romanovs.

This is the hall of personages—behind each of these statues is a chamber of events, loaded also with images. When I was a child, all this was overwhelming, and I dreaded my janitorial visits to the Ypres room or the Verdun exhibit—even a few seconds was too long to spend in there, and I would barely open my eyes.

Now that I consider it, I suppose some of the images, though obviously not these ones, in this section of the city antedate my father. I suppose some of them, perhaps some of the most grotesque and archaic ones from the Avenue of 1800 Gargoyles—that line of naked women disemboweling each other, for example—were his inheritance from the priest who was his teacher. I remember my despair as some of these streets went in: at the time I was afraid that this section of the city, this chaotic section of my father's, would prove infinite. Then he was building antechambers and additions off of every room. But it is not; moving out from Central Records, one comes quite quickly to more ordered streets, laid out by myself without his help. Already when I was six there were huge vacant places in his memory where whole blocks of his city, perhaps whole neighborhoods, had collapsed. It was for this reason, I soon realized, that he was so desperate to effect this transfer of material, to drag these statues down out of his crumbling buildings and reinstall them in my new ones. Perhaps in my encroaching blindness he saw a similarity to the darkness that was overtaking him.

Though we never discussed it, I imagine his city was constructed in Victorian gothic style, full of 19th century homages to castles and chateaux. I imagine something northern, something dark; my city is dark too. In school that year when I was six, before my father took me out, my teacher was reading to us a child's adaptation of Prescott's *History of the Conquest of Peru*, and my mind was full of visions of old Cuzco. Therefore when I planned my city, I conceived of it as the lost capital of an Inca prince, and I located it underground in a vast system of caverns. This was partly due to my illness and my father's influence, but partly also because in this way I hoped to hide my city from Pizarro and his soldiers.

The city streets are lit with gas. From the summit of the Ziggurat of Viracocha, a traveler can see the whole floor of the cavern picked out with light, blurring finally in the dark distance. Beyond this cavern there are others, one of which includes the tomb of the Inca Huascar Capac. It was during the exploration of this tomb, which I had known from the beginning was located somewhere in the city, that I quite suddenly regained my sight in January of 1954.

I have returned often to that court in Central Records, for it was during January also that my father died. I recovered my vision in the group home for Catholics where he had placed me during the previous November, and where he came to see me every day. After his death, I continued on in the group home, as a nine-year-old orphan instead of as a blind boy. I went to school there, storing the contents of my education in my memory city, in images, as my father had taught me. There also I learned the rudiments of photography, which was to become my profession.

Perhaps this was inevitable, but I prefer to think that I had undergone a change during the time of my blindness, when I had lived almost exclusively underground. Blind, I had played among the images, and I prefer to think that my gift of seeing, when it was returned to me, was changed by the experience. When I notice it is easier for me than for others to capture the significance in a pose, or a landscape, or a group of objects, I thank my early training. At certain moments, any image is a memory image, as packed with significance as any montage in my city, and the trick is to isolate it then.

A photographer will discard a hundred exposures for each one he keeps. What goes into that decision? When I am working in the darkroom, it is like discovering how to look. The paper is white, and then you put it in the pan. I never get tired of it, because each time it is like opening my eyes that January, when I was a child. First just lumps of shade and color, the way a baby sees. A swirl of colors from a central point. A man. Six men. Sky, and then as the lines resolve an idea resolves with it, because there is a brain behind the eye after all, a brain that knows things. Soldiers.

This is a photograph that I took years ago. Six white soldiers stand in the shade outside a primitive straw hut. I must have shot the scene a dozen times, and the differences are subtle, but this was the only one which made any sense. And it's not because it tells the story better. Other exposures show a jeep and telephone line, which account for the soldiers' presence, and my presence also. But in my photograph—the one I kept—you just see a wall of mud and straw, and the men standing in the shade smoking cigarettes. The ground is cracked into octagons and the line of trees in the background is distorted, but it is something about the cigarettes that makes the heat oppressive.

Three black men dressed in t-shirts sit together in the foreground, and a little to one side. Yet they are not essential. They are not what made the image important to me, and important enough to other people for it to have appeared full-page in *Paris-Match*, opposite a story about Cubans in Angola. It is not, although perhaps the editor would have claimed it was, the stereo-typically Latin attitude of the men against the wall. It is because the pose of two of the six soldiers corresponds to an image in my city, an image independent of the photograph itself, which of course is filed in Central Records and cross-referenced in numerous other places.

Or perhaps a combination of images, I thought. I have thousands of soldiers down there, for my father was a student of military history. In this photograph, only two have seen me. Or at least, only two are reacting to my presence. One has straightened up and is staring at me. For him this is a portrait, and he has chosen the way he wants to appear: cocky, stiff, his cigarette at an improbable angle. The other has been looking at him, and at the instant the photograph was taken, has turned towards me. He must have expected to see something specific from the way his friend had straightened up—something good, perhaps, I don't know what, but evidently not a dirty foreign journalist, for his expression of disappointment is clear, the clearest thing in the photograph. He is young, mustached, handsome, perhaps nineteen years old.

Thirty months after I departed from Angola I discovered, quite by accident, these two soldiers again. As it happened, they were in the Verdun exhibition, and I saw them in the corner of my eye as I was flickering through. Two soldiers—French this time, though clearly of Spanish or Italian origin—are standing in poses identical to the photograph. Their faces, their expressions of cockiness and disappointment, even their uniforms, unlikely as it seems, are identical, and that is what disturbed me. For the first time I contemplated the possibility that each time I printed a photograph there was some movement down below, some tiny change.

It is stupid to become obsessed with these things—I'm sure the images shift and distort over time. Memory is after all a process of the brain. Only one of the processes, but the fact is, by the time I was in my early thirties my journeys underground had taken the place of thinking, even of learning. When I was blind, other senses became more acute, and were able to take over the functions of sight—as time went on my memory was like that.

It is just laziness, as well as a new dissatisfaction with my work. This trip I took hundreds of photographs, not one of which will ever be developed. A crowd, people throwing things, a building on fire. Broken windows. I've never bothered to learn Spanish. I never tried to read the papers. My editor gave me some articles; I didn't look at them. My writer knew it all, she said. She was the brains, and so I thought perhaps my pictures would be like something in a baby's eye. In the last one, a man is shooting someone in the side of the head. Who are they? I don't know. The district commissioner in Callao had warned me. He had given me a list of things I could photograph in safety—the railway station, the municipal post office—and I had thought he meant safety from him. Not that I cared one way or the other; it was hot, and we were staying in an 800 room Hyatt with about seven other guests, all newsmen. At night we sat around the huge neoclassical deserted bar, stinking drunk, listening to a pianist playing show tunes. Except for that first day, only once did I go into town. I staggered up through cold parsecs of lobby. I took a taxi. The streetlights were broken; we drove along a single narrow road. There were no other cars. We went fast at first, then slow, because gradually the street started to fill up with people—dozens, then hundreds: short men with bearded faces and white pants that would snatch at our headlights as we hesitated and went past.

All the windows were open, and from everywhere on the hot wind came smells so delicious they were almost mournful, as evocative as music. Slower and slower we went, for in some places the entire street was blocked by sudden masses of people, and in some places huge constructions of cardboard, which people would pull away to let us pass. And it was lighter, too, as we went on—the hotel was situated among dark acres of trees, but here every window had a light, and in the streets the men were carrying torches. Sometimes when we stopped, people bent down to peer into my window. Some would put their whole heads inside, and I would see their shiny skin, the shirts wet along their necks. At first I would shrink back onto the seat, but they would smile and reach out to touch me with their slippery hands. Soon I was laughing and smiling back, as if I understood what they were saying. My driver smoked a thin cigar. There was a party tonight, he said. He leaned out of his window to spit at a dog pissing against the tire. We had come to a complete stop.

That night I dreamed about the tomb of the great Inca. Though sometimes I have been able to revisit it in dreams, I saw it for the first and last time when I was nine years old, and have never been able to retrace my steps. This is because nothing distinguishes the building from the outside; also because the month I found it was the month of my father's death, my sudden recovery—though this last, I think, cannot possibly have been unrelated. The tomb is at the center of the city. The Incas had no written language, yet even so this tomb is full of books, the only books in the whole city. Fictions, stories. There is a reading room with long tables. There are pens and stacks of paper. And in the middle, in a glass case, the tomb of Huascar Capac, a giant man dressed in a cloak of hummingbird feathers. The corpse is almost twelve feet long.

What are these books, these stories? When I was nine I needed my true eyesight, perhaps, to read them or to write them. I needed my experience of the world.

In my hotel I awoke suddenly, and got up to stand in the darkness, staring out the window. Far away, down in the city, something was on fire.

That night the American consulate burned to the ground. This was news, and news to me until days later, when I heard it on the radio. By morning Rachel and I had already started out into the countryside, to Z—. In this we had accepted the district commissioner's compromise: the town was not in an area specifically claimed by the insurgents. It was in a different kind of turmoil, following the deaths of almost forty miners in a cave-in. The mine had been closed by strikers for a month, but, despite the urgent petitions of Euro-Bauxite and the Belgian mission, the government had not yet sent soldiers.

Possibly the district commissioner believed the miners to have legitimate grievances that deserved the attention of the international press. I don't know, and doubtless I do him an injustice to judge him by appearances, for as I say I speak no Spanish. All this was grudgingly interpreted for me by Rachel, my correspondent for *The Australian*. Probably he just wanted us out of the way; I don't believe that he was deliberately sending us into danger. Certainly he had seemed impressed by our credentials, even asking Rachel to point out Sydney on his globe and then muttering reflectively, "Kangourou."

We left while it was still dark. The road climbed away from the coast as if through common sense; at sunrise it was cooler than the night, and the city was like the clog in the bottom of a basin, the hills around it ringed with residue. There is a world where water is as thin as air. I can imagine standing on a shore, the air curling and lapping at my feet, the valleys of the sea open below me, and above me not one thing, not one thing that could muddy sunlight—in a way that is the foundation of hope. You can go higher and higher. We reached little iron-roofed villages where the air seemed dry to the touch, the sky king-fisher blue. But the people were as confused as ever; we kept on getting lost. At night the mosquitoes kept us from sleeping. Once the front axle sank to the hubs in gleaming sand. I got out my Hasselblad and walked a long way, until I could look back towards the empty hills and see the car like a rock or a stump, something that hadn't budged one millimeter in a thousand years. Why am I telling you this? Why am I finding new ways to delay? We came to Z— all right in the end, of course. As it turned out, we could have taken a bus. But that would have been too fast. Because I am avoiding this part. Because even though I was there, my thoughts are the way my pictures would have been—focused on things perhaps only inches beside the point. None of them would have been worth keeping.

One of my cameras has an attachment so that you can appear to be shooting in a different direction from the one you actually are. It was as if the thing worked in reverse: you would line up your shot, and the picture would squirt out to one side. Even the last picture, the one of the man getting shot—when they smashed my camera, it was frustrating because I knew I hadn't seen what they thought I had. The photograph would have shown the man's head, his face strong and still. He knew what I was trying to see. Perhaps he knew already he was just a memory image. The gun is poking at him from the side. You can just see part of its black snout in the middle of a grainy cloud; you can see the man's hair billowing, and the side of his head distended. I'm sure they thought the picture was some kind of evidence, but if they had asked me to point out which one had pulled the trigger, I wouldn't have known.

The man was kneeling in the street outside the movie theatre, his hands tied in front of him. Early in the morning he had been released from the tree where I had seen him first, and brought into the square. He had been allowed to wash and feed himself. Nevertheless, he made a show of sitting with his back to his guards and ignoring what seemed to be friendly and solicitous remarks. He looked towards the mine, whose tower rose from a hill of rubble a mile away. I had been up there the day before, and I had as many pictures as I needed; Rachel was up there still. At around six o'clock, a man came down with news that panicked everyone. People came out of the adjoining buildings and made a semicircle around the prisoner. That was when they bound his wrists together. An hour later, a siren went off in the mine. It meant nothing to me, but at the sound, the group around the kneeling man went into some kind of a dance—some ran back and forth, others gesticulated and slapped their chests. This went on for a minute or more; I was taking photographs, and they did nothing of substance until some other men appeared at the far end of the square, yelling and throwing stones. But then they pulled the kneeling man to his feet and tried to drag him away. He stumbled and fell on his face in the dust, and by that time some of the people from the new group were almost upon them. No one had paid any attention to me, and I had shot almost a roll of film from a safe distance. But I needed a close-up of the man's face with dust on it. I had no time to change lenses, so I ran forward cursing and went down on my knees about fifteen feet away. The man raised his eyes to me, and I knew he was thinking about how he looked. If his hands had been free, he would have brushed back his hair. I saw his face out of focus through the viewer. Was that a frown, a sneer? I twisted the barrel savagely but the expression was gone, resolved into fixed staring. You could no longer see the thoughts. Then I saw the pistol coming into the picture from the right-hand side, and I pressed the shutter once, twice. The aperture closed, opened, closed, but in that fraction of a second, I saw his breaking head, perfect, framed. I heard the shot. The men around him scattered. For an instant I was alone with him, and then the square was full of people. I got to my feet, looking for Rachel, looking for a face I recognized, and I had a brief impression that there were no longer any patterns of movement in the square, no clumps of people, and everyone was standing still, posed, equidistant, repetitive, like figures on wallpaper. The man was shot to death right there, and I think I must have gotten up too fast because I bent over and put my hands to my head.

One man was dressed differently from the others—his clothes looked vaguely military. From this and from his beard I guessed he was not from that locality, a real revolutionary perhaps, or else someone from the Shining Path. But he was an idiot just the same, because he stood in front of me and pulled at my camera, as if he expected the leather strap to give way in his hand. I staggered forward and we knocked our heads together; perhaps it is because dignity is important to such a man that after I had handed him the camera, he turned and hit me in the mouth. Or perhaps he really thought I was American. He said, "American," and then he hit me in the mouth, making me sit down. How could I deny it? My mouth was full of blood. Somebody kicked me from behind, several people—not hard, but no accident either. I had not been touched in anger since I was a child, when my father and I were building the memory city, and I was too stupid and too young. But these men were strangers.

I did not resist. In time they left me, and I settled with my back to a small tree. I sat and watched the square empty out. A policeman, a priest, and a doctor were gathered around the corpse, along with some women. They carried it to a waiting car, and then they came towards me. They said something, but I waved them away. Their accents sounded phony. If an actor on stage turns to ask you a question, no matter how pertinent, you feel no compulsion to answer. You are sitting in judgment, always.

Some olive shreds of film blew across my legs and blew across the street. A white dog came and sat beside me.

And gradually as I sat there the town came back to life. Shops that had been closed and shuttered all day opened their doors, and there were lights on inside, now that it was getting dark. The streetlights in front of the municipal building turned on, and some kids smoked cigarettes on the steps. Young men and women, some elegantly dressed, stood under the movie marquee—it shed a silver radiance. "Thunderball." On a side street, men in soft hats played dominoes, perhaps, outside the place where I had eaten lunch. I could see the entrance to our hotel, our car parked along the curb. Someone standing on the porch looking out.

It got dark. I thought the town was making itself soft again, the way some brainless anemone or crab will stretch out after a small trauma. And I didn't want to make it clutch up tight again. So that when I stood up, I did it slowly. And in fact there was no shiver of movement, not from the kids on the steps, not from the woman on the porch. It was as if I didn't exist, and the whole way up to the mine, as I was walking I saw no one. There was no one at the gate—it was securely fastened with shiny padlocks, but to the right the chain-link fence had been trampled flat. Farther up, everything was in shadow, the cage, the showers, the pit: I had been on a tour the day before. And if I make it sound as if all these distances were short, and all these places easy to find, I am giving the wrong impression. But why drag it out? I knew what I was looking for, a place among the sidings where the rails ran straight into the rock, lit by an endless line of naked fluorescent bulbs. It was the supply shaft, and I walked in under the lights, between the tracks. I picked my way through a barricade of smashed machinery—a broken generator, a line of smashed electric cars. Huge pieces of the roof had fallen in, and in one place the floor had subsided four feet in a single step, bending the rails into greasy bows. The walls were rent and fissured, but still the line of light stretched unwavering—it was my comfort, and it buzzed and whispered as if conspiring against the dark.

I stood in a puddle of inky water. Just ahead, the tunnel had collapsed completely, and the line of lights lay buried like a vein of ore. Above, the fall had opened up a cavern, and a wall stood thirty feet high. Along its uneven surface someone had painted a huge red cross, smeared and clunky, and beneath it on a ledge stood an assortment of candles in blue and red glass jars: stubs of wax, mostly, but some still burned. Below, personal effects were gathered in careful heaps—gloves and shoes, orange helmets, framed photographs. A young man with a bad complexion. His tie is stupid, and he is looking away from the camera, but the older woman beside him is staring into it. This must have been the only picture she could find of them together, for it is flattering to neither. But it must have been she who left his clothes washed and folded in a little pile. The woman looks too old to be his wife, too young to be his mother. His sister, perhaps. In the photograph he is not touching her. I borrowed his coat, and the flashlight of another man, the father of five children.

When the tunnel collapsed, it had opened a horizontal gash in the rock above it. Into this I shined my light, and I must have seen some evidence of an opening, because I climbed into it and crawled forward on my hands and feet. I think I wanted to discover a dead body or something. But in fact there was no place to go. One lip of rock had drooped away from another, and I crawled along the gap, flashing my light. It was cold—I could see my breath—and dark too. I had clambered over an outcrop that hid the tunnel from my sight. It was a glow behind some rocks, and looking back all I could see was the outline of the square cross on the wall, thirty feet high, with spots of candlelight beneath it. In front, the beam of my flashlight illuminated quick sections of the rock.

I crawled forward into the dark, and it was only by looking back that I discovered that the ledge I crept on had curled around me. I saw the glow behind me outlined by the shadow of a circle, and I found myself in a volcanic tube almost six feet in diameter, curving gently upward, and there was no reason to be cautious, either, because the rock around me was level and clean. The passage continued in the direction of the buried tunnel, but above it. But already I suspected that the passage I was in had no communication with the modern mine. Perhaps I had read somewhere that the sources of precious metals in these mountains had dried up at the end of the sixteenth century, and that Z— was built on the ruins of a much older town. When I put my light up, I saw that smoke had been cooked into the stone the length of the ceiling. It made no mark on my fingers.

I climbed this passageway for hours, I think, moving quickly because it was so cold. I walked with my neck and shoulders bent, because of the low roof. But the floor was level under a layer of crushed rock, and the air was good. Twice I had to go down on my hands and knees under a gallery of wooden supports. In the beginning, these were the only artifacts I saw: blackened chunks of wood, the mark of the axe still on them. And once I passed a crude stick figure carved into the wall. A man on a horse. There may have been others. For of course I was in total darkness, except for my flashlight, and this I used to keep myself from stumbling or from bumping my head. In front and behind, the light seemed to diffuse very quickly, although it was a strong one. But I explored only when I stopped to negotiate some difficult section, or to rest. So that this part of my trip exists for me only as a series of images a few inches from my eye. The man on horseback with the light in a circle around it. A fat drop of water with the light glistening in the spray. I had stopped where I could stand and stretch, where a narrow shaft opened above me, and I could stand in a ring of wooden posts and stretch my back and knees. It was warmer here. Warm air came from above me.

At every step I had expected to turn back without thinking, before my light failed, before I got lost, but in the warm air the difficulties seemed less urgent. It seemed far to return. Here, something was close by.

* * *

I came through a big chamber. The roof was lost in darkness. But high up along the walls I detected the outlines of painted figures, up where my light was too vague to touch. Even here, things were escaping me, I felt. Again, closer to hand, the wall had been chipped clean of significance. Is that too much to ask, I thought, to hold something in your hands for sure? Now, I don't understand what made me so dissatisfied. But I rushed forward like a drunk, hoping to catch up. It is that hope, you see. I am convinced of it. It is that drunkenness. Because I had passed holes in the floor before, places where the floor had collapsed. I had shone my flashlight into them cautiously. But this one, I must have fallen several feet. I hurt myself, and the light snapped out. But I didn't even care, because I knew at once that I had fallen onto something real. A stone sphere the size of a bowling ball. A stone sphere covered with carvings and bumps my fingers couldn't interpret. No, it was a head, the head of an animal. The head of an animal, with something in its mouth. It was cold and heavy; I lifted it into my lap and put my cheek against it.

As it happens, the flashlight fell close to where I sit. Yet I was prevented from reaching for it by a confusion of hopes. Because like a child I was not helped to action by knowing certain things. And there was something relaxing about sitting here like a blind man, reading the cold stone in the ringing, breathing darkness.

And in any case, in a little while I could see. In my lap is a tiger's head. It is unusual because the sculptor has chosen to work from the outside in. Does that make sense? I mean the rock still holds its natural contours, though it looks as if it had been rolled in skin. The carving has no structure of its own. And yet the artist has taken care to select a rock that did not require much

134

shaping. There are two holes for its eyes.

The head has broken from a larger piece, a stone image standing erect. It is carved in the same superficial style. I am going to use it now, because I know too little to make stone bones for this stone flesh. What is there to know? Only that I am sitting in the fifty-first chamber of the nineteenth court of the imperial treasury of Huascar Capac, and it is years since I have passed this way.

What is there to know? Only that in time I will get up. I will move forward. I will search among the images with ever-increasing eagerness; I will find the tomb of the great Inca, and I will sit down at the table at his feet.

the last homosexual

At my tenth high school reunion at the Fairmont Hotel, I ran into Steve Daigrepont and my life changed.

That was three years ago. Now I am living by myself in a motel room, in the southeast corner of the Republic of California. But in those days I was Jimmy Brothers, and my wife and I owned a house uptown off Audubon Park, in New Orleans. Our telephone number was (504) EXodus-5671. I could call her now. It would be early evening.

I think she still lives there because it was her house, bought with her money. She was the most beautiful woman I ever met, and rich too. In those days she was teaching at Tulane Christian University, and I worked for the *Times-Picayune*. That was why Steve wanted to talk to me.

"Listen," he said. "I want you to do a story about us."

We had been on the baseball team together at Jesuit. Now he worked for the Board of Health. He was divorced. "I work too hard," he said as he took me away from the bar and made me sit down in a corner of the Sazerac Room, under the gold mural. "Especially now."

He had gotten the idea I had an influence over what got printed in the paper. In fact I was just a copy editor. But at Jesuit I had been the starting pitcher on a championship team, and I could tell Steve still looked up to me. "I want you to do a feature," he said. "I want you to come visit us at Carville."

He was talking about the old Gillis W. Long Center, on River Road between New Orleans and Baton Rouge. Formerly the United States National leprosarium, now it was a research foundation.

"You know they're threatening to shut us down," he said.

I had heard something about it. The New Baptist Democrats had taken over the statehouse again, and as usual they were sharpening the axe. Carville was one of the last big virology centers left in the state. Doctors from all over Louisiana came there to study social ailments. But Senator Rasmussen wanted the buildings for a new penitentiary.

"She's always talking about the risks of some terrible outbreak," said Steve. "But it's never happened. It can't happen. In the meantime, there's so much we still don't know. And to destroy the stocks, it's murder."

Steve's ex-wife was pregnant, and she came in and stood next to the entrance to the lobby, talking to some friends. Steve hunched his shoulders over the table and leaned toward me.

"These patients are human beings," he said, sipping his orange crush. "That's what they don't understand." And then he went on to tell a story about one of the staff, an accountant named Dan who had worked at Carville for years. Then someone discovered Dan had embezzled two hundred and fifty thousand dollars from the contingency fund, and he was admitted as a patient. "Now I'll never leave you. Now I'm home," he said when he stepped into the ward.

"Sort of like Father Damien," I murmured. While I wasn't sure why my old friend wanted this story in the newspaper, still I admired his passion, his urgency. When we said goodbye, he pressed my hand in both of his, as if he really thought I could help him. It was enough to make me mention the problems at Carville to my boss a few days later, who looked at me doubtfully and suggested I go up there and take a look around on my day off.

"People have different opinions about that place," he said. "Although these days it would be hard for us to question the judgment of a Louisiana state senator."

* * *

I didn't tell Melissa where I was going. I drove up alone through the abandoned suburbs and the swamps. Once past the city I drove with the river on my left, behind the new levee. I went through small towns filled with old people, their trailers and cabins in sad contrast to the towers of the petro-chemical and agricultural concerns, which lined the Mississippi between Destrehan and Lutcher.

Carville lay inside an elbow of the river, surrounded by swamps and graveyards and overgrown fields. In the old days people had grown sugar cane. Now I drove up along a line of beautiful live oaks covered with moss and ferns. At the end of it a thirty-foot concrete statue of Christ the Redeemer, and then I turned in at the gate beside the mansion, a plantation house before the civil war, and the administration building since the time of the original

IF LIONS COULD SPEAK

leprosarium.

At the guardhouse they examined my medical records and took some blood. They scanned me with the lie detector and asked some questions. Then they called in to Steve, and I had to sign a lot of forms in case I had to be quarantined. Finally they let me past the barricade and into the first of many wire enclosures. Soldiers leaned against the Corinthian columns of the main house.

I don't want to drag this out with a lot of description. Carville was a big place. Once you were inside past the staff offices, it was laid out in sections, and some were quite pleasant. The security was not oppressive. When he met me at the inner gate, Steve was smiling. "Welcome to our Inferno," he said, when no one else could hear. Then he led me down a series of complicated covered walkways past the hospital, the Catholic and Protestant chapels, the cafeteria. Sometimes he stopped and introduced me to doctors and administrators, who seemed eager to answer questions. Then there were others who hovered at a respectful distance: patients, smiling and polite, dressed in street clothes. They did not shake hands, and when they coughed or sneezed, they turned their faces away.

"Depression," murmured Steve, and later, "alcoholism. Theft."

It had been around the time I was born that Drs. Fargas and Watanabe, working at what had been LSU, discovered the viral nature of our most difficult human problems. I mean the diseases that even Christ can't heal. They had been working with the quarantined HIV-2 population a few years after independence, during the old Christian Coalition days. Nothing much had changed since then in most of the world, where New Baptist doctrine didn't have the same clout as in Louisiana. But those former states which had been willing to isolate the carriers and stop the dreadful cycle of contagion, had been transformed. Per capita income rates showed a steady rise, and crime was almost non-existent. Even so, thirty years later there was still much to learn about susceptibility, about immunization, and the actual process of transmission. As is so often the case, political theory had outstripped science, and though it was hard to argue with the results, still as Steve Daigrepont explained it, there was a need for places like Carville, where important research was being done.

"If only to keep the patients alive," he muttered. His voice had softened as we progressed into the complex, and now I had to lean close to him to understand. After the second checkpoint when we put our masks on, I had to ask him to speak up.

We put on isolation suits and latex gloves. We stood outside some glassed-in rooms, watching people drink coffee and read newspapers, as they sat on plain, institutional couches. "Obesity," whispered Steve, which surprised me. No one in the room seemed particularly overweight.

"These are carriers," he hissed, angry for some reason. "They aren't necessarily infected. Besides, their diet is strictly controlled."

Later we found ourselves outside again, under the hot sun. I stared into a large enclosure like the rhinoceros exhibit at the Audubon zoo. A ditch protected us, and in the distance I could see some tarpaper shacks and rotted-out cars. "Poor people," mumbled Steve through his mask. "Chronic poverty." Children were playing in the dirt outside one of the shacks. They were scratching at the ground with sticks.

Again, I don't want to drag this out. I want to move on to the parts that are most painful to me. Now it hurts me to imagine what a terrible place Carville was, to imagine myself walking numbly through. That is a disease as well. In those days, in Louisiana, we were all numb, and we touched things with our deadened hands.

But for me there was a pain of wakening, as when blood comes to a sleeping limb. Because I was pretending to be a reporter, I asked Steve a lot of questions. Even though as time went on I hoped he wouldn't answer, but he did. "I thought this was a research facility," I said. "Where are the labs?"

"That section is classified. This is the public part. We get a lot of important guests."

We were standing outside a high, wrought-iron fence. I peered at Steve through my mask, trying to see his eyes. Why had he brought me here? Did he have some private reason? I stood in the stifling heat with my gloved hands on the bars of the fence, and then Steve wasn't there. He was called away somewhere and left me alone. I stood looking into a small enclosure, a clipped green lawn and a gazebo. But it was dark there, too. Maybe there were tall trees, or a mass of shrubbery. I remember peering through the bars, wondering if the cage was empty. I inspected a small placard near my eye. "Curtis Garr," it said. "Sodomite."

And then suddenly he was there on the other side of the fence. He was a tall man in his mid-fifties, well-dressed in a dark suit, leaning on a cane. He was very thin, with a famished, bony face, and a wave of grey hair that curled back over his ears. And I noticed that he also was wearing gloves, grey leather gloves.

He stood opposite me for a long time. His thin lips were smiling. But his eyes, which were grey and very large, showed the intensity of any caged beast.

I stood staring at him, my hands on the bars. He smiled.

Carefully and slowly, he reached out his gloved forefinger and touched me on my wrist, in a gap between my isolation suit and latex hand.

Then as Steve came up, he gave a jaunty wave and walked away.

Steve nodded. "Curtis is priceless," he muttered behind my ear. "We think he might be the last one left in the entire state. We had two others, but they died."

* * *

Last of all, Steve took me back to his air-conditioned office. "We must get together for lunch," he said. "Next time I'm in the city."

Now I can wonder about the Father Damien story he had told me at the Fairmont. I can wonder if in some way he was talking about himself. But at the time I smiled and nodded, for I was anxious to be gone.

I didn't tell Steve the man had touched me. Nor did I tell the doctors who examined me before I was released. But driving back to New Orleans, I found myself examining the skin over my left wrist. Soon it was hot and red from rubbing at it. Once I even stopped the car to look. But I didn't tell Melissa, either, when I got home.

She wouldn't have sympathized. She was furious enough at what she called my "Jesuit liberalism," when I confessed where I had been. I hated when she talked like that. She had been born a Catholic like me and Steve, but her parents had converted after the church split with Rome. As she might have explained it, since the differences between American Catholic and New Baptist were mostly social, why not have the courage to do whatever it took to get ahead? No, that's not fair—she was a true believer. At twenty-eight she was already a full professor of Creationist biology.

"What if somebody had seen you? What if you had caught something?" she demanded as I rubbed my wrist. I was sitting next to the fireplace, and she stood next to the window with the afternoon light in her hair. All the time she lectured me, I was thinking how much I wanted to make love to her, to push her down and push my penis into her right there on the Doshmelti carpet—"I don't know how you can take such risks," she said. "Or I do know: It's because you don't really believe in any of it. No matter what the proofs, no matter how many times we duplicate the Watanabe results, you just don't accept them."

I sat there fingering my wrist. To tell the truth, there were parts of the doctrine of ethical contagion that no educated person believed. Melissa herself didn't believe in half of it. But she had to pretend that she believed it, and maybe it was the pretense that made it true.

I didn't want to interrupt her when she was just getting started. "Damn those Jesuits," she said. "Damn them. They ruined you, Jim. You'll never amount to anything, not in Louisiana. Why don't you just go on up to Massachusetts, or someplace where you'd feel at home."

I loved it when she yelled. Her hair, her eyes. She loved it too. She was like an actress in a play. The fact is, she never would have married one of those Baptist boys, sickly and small and half-poisoned with saltpeter. No matter how much she told her students about the lechery vaccines, no matter how many times she showed her slides of spirochetes attacking the brain, still it was too late for her and me, and she knew it.

The more she yelled at me, the hotter she got. After a while we went at it like animals.

* * *

Two months later, I heard from Steve again. I remember it was in the fall, one of those cool, crisp, blue New Orleans days that seem to come out of nowhere. I had been fired from the paper, and I was standing in my vegetable garden looking out toward the park when I heard the phone ring. I thought it was Melissa, calling back to apologize. She had gone up to Washington, which had been the capital of the Union in the old days, before the states had taken back their rights. She was at an academic conference, and lonely for home. Already that morning she had called me to describe a reception she had been to the night before. When she traveled out of Louisiana, she always had a taste for the unusual—"They have black people here," she said. "Not just servants; I mean at the conference. And the band! There was a trombone player, you have no idea. Such grace, such raw sexuality."

"I'm not sure I want to hear about that," I said.

She was silent for a moment, and she'd apologized. "I guess I'm a little upset," she confessed.

"Why?"

"I don't like it here. No one takes us seriously. People are very rude, as if we were to blame. But we're not the only ones"—she told me about a Dr. Wu from Boise who had given a paper the previous night on Christian genetics. "He showed slides of what he called 'criminal' DNA with all the sins marked on them. As if God had molded them that way. 'With tiny fingers,' as he put it."

I wasn't sure what the New Baptists would say about this. And I didn't want to make a mistake. "That sounds plausible," I murmured, finally.

"You would think that. Plausible and dangerous. It's an argument that leads straight back to Catholicism and original sin. That's fine for you—you want to be guilty when everybody else has been redeemed. But it completely contradicts Fargas and Watanabe, for one thing. Either the soul is uncontaminated at birth or else it isn't. If it isn't, all our immunization research is worthless. What's the point of pretending we can be healed, either by Christ or by science? That's what I said during the Q&A. Everybody hissed and booed, but then I found myself supported by a Jewish gentleman from New York. He said we could not ignore environmental factors, which is not quite a New Baptist point of view the way he expressed it, but what can you expect? He was an old reactionary, but his heart was in the right place. And such a spokesman for his race. Such intelligence and clarity."

That was the last time I spoke to Melissa, my wife. I wish we had talked about another subject, so that now in California, when I go over her words in my mind, I might not be distracted by these academic arguments. Distracted by my anger, and the guilt that we all shared. I didn't want to hear about the Jewish man. So many Jews had died during the quarantine—I can say that now. But at the time I thought Melissa was teasing me and trying to make me jealous. "That's the one good thing about you getting yourself canned," she said as she hung up. "I always know where to find you."

Sometimes I wonder what might have happened if I hadn't answered the phone when it rang again a few minutes later. I almost didn't. I sulked in the garden, listening to it, but then at the last moment I went in and picked it up.

But maybe nothing would have been different. Maybe the infection had already spread too far. There was a red spot on my wrist where I'd been rubbing it. I noticed it again as I picked up the phone.

"Jimmy, is that you?" Steve's voice was harsh and confused, and the connection was bad. In the background was a rhythmic banging noise. Melissa, in Washington, had sounded clearer.

After Steve was finished, I went out and stood in my vegetable garden again, in the bright, clean sun. Over in the park, a family was sitting by the pond having a picnic. A little girl in a blue dress stood up and clapped her hands.

What public sacrifice is too great, I thought, to keep that girl free from contamination? Or maybe it's just now, looking back, that I allow myself a thought. Maybe at the time I just stared numbly over the fence, and then went in and drank a Coke. It wasn't until a few hours later that I got in the car and drove north.

Over the past months I had looked for stories about Carville in the news. And Melissa had told me some of the gossip—there were differences of opinion in Baton Rouge. Some of the senators wanted the hospital kept open, as a showpiece for foreign visitors. But Barbara Rasmussen wanted the patients shipped to a labor camp outside of Shreveport, near the Arkansas border. It was a place both Steve and I had heard of.

Over the phone he'd said, "It's murder,"—a painful word. Then he'd told me where to meet him. He'd mentioned a time. But I knew I'd be late, because of the slow way I was driving. I wasn't sure I wanted to help him. So I took a leisurely, roundabout route, and crossed the river near the ruins of Hahnville. I drove up old Route 18 past Vacherie. It was deserted country there, rising swamps and burned-out towns, and endless cemeteries full of rows of painted wooden markers. Some had names on them, but mostly just numbers.

I passed some old Negroes working in a field.

Once I drove up onto the levee and sat staring at the great river next to a crude, concrete statue of Christ the Healer. The metal bones of His fingers protruded from His crumbling hands. Then over the Sunshine Bridge, and it was early evening.

I first met them on River Road near Belle-Helene plantation, as they were coming back from Carville. There was a patchy mist out of the swamp. I drove slowly, and from time to time I had to wipe the condensation from the inside of my windshield.

In the middle of the smudged circle I had made with my handkerchief, I saw the glimmer of their Coleman lanterns. The oak trees hung over the car. I pulled over to the grass and turned off the ignition. I rolled down my window and listened to the car tick and cool. Soon they came walking down the middle of the road, their spare, pinched faces, their white, buttoned-up shirts stained dirty from the cinders. One or two wore masks over their mouth and nose. Some wore civil defense armbands. Some carried books, others hammers and wrecking bars.

The most terrifying thing about those New Baptist mobs was their sobriety, their politeness. There was no swagger to them, no drunken truculence. They came out of the fog in orderly rows. There was no laughter or shouting. Most of the men walked by me without even looking my way. But then four or five of them came over and stood by the window.

"Excuse me, sir," said one. He took off his gimme cap and wiped the moisture from his bald forehead. "You from around here?"

"I'm from the *Times-Picayune*. I was headed up to Carville."

"Well," said another, shaking his head. "Nothing to see."

"The road's blocked," offered a third. He had rubber gloves on, and his voice was soft and high. "But right here you can get onto the interstate. You just passed it. Route 73 from Geismar. It will take you straight back to the city."

Some more men had come over to stand next to me along the driver's side. One of them stooped to peer inside. Now he tapped the roof lightly over my head, and I could hear his fingernails on the smooth plastic.

"I think I'd like to take a look," I said. "Even so."

He smiled, and then looked serious. "You a Catholic, sir? I guess New Orleans is a Catholic town."

I sat for a moment, and then rolled up the window. "Thank you," I murmured through the glass. Then I turned on the ignition, and pulled the car around in a tight semi-circle. Darkness had come. I put on my headlights, which snatched at the men's legs as I turned around. Illuminated in red whenever I hit the brakes, the New Baptists stood together in the middle of the road, and I watched them in my rear view mirror. One waved.

Then I drove slowly through the crowd again until I found the connecting road. It led away from the river through a few small, neon-lit stores. Pickup trucks were parked there. I recognized the bar Steve had mentioned, and I slowed up when I passed it. I was too late. From Geismar on, the road was deserted.

Close to I-10 it ran through the cypress swamps, and there was no one. Full dark now, and gusts of fog. I drove slowly until I saw a man walking by the side of the road. I speeded up to pass him, and in my high-beams I caught of glimpse of his furious, thin face as he looked over his shoulder. It was Curtis Garr.

* * *

I wish I could tell you how I left him there, trudging on the gravel shoulder. I wish I could tell you how I sped away until the sodomite was swallowed up in the darkness and the fog, how I sped home and found my wife there, unexpectedly waiting. The conference might have let out early. She might have decided to surprise me.

These thoughts are painful to me, and it's not because I can never go back. My friend Rob tells me the borders are full of holes, at least for white people. Passports and medical papers are easy to forge. He spends a lot of time at gun shows and survivalist meetings, where I suppose they talk about these things.

But I left because I had to. Because I changed, and Curtis Garr changed me. Now, in California, in the desert night, I still can't forgive him, partly because I took such a terrible revenge. If he's dead or in prison now, God damn him. He broke my life apart, and maybe it was fragile and ready to break. Maybe I was contaminated already, and that's why I stopped in the middle of the road, and backed up, and let him into my car. Melissa's car.

He got into the back seat without a word. But he was angry. As soon as we started driving again, he spoke. "Where were you? I waited at that bar for over an hour."

"I thought I was meeting Steve."

"Yes—he told me. He described your car."

I looked at him in the rearview mirror. His clothes were still immaculate, his dark suit. He was a fierce, thin, handsome man.

"Where are you going?"

He said nothing, but just stared on ahead through the windshield. I wondered if he recognized me. If he felt something in me calling out to him, he didn't show it. At Carville I'd been wearing a mask over my eyes and mouth.

But I wanted to ask him about Steve. "You're Curtis Garr," I said.

Then he looked at me in the mirror, his fierce eyes. "Don't be afraid," I said, though he seemed anything but frightened.

"I thought I was meeting Steve," I said after an empty pause. "He didn't say anything about you."

"Maybe he didn't think you would come." And then: "We had to change our plans after Rasmussen's goons showed up. Don't worry about Steve. You'll see him later. No one on the staff was hurt."

Garr's voice was low and harsh. I drove with my left hand. From time to time I scratched the skin over my left wrist.

Soon we came up to the Interstate. The green sign hung flapping. I-10 was a dangerous road, and ordinarily I wouldn't have taken it. Most of the way it was built on crumbling pontoons over the swamp. In some places the guard-rail was down, and there were holes in the pavement. But it bypassed all the towns.

Curtis Garr rolled down his window. There was no one on the road. In time we felt a cool draught off the lake.

Once past the airport we could go faster, because the road was carefully maintained from Kenner to the bridge. The city lights were comforting and bright. We took the Annunciation exit and drove up St. Charles, the great old houses full of prosperous, happy folk.

In more than an hour, Garr and I had not exchanged a word. But I felt a terrible tension in my stomach, and my wrist itched and ached.

I kept thinking the man would tell me where to drop him off. I hoped he would. But he said nothing as I drove down Calhoun toward Magazine, toward Melissa's house on Exposition Boulevard.

"Where are you going?" I asked.

He shrugged.

I felt my guts might burst from my excitement. My fingers trembled on the wheel. "Can I put you up?" I said. "It's past curfew. You'll be safer in the morning."

"Yes. I'm meeting Steve at ten."

And that was all. I pulled into the parking slip and turned off the car. Then I stepped outside into the cool, humid night, and he was there beside me. I listened to him breathe. Almost a hissing sound.

"Nice house."

"It's my wife's. She's a professor at Tulane."

Again that harsh intake of breath. He looked up at the gabled roof. For a moment I was afraid he might refuse to come inside. Something in him seemed to resist. But then he followed me onto the porch.

"You don't lock your doors?"

"Of course not."

"Hunh. When I was in school, New Orleans was the murder capital of the entire country."

"It hasn't all been bad," I said.

Then he was in the living room, standing on the Doshmelti carpet. I excused myself to wash my face and hands in the kitchen bathroom, and when I returned he was looking at the bookcase. "Can I get you something to eat?" I asked. "I'm famished."

"Something to drink," by which he meant alcohol. So I brought out a bottle of white bourbon that we had. I poured him a glass. I really was very hungry.

I'd scarcely eaten all day.

"How can you stand it?" he asked suddenly. He had moved over to a case full of biology and medical texts, a collection Melissa had gathered during her trips.

He had one of the books open in his hand. With the other, he gestured with his glass around the room. "All this. You're not a fool. Or are you?"

He put down the book and then walked over to stand in front of me, inches away, his face inches from my own. "I was at Carville," he said. "People died there. Aren't you afraid you're going to catch something?"

But I knew I had caught something already. My heart was shuddering. My face was wet.

I looked up at him, and I thought I could see every pore in his skin. I could see the way his teeth fit into his gums. I could smell his breath and his body when he spoke to me, not just the alcohol but something else. "This state is a sick joke everywhere," he said. "Those people who attacked the Center, they didn't have a tenth-grade education between them. How can you blame them?"

Curtis Garr had black hair in his ears. His lower face was rinsed in grey—he hadn't shaved. I stood looking up at him, admiring the shapes his thin lips formed around his words. "What does your wife teach?"

"Biology."

At that moment the phone rang. It was on a table in a little alcove by the door. I didn't answer it. Garr and I stood inches apart. After three rings the machine picked up.

"Hi, sweetie," said Melissa. "I just thought I'd try to catch you before you went to bed. Sorry I missed you. I was just thinking how nice it would be to be in bed with you, sucking that big Monongahela. Just a thought. I'll be back tomorrow night."

The machine turned off, and Curtis Garr smiled. "That sounds very cozy." Then he stepped away from me, back to the bookcase again, and I let out my breath.

"A third of the population of Louisiana died during the HIV-2 epidemic," I said. "In just a few years. The feds told them not to worry. The doctors told them it couldn't happen. The New Baptists were the only ones who didn't lie to them. What do you expect?"

"Sin and disease," he said. "I know the history. Not everybody died of HIV. I knew some biology too—the real kind. And I said something about it. That's why I was at Carville in the first place. The other thing's just an excuse."

He was staring at the books as he spoke. But he must have been watching me as well, must have seen something in my face as he sipped his whisky, because he lowered the glass and grinned at me over the rim. "You're disappointed, aren't you?"

And then after a moment: "Christ, you are. You hypocrite."

But I was standing with my hands held out, my right hand closed around my wrist. "Please," I said. "Please."

He finished his drink and gave a little burp. He put his glass on one of the shelves of the bookcase, and then sat down in the middle of the couch, stretching his thin arms along the top of it on either side. "No, you disgust me," he said smiling. "Everything about you disgusts me."

* * *

Often now I'll start awake in bed, wondering where I am.

"Melissa," I'll say, still half-asleep, when I get up to go to the bathroom. So Rob tells me on the nights he's there. I used to sleep as soundly as a child. That night, when Curtis Garr stayed in the house on Exposition Boulevard, was the first I remember lying awake.

After I had gone upstairs, he sat up late, reading and drinking whisky on the couch. From time to time I would get up and stand at the top of the stairs, watching the light through the banisters, listening to the rustle of the pages. Near dawn I masturbated, and then after I'd washed up I went downstairs and stood next to him as he slept. He had left the light on and had curled up on the couch, still in his suit. He hadn't even taken off his shoes.

His mouth was open, pushed out of shape by the cushions. I stood next to him, and then I bent down and stretched out my left hand. I almost touched him. My left wrist was a mass of hectic spots. The rash had spread up the inside of my arm.

In my other hand I carried a knapsack with some clothes. My passport, and a few small personal items. Almost everything in the house that actually belonged to me, I could fit in that one bag. A picture of Melissa, which is on my bedside still. I had the card to her bank account, and I stood by the couch, wondering if I should leave a note.

Instead I went into the kitchen, and from the kitchen phone I dialed a number we all knew in Louisiana, in those days. Together with the numbers for the fire department and the ordinary police, it was typed on a piece of paper which was thumbtacked to the wall. The phone rang a long time. But then finally someone answered it, and there was nothing in his tone of voice to suggest he'd been asleep.

Within a few minutes I was on my way. I walked up to St. Charles Avenue just as it got light, toward the streetcar line. The air was full of birds, their voices competing with the soft noise of the cars as they passed a block away, bound toward Melissa's house or somewhere else, I couldn't really tell.

bukavu dreams

At the ten o'clock mass, Father Bizima takes a collection for the survivors of Lyons. He lived in Europe for half his life, and there are tears in his eyes when he makes his appeal. Alphonsine puts two francs into the bowl, and Sergeant Kengo nods his head. He understands her feelings, though money is scarce.

Outside Notre Dame cathedral it's a bright September day. Kengo and his wife walk down the hill, followed by his older daughters. He kisses Alphonsine as they reach the Avenue de l'Athenee, where she turns off to the market with the girls. One of the new men pedals past, ringing his bell. Kengo waves, then follows him down toward the lake.

The prefecture fills half of the old Riviera Hotel, right at the junction of the Botte. Kengo enjoys the walk down through the center of town along Kabila Boulevard. This week it has rained every morning and the streets are clean. Now at midday the small vendors are opening up, and they smile and offer cigarettes. After Bizima's sermon, the sergeant feels thankful and sad. Bukavu is a beautiful city still. Five years of peace since Independence, thank God. One has seen photographs of Paris and they turn the stomach.

He's humming a small tune as he passes the Lumumba Monument. He peels off his white gloves, puts them into his armpit, rubs his hands. His uniform is newer than his suit, so he's worn it to church. Besides, he's promised to stop by the station before joining Alphonsine at her mother's house for dinner. These days there's often some catastrophe, and they are undermanned.

He's right; there's someone in the holding pen. A man in his forties, wire glasses, long stringy blond hair, dull eyes, emaciated. No French, no Kiswahili, unless he's pretending. He's been arrested for selling dagga, after all.

Kengo talks to Jean-Marie, who's on the desk. He's from the hills between Walikale and the Congolese border, so they speak French. "Pas de passport?"

"Non. Deux kilos de contraband, neuf dollars, et un billet de cinquante mille Deutschmarks. Rien de valeur."

Kengo shrugs. "Sauf que le sentiment." He walks over to the cage and grasps one of the bars. "Sprechen sie Deutsch?" Though if the man responds, what then? But he says nothing. He's sitting on the bench, drunk on banana beer, clutching an empty packet of Sportsmans.

"Quelle pagaille," mutters Sergeant Kengo. These refugees are a new development. They've been drifting in over the past six months, crossing through the forest or in small boats from Rwanda over the lake. They stand outside the Marché d'X, showing off their burns or missing fingers. Now there are women too, French and German, begging or prostituting in the villages. How did they get this far? Or is this where all the money finally runs out for everyone, in his poor country? Nine dollars, my God. But a sum like that might easily get mislaid.

Now the man stirs. He stands up in the middle of the cage. "You fucking kaffir bastards," he says. "I've got to piss."

Kengo knows no English, though the man's meaning is obvious. The more so after he unzips his pants and, wonder of wonders, urinates right there in the middle of the cage. His penis is very long, very thin, Kengo notices before he turns away.

He leaves Jean-Marie to call for the concierge, and walks down the hall to the office he shares with Lt. Souza and two others. Today he has it to himself. He throws his kepi and gloves onto the desk, sends the boy out for coffee, and stands looking out the window, a wall of small glass squares. An overgrown garden descends through pines and eucalyptus to the shore. Clouds of mist still linger on Lake Kivu. The water is striped blue and white.

The hotel was built in the 1930s for the families of Belgian civil servants on vacation. In Kengo's childhood it was full of engineers and mzungu tourists. There are glass bricks, yellow zig-zags in the plaster in the art-deco style. The whole Botte, the part of town built on the peninsula, was more or less whites-only even in Mobutu's time. Or else it had seemed that way to him when he was young—dilapidated villas full of ghosts.

He stands listening to the muffled shouting in the hall. Then he turns on the short-wave on the lieutenant's desk and finds a station in Kigali which plays classical music on Sunday afternoons. It's an orchestral piece which he recognizes but can't name, and for a moment he stands irritated at himself, tapping his fingers on Souza's blotter. But then the boy comes in with coffee and the paper.

Now finally everything is calm. The prisoner seems to have been subdued.

Kengo sits down at his desk, rubs his face, smells his fingers. He loves these afternoons when he can be here by himself. His house is so small. He reads some old magazines and then leafs through the rough, smudged pages of Kivu-Match. Again there's a report of poachers in Kahuzi-Biega, which can't be tolerated. He puts his feet up on his desk, listening to the music on the radio. By the time the international news comes on, he's already asleep.

But some of the images from the broadcast work their way into his dream. There's a storm over the lake. Lightning strikes the tallest trees, while others are bent double in the shuddering gusts of wind. Thunder buzzes like a distant aircraft, too high up, too far away to see.

At first there's no rain. Kengo walks along the Avenue du Lac as darkness gathers. He sees the outline of a big house near the old tennis club, and when the first drops come he opens the gate and walks down the overgrown path. He climbs the rotting stairs onto the porch.

The house is empty. There's no furniture in the big rooms. White curtains blow in from open windows on the ground floor. Now the breeze off the lake is wet. Raindrops streak the glass.

Because this is a dream, he smells nothing, hears nothing. He stands with his back to the wall in one of the big rooms, watching the rain spatter in over the window sill, watching it darken the wooden floor. He leans against the blue and silver paper. When she comes in, she doesn't know he's there. She stands in the center of the room. Her raincoat drips. She wears a scarf over her yellow hair. She takes off the coat, the scarf, and hangs them over the top of one of the open glass doors. She kicks off her wet shoes, and when she turns on the electric chandelier, he can see the wet marks of her stockings on the floor.

She wears wire-rimmed glasses, which are fogged up, and she pulls her shirt-tail out to wipe them. She is nineteen or twenty—no more. Now, even though he's moving toward her, she can't see him with her glasses off. Or if she does, she takes no notice. She turns and walks away.

When he wakes up, he finds he has fallen forward with his cheek on his desk. His neck hurts and he has an erection. He feels as if he's been watching an old silent film, and then suddenly the stock has shattered in the department's ancient reel-to-reel.

He knows he must go meet his family at his mother-in-law's house, but for a moment he just sits and listens to the rain outside his office window.

Before they were married, he and Alphonsine used to make love many times a day. Sometimes he would meet her in her mother's house. She would visit him where he was working. She had no shame. She would put her tongue into his ear, lick and kiss him in many places. She rarely kissed him on the lips.

As time goes on, it gets harder and harder to be yourself, express yourself to those you love the most. Too much is at stake. Now like most men in an official position he has a woman he goes to every Friday afternoon. It's a waste of money, for one thing. And now at night with Alphonsine he's like a boy. He doesn't know what to do.

He puts his feet on the desk again. Later, not quite half-asleep, he sees himself picking up an allotment of petrol at the station on the Avenue de la Brasserie. The custodian of the park has sent a boy to ask for police assistance. A gorilla has been found decapitated, shot through the chest, part of the body cooked and eaten. His father, an old silverback named Coco, comes to the Tshivanga station at five o'clock on Saturday morning and leads the guides to a clearing in the bamboo forest on Biega Mountain. His wives and other children hide in the bush.

Kengo wheels out the velo onto the Katana road. He wonders whether he should let the messenger ride behind him. It is a distance of thirty kilometers, all uphill. But dignity is important in these cases. Besides, what would the boy do with his bicycle?

He takes the turn toward Kisangani and climbs west away from the lake, through abandoned plantations of cinchona, coffee, tea. And then into the high forest.

The station house was built for Father Paul d'Alembert, a Belgian primatologist who lived there off and on for seventy-five years, until finally he was murdered by the Hutu militia. His grave is in a garden of ficus trees behind the house. On Sundays, Coco and his family bring long flowering vines out of the forest and twist them round the stone. This behavior is not typical. There was a story about it in the final issue of National Geographic, several years before. Lt. Souza keeps the pages pinned together in his desk.

Because the money and the tourists are all gone, the gorillas have retreated into the forest. Only Coco stays, an evil-looking brute two meters tall, two hundred and fifty kilograms. His portrait is on the five franc note. And he was always the most remarkable, with his vocabulary of over seven hundred signs and phrases, his familiarity with such concepts as freedom and God. D'Alembert used to talk to him for hour after hour in a language no one else learned how to speak. Still he comes round most afternoons, hoping to find somebody to talk to. The village boys who live at Tshivanga now, they're not the ones, thinks Kengo as he rides up through the banana trees. It's evening, and the sun's already down behind the leaves.

He parks in the overgrown lot, walks through the shadows to the house. Three boys dressed in shorts and t-shirts are smoking a hand-rolled cigarette on the porch. They pass it back and forth among themselves, then to a chimpanzee who is tethered to the steps, a chain around its collar. Its wrist is long and limp. It smokes expertly, staring up with bleared, red-rimmed eyes.

Kengo rubs his gloves together. He stands before them with his feet apart, shrugging and gesturing, though no words are spoken. One boy points with his machete to an opening in the bush. A path has been hacked out through the undergrowth.

Kengo has nothing, no food, no water, no stick. He's wearing his hat, his uniform, his white gloves. In the welling twilight he starts down the path. Hyraxes scream. Insects chatter and whine.

Now perhaps there's a big moon or a strange light from the stars, but even after several hours it is not completely dark. The track is cut close to the ground, easy to follow. And there is an animal moving parallel to him fifty meters to his left. When he stops, it stops. It disappears for a moment, and then he sees it up ahead, a motionless shadow. It's not Coco, but a smaller gorilla, perhaps a baby or an unattached male.

For several minutes Kengo stands still. There are mosquitoes around his head. He tries walking back the way he came, but the gorilla follows him. When he stops, it stops.

Kengo's white gloves shine in the darkness. He thinks if he rushes forward, the gorilla will flee away. So he runs toward it up the track, waving his arms. He cries out, but doesn't make a sound.

And the gorilla starts running too, not into the bush, but toward him. In a moment it has jumped into his arms. It locks its legs around his waist, its arms around his neck.

He has to spread his legs, hold onto a vine to support its weight. He turns his head, and he can see its long eyelashes, its black eye. Sweat is running down his neck, and he feels the soft lips of the animal as it nuzzles him. He feels its soft tongue on his neck.

Then it clambers down his legs and takes him by the hand. It leads him away from the track into the sheer forest. Yet Kengo follows easily. A fire is burning up ahead.

Three Europeans are sleeping in a clearing beside a small circle of embers. A plume of smoke drifts up. Kengo can see the stars.

He turns around, but the baby gorilla has disappeared. It has lumbered silently into the bush. Kengo walks around the clearing, and then approaches the sleeping figures from the side nearest their heads, which lie close together. He squats down to examine them.

So young, my God. Two boys and a girl, all in their teens. The girl lies on her back in a green sleeping bag, which she has unzipped in the warm night. Mosquitoes gather on her yellow hair. Kengo moves his hand to chase them away.

Her wire-rimmed glasses are on a cloth beside her head. Her mouth has fallen open, and he can see her teeth. She has a beautiful, wide mouth. For several minutes he squats over her, admiring her neck, her collar bone, her breasts, which he can see under her checked flannel shirt, unbuttoned at the top. He moves his gloved hand back and forth over her face, keeping the mosquitoes away.

Kengo is a burly man, and it's uncomfortable for him to squat like this. When he shifts his weight, his joints crack. Suddenly one of the boys has woken up. He rolls away, then comes to his knees holding a gun.

He calls out in a language Kengo doesn't understand. The other two sit up. The boy with the gun is standing now. Kengo rises with his hands held out; he hopes the uniform will protect him. Surely it's a serious thing to fire on a policeman, no matter where you're from, what horrors you've seen. In fact he disarms the boy quite easily.

Or in another moment he imagines differently. The gun is in his hand. He's taken it from the boy, but not before two silent shots were fired. A bullet has hit him in the shoulder.

It's an unpleasant feeling. For a while he can still move his left arm, but then the muscles stiffen. Blood drips down his chest under his shirt.

The two boys run away into the darkness. They crash through the undergrowth, and he can hear them for a long time. With his right hand he probes the left shoulder of his jacket, and his glove comes away with blood on it.

He hears a whimper in the darkness, and he goes back to where the girl is lying. Kneeling down, in a moment he sees she's been shot through the chest. The wound is hopeless and she knows it. Her eyes are big, shining in the strange light. He takes her in his arms, and she bleeds to death in spite of all his efforts. Grateful, she whispers to him, though he doesn't understand. Perhaps she's giving him a message for her family. "Sprechen sie Deutsch," he murmurs, though if she does, what then? Then he wakes up, and he's fallen forward onto his desk again. His mouth feels big and swollen, pushed out of shape by the pressure of the damp wood.

He's been roused by the sound of a disturbance. Jean-Marie is shouting his name, so Kengo goes out into the hall. Inside the cage, the prisoner is holding onto the bars and banging his head against them. "Fuck, fuck, fuck," he says.

Kengo pulls open the lock and walks into the cage, holding out his hands. "S'il te plait," he murmurs, but the prisoner comes forward with his fists raised. Blood runs from his forehead over his cheeks. Kengo is stronger than this drunken mzungu, but he's still groggy from his nap. Before he's able to wrestle the man down, his eye has been blackened, his lip split.

Then Jean-Marie is there and another patrolman. They take turns slapping the white man's face. Then they pull him to his feet. Kengo watches for a moment as they take him down the hall toward the door into the yard. They will beat him, Kengo's sure.

But it's time to meet Alphonsine and the family. He goes into the cabinet behind the desk and washes his face in the sink. Then he stares at himself in the cracked mirror. The skin over his eye has begun to swell. He dabs at his lip with a wet rag.

Outside it's dark already, and he's late. What a beautiful cool evening. Over the past year people have been predicting radiation storms and terrible weather out of the north, but so far none of that has come. Walking uphill toward Ibanda, at moments he feels anxious and depressed, at moments happy and calm. The air seems to hold currents of sadness, currents of possibility, and he moves through them past the old Residence Hotel, the broken buildings of the Belgian commercial center. An empire of the mind has come to dust.

Alphonsine is waiting at the corner of the dark street. She's a big woman, and he recognizes her from far away. She paces back and forth along the broken sidewalk, a shawl over her shoulders. Reflexively, he allows a stagger of weariness into his step, and she runs toward him. With one hand she holds her flowered shawl closed on her breast, and with the other she's touching his eye, his face. She pulls him under the dim streetlight, making small sounds under her breath. "I was worried," she says. "I heard there was a fight in Nyamugo and some looting. When you didn't come . . . "

He pats her hand. He smiles. "Don't be afraid."

rangriver fell

There had been others before, of course, traders and travelers—our house was full of things only barbarians could make: glass and steel, products of slavery and the burning South. The first one I saw with my own eyes, my brothers and sisters were coming back from somewhere, down from Rangriver where we lived in those days when we were still free, before the soldiers burned us out. That's not fair. We would have gone anyway, soldiers or not. The world was changing and we changed freely—from the time I speak of, I cannot now remember anything but snow. From farther north whole households had already ridden through, searching for food.

This barbarian was on muleback and alone. We followed him along the cliff's edge, singing and throwing snowballs. He was taller than I expected, though not so tall as a man, and he smiled and gave us sugar candies wrapped in real paper. His teeth were black. There are barbarians who pull their children's teeth in babyhood, canines and incisors—they leave gaps on both sides, and later they smoke cigarettes. Their speech is slurred and indistinct. Because they are closer to beasts, they love them more. They eat no meat, raw or cooked. They wear no leather or wool, for their own bodies are hairy past belief. How can they live where it is hot? When I was young I never asked. I was still free, nothing in my mind, wisps of things, snatches of songs, clouds in the sky. We danced around him, grabbing at his stirrups and the heels of his rubber, spurless boots, looking for his tail. "Is it a rat's, a rabbit's, or a dog's?" we sang, each in a different mode. He reached down to pat our heads. He was keeping it hidden in his pants.

At the top of the gorge we came up through cinder pines onto the fell, and here it started to snow again. Here we found people waiting, in from hunting, the horses steaming and blowing, and kicking at the snow. I can identify the time, because the horses still looked sleek. Later they ate bark from the trees. Bears and lions, unnamed from hunger, came down to find them in their pens.

My sister stood away from the rest, and when she saw us, she turned her horse. Not knowing whether the barbarian had been among us before, I hummed a word of possessiveness and pride, for this was how I would have chosen my people to be displayed before a stranger. A woman on horseback, her shoulders wrapped in bearskin, the rifle on her back, her long hair matted and tangled, she looked so free, so quickly gone. The dead buck hanging from her saddle. Child as I was, I felt something loosen in my heart. But barbarians are a practical people, and this one felt nothing. He got down from his mule and walked towards her, talking, and we could hear behind the words of her reply a hint of music, tentative welcome as was proper, in a mode of strength to weakness. Not that it mattered, because though like all barbarians he knew everything, there was something the matter with his ears. He could hear our speech but not our music. In his country the sun has bleached out melody from rhythm—they know all languages, and speak them in dry cadences that mean nothing to us. They hit the bald words like drums. They never try to listen, they only try to understand. He looked puzzled. He couldn't hear that in her music she was offering a place for him to stay, freely, gladly. She meant no harm. Our town was close by, over the ridge. It seemed so easy in those days.

Two ponies pulled a sledge piled with gutted animals, and when he saw it, the barbarian spat, and touched his nose with the heel of his hand, and ducked his face down into his armpit. It is your ritual of hatred. Seeing it for the first time, standing in the snow, I found it funny. My brother had climbed onto the mule, and he was kicking his boots into its ribs while I kicked its backside. "Look how he hates death," sang my brother as the barbarian muttered and prayed. "He hates the sight of it." A strutwing goose trailed its beak along the snow from the back of the sledge, its feathers dripping blood. "He hates it," sang my brother.

* * *

My lords, how hard it is for me to tell you this. To tell a story in the mode of truth from beginning to end, a man is chained like a slave. We were a free people then. This means nothing to you, I know. To me it means my memories from this time are wordless. The beast on the mountain, what is in its mind but music? Chained, it understands each link. It fingers them, it memorizes the feel. Barbarians have their prayers, their work, their things, their names, their families to think of. But we had nothing. No names for ourselves. No words for so many things. No future and no past. Good—here, now, I can be proud of that. But it makes it difficult to begin. Difficult to remember a whole world.

But I remember the death of this barbarian, because that was the beginning of a change in me, the first piece of what is now a burden of memory, and the end of—what? He was the first I had seen. He was a scholar, I know now. He was studying a place familiar to us all, unnamed in our tongue, Baat—or Paat—Cairn, something like that, in his: an empty city high up between the mountain's knees, where the river runs out. I used to go so often. And of all the places of my childhood I remember it the best, because I know that now, right now as I speak, it is there unchanged—the great stone walls and stair-cases, the fallen columns and carved figures many times my height—un-changed, just as I remember it, in that eternal snow. We were a transient peo-ple then, dancers, musicians, hunters on horseback, sloppy builders. We were in love with things that disappear: the last note of the flute, the single flutter of the dancer's hands. In that old barbarian city, people had lived and disap-peared. They would never be back.

The scholar went there every day. At night he stayed in our town and stud-ied us, stayed in our houses, took up no room, made no trouble. He played with his books and papers, his camera and tapes. He had brought his own food, dried vegetables and fruits. Real food disgusted him. And at first my sisters were careful where they slept and how they dressed when he was by, for they had heard barbarians were sensitive to human women, and they had no wish to kill him. But nothing came of that; he slept heavily on the mats and rugs we gave him. And by nightfall he was always drunk. Every evening he would find a corner in the longhouse, and watch and drink until his eyes burned. And I paid close attention. I said to him, "Stranger."

"Yes, boy," his voice a dry drumbeat.

"Stranger, what do you see?"

But one night I thought he hadn't heard. I was squatting beside him. He lay in the dark among the outer circle of watchers, among the children and the cripples. Although it was a frozen night, he wore only a cloth shirt, slavishly embroidered, open at the neck, his chest hair like a blanket, I hoped. The li-quor numbs your senses, I know now. He was very drunk. My face, so close to his, ignited nothing. I saw nothing in the mirror of his face. Fascinated, I stuck my hand in front of his nose. Nothing. His mouth sagged, and I could smell his ruined teeth.

In the silence behind me, in a circle of torchlight, my sister started to dance.

She was new to it, and nervous, her gift just large enough to hide her nervousness. And she danced passionately, as if she were looking to deny what we all knew, that she had not yet heard the song of her own self, that her movements were stolen, mixtures of copies, and she was too young and hot to be anything but formless, anything but molten in her heart's core. She danced, and from time to time in her flashing hands and feet an older dancer in the hall might catch the flicker of something as personal to him as his own body, performed with a dextrousness that he, perhaps, no longer maintained. This was why old and younger dancers were able to gather up the pride necessary to perform. Their greenness or their dryness gave their work a tension missing from more perfect work, the tension of their bodies and their spirit in unequal struggle. When later we would watch a dancer in full flower, her death would dance around her as she danced.

I saw this without looking, but the barbarian stared and stared. My sister raised her naked arms. What did he see? I had heard wonders of drunkenness, stories of hallucinations, burning fires, men turned into beasts, whispers to thunder. I had seen a woman so in love with death that she had cut her foot off and died of the wound, not allowing the biters to come near. But this man didn't look at me. Impatient, I stuck my fingers into his face, poking his uneven cheek. He jerked his head away.

Behind me a musician had begun to play. She had built a new instrument, a kind of guitar that I had never seen before. Envious, I turned to listen, but she had just started when the barbarian got up and stumbled forward under the lamps. Ignoring me, he pushed his way into the center of the hall. My sister crouched over her guitar. The barbarian covered her shoulder with his hairy fingers, and she looked up at him and smiled. The rest of us were too surprised to move, though some of my brothers and sisters were violent and loved bullying. Others had not forgiven him for having brought his camera into the hall one night, or for having tried to sketch them. But most of us were free from that, and we would have been happy to hear him out. And I especially, for some reason, I felt my heart beating as I watched him in the torchlight, leaning on my sister's shoulder, closing his drunken eyes. And when he started to sing, I was caught by a kind of sound that I had never heard before, the uncouth melody, the words like vomiting. His voice was harsh. It made me listen and remember, so that much later I would recognize, in a language that I didn't know, the beginning of the Song of Angkhdt, which is barbarian scripture. "Oh my sweet love, oh God my love, God let me touch you, and feel the comfort of your kisses, for you are my light, my life, my joy, my cure, my heart, my heartache . . ." The language was dead before time began, abandoned by decree. Your bishop said it was a sacrilege to use the holy words for common purposes. Now no one can tell how they were once pronounced, and you fight wars over their meaning.

Of all that I knew nothing yet. But I heard the conviction in the drunkard's voice; it rang the rafters. This was the first song I remember—I mean with words. Among us words were thought to muddy music, for the notes themselves can mean so much. That was not at issue here, in a language none of us could understand. But some could not endure even the sound of your religion, the vicious ecstasy, the sound of faith. I didn't mind it. I thought they were jealous of a new way. Anyone should be able to stand up and sing. But we had habits, though it hurts me to say it, for yes, that was slavery too, of a kind. You must understand, not all of us were clever. But some sang every night, and their music and their pride was the only law we had. One of my brothers, a bully and a dancer, took the barbarian by the throat and struck him down, and threw him out into the snow.

Late at night I got up from the sleeping room and went out. He was lying in a snowbank, breathing softly. I thought his body hair might keep him warm. There was no wind. The stars hung close. I had brought a bearskin, and hoped not to offend him, but I did. By morning he had thrown it off. I suppose he smelled the leather even in his sleep. By morning he was frozen dead.

* * *

My lords, our world must appear cruel and incomplete. We knew nothing about love. That is a barbarian lesson I learned later. But at that time we were a free people. We called each other brother and sister, but we were always alone. Because what is freedom more than that—the need to hear your own music always, even in a crowd? When the barbarian died, I felt stifled, watching the biters cut off his tail on the high ground above the river, watching them cut his body into pieces for the wheeling birds. In the morning I took a pony and some skis, and rode out through the gates of our town, out over the hills, far out towards the abandoned city, where the barbarian had had a camp. I was unhappy, but not for long. The snow stretched unbroken all around me, and in a little while I had forgotten. My mind felt empty as the snow, and I found myself humming and making little gestures with my hands, because I loved that journey. You rode in over a high span of stone, the river booming far below you at the bottom of a gorge. Birds flew underneath the arch, and at the far side the remnants of a huge bird-headed statue broke the way. Its head lay in a rubble of chipped stone, as long as my body, intricately carved, its round eye staring upward. I had to lead my pony over it, and in through the shattered gateway where the bridge met the sheer cliff face, the clifftops high above me. I rode up through a steep defile cut into the rock, lined with broken columns in the shape of trees. Their stone branches mingled into arches, and I rode up through another gateway where the walls around me rushed away, and out into a great open space where the wind pulled at my clothing and swept the stones clean. From here you could see the sun, rising as if behind a paper shield, the sky as white as paper. And in the middle of this stone expanse rose up an enormous pitchrock fountain, a giant in chains; that city must have been a great center of slavery, the stonework is so good. His hands and feet are chained behind him, his eyesockets are hollow. The water must have come from there and dribbled down from wounds cut in his chest and arms and thighs. In the old days, he must have stood in a pool of tears and blood.

I went on and entered streets of empty palaces, their insides open to the weather, their doorways blocked by drifting snow. I turned the corners randomly and wandered in and out of being lost, but the pony knew the way, slave to habit. So I got down and left it sheltered in a ruined porch, and climbed up into an older section of the town, where massive pyramids and temples of an older, gentler design stood like a ring of snowy hills. And in an open space near the largest of these, a tumbled hill of masonry, I found the barbarian's camp. He had discovered something, a hidden temple where the rock seemed solid, and he had come up every day to work on it, and come back every night to live with us and drink and sleep in our houses in the valley. He had kept maps and papers here, in a black tent standing in a ruck of fallen stones. He had kept a fire outside, the black smoke visible from far away. Once I had come to watch him work.

Now the fire was scattered, but there was a horse tethered outside. I had seen its footprints in the snow, and dog prints too. I could hear dogs barking, and in a little while they came running towards me over the snow, long-legged hunting dogs, but the tent was empty. I stood outside, the dogs jumping and cleaning my hands. I opened my coat to the white air and sucked the cold air through my teeth. I was so happy. I had no way of guessing then, my lords, that the future of my people lay in a barbarian city like that one had been, full of sweat and noise and slavery. Our tails would grow long, and we would never eat meat anymore. My lords, here in your hard streets, hunger forces me to make up answers to your questions and sell my memories for food. It is a biting habit to think about the past. But I have no pride left; it hurts me to say it, for humility was something far beyond my childlike imagination as I stood in that abandoned city in the snow. Then my heart was empty as the air. I stamped my feet and shook my arms, and saw as if for the first time where the barbarian had found a flaw in the gradual surface of the pyramid, and rubbed it with gasoline and blasted out a hole the size of a man.

He had discovered a rough passageway into the heart of the stone hill; I entered it, and stopped on the threshold of a round chamber. To my right and to my left around the wall stretched a row of statues in a ring, facing inward to the room. They sat and stood in lifelike poses, some stiff, some slouching, and some leaned together as if talking. Some were gesturing with open mouths, as if they had been cut off in the middle of a word. The one beside me touched his neighbor lightly on the arm, as if to draw his attention to something happening across the room. And they had all been carved by the same hand, that much was clear, a hand that took delight in complicated clothes and simple faces. For though some were old with stringy necks and some were young, they all had qualities in common. Their faces were unmixed. Each had hardened over a single mood—pride in one, stupidity in another, malice, innocence. An old man was biting on a coin. Another pulled a stone cork from a stone bottle, his face contorted in a drunken leer. Another hid the stiffness in his lap under a fold of cloth and scratched forever at a bleeding sore. For a free man, the joy of living comes from knowing that it won't be long, that all flesh dies and disappears, but these barbarian kings and princes, it was as if the god they worshipped had turned them into stone. They would live forever, as doubtless they had begged him in their prayers.

A man stepped out across the room opposite from where I stood, a biter. I would have known him by his clean clothes even if I had not known his face. He had been a strong musician once, and I have memories of him standing in the torchlight of the hall, bent over his violin, my brothers and my sisters packed like slaves to hear him. Or even when he played alone, by himself in the high pastures, I remember children running out to find him, and they would sit around him in the snow. But by the time I speak of, that was past. A man had cut his hand off in a fight, I don't know why, and he had given up and taken to biting in a house by himself. Let me explain. Our kind of life was not for everyone. Some found it hard to give up everything for freedom's sake. They had things to occupy their minds. They were addicted to some work, or they had friends and children. We had given them a name. We called them betrayers, literally "biters" in our language, and we hated them. The pride of our race was so hard to sustain. The rest of us had sacrificed so much to music, to emptiness and long cold wandering, that we could only hate them. And we hated them the more because we needed them. The biters were our doctors, builders, makers, parents. It gave them happiness to do things for themselves and other people. Without that, life falls apart, no matter what your gifts. Babies die, houses fall down. We needed someone to preserve us, to preserve a spirit they themselves could never share, a spirit to fill us with hunger every morning as we broke snow on the mountains with our horses and our dogs, a spirit to fill us every night and every morning with reasons to be up and to be gone.

But I am wandering: That day, in that stone chamber when I was a child, a biter stood in the middle of a circle of statues with a carbide lantern in his hand. He said, "Is that you?" He said "Is that you?" in an empty voice, and then something else. I didn't understand him. Biters often know peculiar words. But the dead man, the barbarian scholar, had had a name and that was it. Mistaking me for him, the biter called me by his name, a word that referred to him as if he were a thing, fit to be used, like a blanket or a bed. My brothers and my sisters had no names.

I took up a loose piece of tile and skipped it across the floor. It made a circle round the biter's feet. He laughed. "Little brother," he said, and he came towards me. "Little brother, what are you doing here?" This was common biting, not worth a reply. I spat onto the floor and turned away. There was a statue in the center of the room, different from the rest—a stone table and the figure of a man astride it, his legs hanging down on either side. He had a dog's head, dog's teeth, dog's eyes, and the hair ran down his back under his rich clothes. From his groin rose up a stiff, enormous phallus which he held in front of him between his hands. It was so thick his fingers couldn't close around it, and so tall it protruded to his chin. Along its naked sides long lines of words were cut into the stone, and single words into the spaces between his knuckles.

The biter stood behind me and reached out to touch its bulbous head, where it swelled out above the statue's hands. "It is Angkhdt," he said softly. "Prophet of God. The dog-headed master. It's sad, isn't it, that it would come to this?"

Questions, hard tenses, gods. I hated him. I hummed a few phrases of an anger song, a melody called "I'm warning you," but the biter took no notice. "Where is he?" he asked.

I turned to face him, furious. How could he force me to remember? The man was dead, gone, vanished out of mind. Time had closed its hand. In those days we were in love with a lie, that objects could disappear into the air, that there was no past, no future, that people needed the touch of my hand in order to exist, the image in my eye.

It was a lie I cherished rather than believed. In fact, I remembered very well. And I wanted him to know what had happened. I wanted him to know the man was dead. And so, though I said nothing, through music I put a little death into the air, a song called "now it's gone," but in a complicated rhythm because I could not cover in my voice a small regret.

The biter listened carefully, tilting his head. With his forefinger, he stroked the underlip of the stone phallus, and his face took on a strange gentle statement. "They murdered him," he said. "Which one?"

How I hated him! Him and his past tense. Him and his questions. Yet there was a power in his hawklike face that made him difficult to resist, a keenness in his eye. I dropped my head and muttered part of a song, my brother's music, the man who had first struck the barbarian down.

He recognized it. It was a beautiful song, spare, strong, proud, like the man himself. At the second change, I heard the biter hum a part of it. He brought his wrists together, and with his whole hand he caressed the angry stump where his other hand had been. "It is he," he said softly. "It is always he. Little brother," he said, and stretched his hand out to touch me, only I ducked away. "Little brother," he continued. "Don't you see how men like him can kill us all?"

I started away, my face full of disgust, but he smiled and called out to me: "I'm sorry. I apologize. No biting. Or at least, only a little. Because I am talking about the future. Don't pretend you never think of it."

I turned to face him, because I was pretending. He was right. He said: "I see you. You are different from the rest. I see you. Before. I saw you. The others do not think, do not remember. You can."

I stood fascinated. He was trying to seduce me, I could tell. It was the biter's slough of reason, of cause and effect, so easy to fall into, so hard to climb back out. I could feel tears in my eyes, and I bent to pick up a loose stone.

The biter smiled. "I'm insulting you," he said. "Listen. Use your thoughts. We are starving. There is nothing left in these mountains. Every day the hunters bring in less. There is none left."

I listened, hardfaced.

"Don't you understand?" he said. "We have to do it. Something. All together."

I stared at him.

"South of here," he said. "Way south, there is no snow. There are deer on the hill. Fish in the water. Listen—every day I talk to the barbarian. Every day I come here. I listen to his stories. He is teaching me. Now he is dead, yet it is still the truth. He was . . . He told me about it. There is food to eat."

"Yes I starve. I want it."

"That's not true."

"Yes," I cried. "But I am not a slave to my own mind. I am not. I prefer to die. My brothers and sisters are too proud."

"I don't mean that," he said. "We are not slaves. I mean to take what we want. Take it. These barbarians are hairy dwarves. We are free. He was teaching me a trick. A way of singing—let me tell you."

Bored, I turned away. But there was a peculiar music in his words. He brought his fist crashing down on the tabletop. "I can hurt you," he shouted. "I can force you. There is a strength in this room if I knew how. There is strength in these gods." He came towards me, grinning, and I backed away. "I will do it," he said. "I hate your stupidness. And I hate myself."

He lied. His self-love rang in every word. His voice was like two instruments in conflict, one ferocious, one insinuating. He had been a strong musician, and this music was a storm in him. "Do not laugh at me!" he shouted, and shook the stump of his arm in my face as if it were a weapon. He was a little crazy, too, I thought, with his bony face, his eyebrows, his dark eyes. In the light of the carbide lantern his shadow made a giant on the wall, reeling drunkenly in the light of the carbide lantern.

In those days I was easily bored. I knew so few words. This biter was talking about something. He was using words as a kind of movement, and that made me uncomfortable. So I left him, and outside it had begun to snow again. The sky was full of wordless snow. It blunted the edges of the mountains and the buildings, blunted everything, relaxed and calmed me. The dogs were stifled as I slogged away. It was very cold.

* * *

My lords, that night a volcano burst up on the ridge somewhere, and my brothers and sisters and I went up to see—nothing, as it turned out, nothing but smoke and steam. It rained, and in the valley you could hear the trees exploding like distant gunshots, like gunshots where the hot stones spattered on the ice. The clouds reflected a dull glow from far away, that was all. We froze. I thought the night went on forever. That night I thought the world had changed, and perhaps it had, because in the morning the sun was late in coming, I could tell. It rose late out of a smelly mist, and we shivered and whispered, coming home over the ice. From far away we could see a fire burning in our town, and we laughed and ran down the last ridge, in through the gates, under the belltower, up past the longhouses and barns. In those days before the soldiers came, our town was built of logs and mud among the ruins of an older place. The stone walls, the tower, the eternal well, all that was ancient barbarism. We had built our windowless, dark halls on its foundation.

Outside the dancing hall, the biter had made a bonfire. With biter friends he had slaved together a wooden wagon with heavy wooden wheels and had pulled the stone table and Angkhdt's statue from the mountainside, all the way down from the empty city. He had drawn his cart up to the bonfire, the open end facing outward, and the firelight shining through the braces and the wooden spokes. He stood in it as if on a stage, the fire at his back. Beneath him my brothers and my sisters shambled around the stone table, and they admired its blunt surface and the lewd god astride it.

We heard the biter's voice. He had been a strong musician once, but now he used his voice to bite us. He used the thing that he had learned. He had made a barbarian way of singing. With words he could make new pictures in the air. And he was using them to bite us, for in those days nothing could bind my stupid family like fire, like dancing; he capered above them in a black flapping robe, his mutilated arm held crazily aloft, and they stood in the slush with their mouths open. At first I didn't listen. I was watching for the sunrise, and as I stood at the outskirt of the crowd, pushing towards the heat, I saw a little way in front of me the neck and shoulders of my sister, wedged in between some others. She was close enough to touch, almost, a girl almost ripe, older than I. I could only see part of her head, but I knew that it was she, because around her I always felt a sad mix of feelings, so I wriggled forward until I stood behind her. Her yellow hair ran down her back. My mind was full of it, full of the barbarian luxury of it. Yet even so the biter's melody broke in, and I looked up to see him dancing and reeling. He was a powerful man. In his singing I could see the barbarian city on the mountain as it was when men still lived there, the paint still fresh on the buildings. His voice was full of holes. Yet even so I saw that barbarian city, and a crowd of people standing in the square. I saw the colors of their clothes and the lines of their faces. In a central square of yellow stone, of high, flat buildings, lines of open windows, hanging balconies, a group of huntsmen dismounted. They were dressed in leather and rich clothes, red and brilliant green. A huge horse stood without a rider, and beside it, chained by one wrist to the empty stirrup, naked and dusty, his great dog's head bent low, knelt the barbarian god. He had careful, yellow, dog's eyes. Nearby, a pale boy, wounded in the chase perhaps, lay dead or dying on the stones, surrounded by slaves and sad old men. The sun burned, and the god waited, sweating in the dirty shade around the horse's legs, until they brought a wooden cage and chained his hands and feet, and prodded him inside with long thin poles; he lay in one corner and licked along his arm.

This is a story from the Song of Angkhdt. As we listened, standing near the fire with our mouths open, people said they saw the statue move, and some claimed that the lines of symbols on its swollen penis seemed to glow. I know nothing about that. But as stupid as it sounds, my lords, I did hear a voice out of its stone head, for the music had stopped suddenly, and the vision had disappeared. It was a curious, airless kind of voice, and either the language was unknown to me or else I was too far away to understand. But I understood the biter. He was speaking too. "Listen to God's laws," he said. "Love freedom. Love freedom more than death. Be kind to one another," things like that, laws and hateful rules. That biter was a crazy man. So much loneliness, so much gnawing on his biter's heart had made him mad. He was searching for a god to make him lead us, force us to follow after him, yet how could he have thought that we would stand still and listen to that kind of song? In fact, he must have quickly realized his mistake, for all around, people were moving and touching themselves, the magic broken. In front of me, the girl had turned away and put her fingers to her head.

I was bored and angry, but not for long, because the biter started to sing again. In his voice I saw the god lying in darkness in a wooden cage. It was empty night in the barbarian city, and I saw him raise his silver head just as a dog would have, for towards him over the flagstones flowed a rivulet of water—down one street, down another, out into the open square. He was waiting for it. And as it came, a gentle wind ran through the city, starting out of nothing, then subsiding. The god yawned, and passed his hand along the bars of his cage. He rubbed it slowly, rhythmically, coaxing some greenness back into the dead wood; slowly at first, imperceptibly, he sealed the wounded bark, he rubbed it whole. Under the cage the flagstones split apart as roots spread down. And in the iron joints the first leaves appeared, one, and then more, tiny and weak at first, but gathering strength and number until the cage had disappeared and Angkhdt lay as if in a leafy thicket or a wood, a gentle wind stirring the branches, while in the house women woke next to their sleeping mates, and shook themselves awake and looked around.

Again the vision broke. I heard the statue speak again, louder this time, and this time I could understand, for I was looking for the magic, and so was everybody else. That way it claimed our minds. It said: "You are my people. Free as fire. Like the fire you will grow and spread. For I have chosen a way..." It went on for a long time, telling us to take our things and weapons and leave our town, telling us to follow this biter and make a war with him. In the crowd some stood without listening, warming their hands, but others shouted angrily, and one climbed up into the open cart. He grabbed the biter from behind, one arm across his stomach, the other on his throat. He lifted him off his feet, lifted him up kicking, and dropped him over the side of the cart into the crowd. Then there was quiet. My brother was in the cart, standing up alone. We were used to him, watching him dance, so we just stood there, watching. He raised his arms above his head and clenched his fists, and leaped the distance from the cart onto the tabletop. He kicked the dog-headed statue in the chest, and it turned on its base and fell heavily to the ground, legs in the air. The biter cried out and struggled forward through the crowd, but nobody looked at him because my brother, limping and twisting on one foot, had raised his hands above his head and started to dance. It was tentative and slow, a dance we all knew, a dance which belonged to us, part of all of us. All of us could dance it in our different ways. It was the song of freedom, of namelessness, the triumph of our race, and so poignant, too, to see him dancing with his broken foot, it gave each step a special transience. My brother danced, and the crowd spread out away from him, because this was the kind of dance that helps you not to stand together in a group, thinking the same thoughts.

My brother pulled a knife out from his clothes and danced with it. Now from the crowd came up a kind of music, hesitant at first, but stronger and stronger as it became clear to us what he was going to do. Our voices, young and old, rough and smooth, searched for a common music, making it out of nothing, and some had carried their instruments with them, and some ran to fetch theirs, and all clapped their hands and sang—we didn't know this music. But like the dance it came together as we sang, more sure with every motion, every note. It sang of freedom, sang of emptiness, and it came together as if out of our own empty hearts. My brother danced a long time. And in the end, everybody knew it; we forced him with our voices, we built him to a climax, and at the end of it he drew the knife around his neck, once, twice, in perfect rhythm to the dance, a scarlet string around his neck—too tight, for he tried to sing then and couldn't, for his mouth was full of blood. He spit it out, and summoning his strength, he sang a song that was not like singing nor like anything.

And as he sang, a shadow rose and it got dark. The sun was hidden in a cloud of frozen dust, remnants of the volcano we had seen the night before. Sticks and pieces of dirt fell from the sky. Horses cried out and kicked their stalls. People gathered together, cursing in the filthy dark. We ran inside out of the storm, and then the biter spoke again, and said in plain language that he was running south with others of his kind, to bring some war into the cities there. He said the storm was the barbarian god. People moved around him, desperate and afraid, but more prepared to go off by themselves, according to our custom of leaving and never coming back. They prepared to ride out north, perhaps, alone. They had no maps. They prepared to ride out into the unbroken snow. For some it was as if they had found a sudden reason to do as they had always wanted. The mud lay inches thick on all the beds. It seemed pointless to clear it all away.

* * *

My lords, a child's mind is not to be relied on. If I thought that you were interested in the truth, I suppose I would keep silent. Yet I have carried these images with me, and now I unpack them, some for the first time. Always I am tempted to describe my life as if to an empty room, as if the words could simply disappear. Tempted and not tempted, for the bitterness is that I have changed and not just gotten older. Here in your sad city I have let a world collect around me, opinions, objects, thoughts; I have found a name. Nor can I claim compulsion. I have made myself a slave, and now I look around me through a slave's eyes, that's all. Therefore I have become very fine in my distinctions, and I think I was mistaken. I think now the volcano and the mudstorm came some other time. Reason tells me now there must have been a period when people came to their own conclusions and rode out, too hungry to stay, but how could we measure time in that blank winter, with our blank minds? When my mothers and fathers were growing up, there were still seasons in the lives of animals, but in that last phase of winter, when I was a child, there were no more fawns, no cubs, no colts, no pups, no calves, no goslings, no sweet lambs, and after that the hills were empty. We went hungry. Why would people stand for it, who had a choice?

I remember a full town and an empty one. And there was a mudstorm, yes. The sky was black; stones fell from the sky. I huddled in my muddy bed. People yelled and ran. And I remember waking up one morning to new snow. New snow was falling. I walked out to the open space in front of my house. The stone table was there, and the dog-headed statue on its back in the new snow. Our town was empty. Or rather, the children were left. Those who hadn't had the strength to go. They came out one by one, my brothers and my sisters, with white, muddy faces. There was not a sound.

I walked over to the gate. Broken instruments littered the ground, sifted over with snow. Departing during the storm, people had stood shouting over the noise of the wind, their baggage around them in fat bags, the horses kicking and stamping in the frozen mud. One by one, men and women had pulled on their knapsacks and swung themselves up into their saddles, leaving what they could not carry. And as they walked their horses through the tower gate, their instruments in their hands, some would bend down and break them on the stone gatepost, and others would stand up in the stirrups and break them on the arch above their heads. I kicked through fretboards, mutes, and reeds.

Some older children had been able to seize the strength to go, and women had taken the youngest ones, their own or someone else's, for tangled reasons. Those left behind were of the age which no one loves, and I was one of these.

We took our blankets from the abandoned halls and all moved into one, except for a few of the proudest. But these soon took horses and rode out, not knowing where, I suppose, or where else but to their deaths. The rest of us lived together in one hall, and kept a fire burning. For nothing reduces people to barbarity quicker than hunger. We developed barbarous habits. We sat together and discussed things. Looking back, that seems like the worst part. Then, the worst part was going to bed hungry, was the interminable waiting to grow up.

There was a girl with yellow hair. How can I describe my feelings? They were a source of shame to me. She lit a fire in the hall and danced for us a little. I scraped the mud away from part of the floor and built a pile of pillows next to her bed. I should have stayed away in the farthest corner. She was not musical or strong, a great hunter or a great dancer. But I wanted something, even though I knew that wanting is a trick of the mind. It is like stooping to believe a lie. For days I would go off alone, hunting in the snow, fishing, yet at night I would sit and watch her shake her hair loose down her bare back. She had a face—how shall I say—unmarked by pride. That is our flaw, in general, the way you barbarians are hairy, with rotten teeth and foul breath. Our men and women had proud faces, and if they laughed it was for a reason: Because after a cold day they had brought a buck down with one shot. Or because another had missed. Or because in the middle of the morning they could hear nothing but their own music. Yet this girl would laugh about nothing. She saw no stain in kindness, and perhaps she was adapting to new circumstances, but I thought rather it was something true to her. The men and women of our race have hungry bodies, but already hers was made for giving. She had full breasts, wide hips, round arms and legs.

The snow went on forever, and then a new season came, a dark, false season. It was the Paradise thaw, the last phase of winter, though how could we have known? The sun barely shone. The snow melted, for a while. The grass grew white and yellow, but it did grow, and in a biter's house we had found a store of corn. The taste was poisonous, but I was glad to be alive, because the world was strangely beautiful during the thaw. The trees never recovered their leaves. In the valleys, in the white grass, they stood up dead with naked arms. And it was always dark, for at this time the sun crept blood-red along the horizon all day, rising and setting between the jagged peaks, the colored clouds like sunset all the morning and midday, the shadows long and heavy. At night it was almost brighter—you could ride all night, because during the thaw a new planet appeared, Paradise, you call it, another world, and it burned with a dead light above our heads. That first night it took up half the sky. The dogs howled and cried out. Barbarians worship Paradise, but I knew nothing of that yet. At first I was afraid.

The air was still. There was not a breath of wind. There was no rain, although the ground was wet with stagnant water everywhere. No dogs gave birth. Plants grew, yes, but the stalks had lost their stiffness—they grew flat and tangled on the ground like the hair on a man's head. The air seemed hard to breathe and full of queasy echoing. There was no nourishment in it. Noises close at hand seemed far away. And in the high pastures our ears buzzed and rang; we walked our horses and held onto their manes. It was a different kind of living. People slept all day, and even awake they were part asleep.

It is easy to describe these things as if the world had died overnight. But soon we remembered nothing different. These changes, though they sound tremendous, came subtly and gradually. I thought I was growing up. My body had changed more than the air. And though every day I was filled with sleepy awe, though in everything I saw the promise of my death—the stark trees, the plants twisting along the ground—I was more concerned with hunger, and more concerned with sleeping next to that girl every night. I wanted there to be a way of touching her, but it was impossible. I would sit awake, looking at the heap of blankets next to me. Perhaps she would have responded to my touch. Yet I was afraid I was not capable. I had seen it often enough. And barbarians can copulate like animals, but I thought I was not yet quite enough of a barbarian for that. There were physical differences, I had heard. Besides, what should I do? Should I say . . . something, should I reach out my hand? Men and women drank to frenzy before they could surrender to this thing. They drank a wine we had, and then they dreamed a numb, erotic dream. In the morning they remembered nothing and could look at each other without shame. Women had no men, children no fathers. The slavery would have been intolerable, for in this act of loving there is always slave and master, victory and defeat. We were too proud for that.

But the temptation made me angry, and I saw her sweating like a pig that season, her and a few others, planting and digging. I told myself she had surrendered to a biter's foresight, finding a biter's comfort in the dirt, the sweat, the feeble grain. It was not food for human beings. But with a biter's caution, she saw that soon we would be so hungry we would be eating dogs and horse meat. She had found a taste for choices. She took corn and ground it to a pulp, and mixed it with hot water—edible, perhaps, but deadly to the heart. We blamed her for it. We would slink up to the pot and put our hands in it, angry and sullen because we found ourselves grateful, I suppose. We would have starved on what human food we had. Or we would have had to kill our animals. Horses, always docile, had learned to eat grass, though it made them sick and listless. But our dogs had higher stomachs. Already they fought one another and devoured the carcasses, and in this we might have seen a wild premonition of ourselves, had not my sister showed us we were more like horses.

And in time I came to admire her for her serenity, her way of laughing at our sulkiness. Besides, I had begun to notice biting tendencies in myself. I discovered the importance of things I never would have noticed. One of the younger children was very sick. He had started to die. He was a sniveling little boy, with a sniveling weak face, but it was as if I found a strange compulsion to memorize everything about him, every sickness, every change. I could feel I was robbing him of his own death, for it was as if I had clenched my hands around his spirit, and as if his spirit was escaping not from another room, not from some private place, but from between my fingers. But finally he escaped from me.

That day the sun shone blood-red on the pale grass, and I was walking with my horse among some trees. I will describe the place. Among dead trees a brook widened into a clear pool, a small thing, water coiling on a cold rock. I found a single, leather, child's boot. A boot like many others, but with the biter's part of my mind I recognized it. It had belonged to the little boy.

In winter, a field of snow stretches unblemished to the horizon, but you have only to look behind you to see your own trampled mark, ephemeral and confused, a dream in the pure wilderness of sleep. I thought, what difference can it make to me where the child is? If he were dead, then he was on that hillside where the snow never broke beneath his feet, not in front of him, not behind. He had become part of the world's intolerable beauty. Where was the sadness in that thought? Where was the sadness in death? Yet I was not happy, because no matter how hard you try to be free—and when I was a child we did try—people have dark in them as well as light. They have deep, biting instincts in their heart of hearts. They are like the dark world with Paradise around it.

I reached for the boot. It was a good one, fur-lined, but with the remnants of some decoration. I held it in my hand, trying to forget, until above me on the hillside, a boy came running down. Dogs were with him, barking and excited. He carried dead animals from the end of a long pole, and now he swung the pole up over their heads and kicked them as they snarled and jumped. He capered down the hillside out of breath, the dogs around him. When he passed me, he stopped and swung the pole.

I saw the naked tail hang down from one of them. "Rabbits," I said.

"Rabbits," he repeated proudly.

"Look what I have," I said.

He seemed doubtful. I held the boot out by the heel, and he took it, saw it was too small for him, cast it on the bank. I admired the sparseness of his mind. "Boot," he said.

I explained what I was feeling as well as I could. He understood me, or rather understood the words, the music, the sense, but not the point. I could tell he thought me strange to concern myself when there must be other children still alive who fit my vague descriptions. But he retrieved the boot, examined it more closely, threw it down again. And, sick of listening, he said, "Come eat," and leapt away from rock to rock, brandishing his pole, humming part of a song called "I forget."

I didn't follow, even though the smell of dead meat swinging near my head had lit in me a burning hunger. I turned and walked up to where I had left my horse. I knelt by the stream and ran my fingers in the water. It had gotten dark, but even in the darkness I could see the shadows of the trees. And when I stood up to lead the horse away, I saw that he held between the cruel ridges of his beak a child's severed hand. He was sucking on it the way barbarians eat candy. I reached up, and he pulled his head away and glared at me; he had been scratching for toads in the flaccid grass and had found something better. I let him be.

The air was perfectly still. The grass grew thick where I stood in a bowl-like indentation in the slope, which was lined with trees and slabs of stone. Paradise had risen, once again, up over the mountain crests, and rinsed the grass with silver light. From one tree there came a drip, drip, drip. Something hung from a rope among the lower branches. It circled quietly in the quiet air.

I walked up the slope until I stood beneath the tree. I reached out and caught some of the drops. In that light they had no color of their own, but it was blood, of course. I knew it by the feel and smell and taste, and like the smell of my brother's rabbits it awakened a hunger in me—blood past its first freshness. I stood admiring the light until a little pool had formed in my palm. Beneath the tree, the grass lay crushed. Animals had rolled in it.

A child's body had been tied up like a package. It rotated slowly at the end of a rope, and I saw the rope was barbarian-made, because of its contemptibly high quality.

I climbed up into the tree. A child had been mutilated, his eyes dug away, his tongue cut out. Only his torso and his head remained; his arms and legs had been severed at the joints and carried away. His strange, empty head fell loosely from side to side as the rope rotated. His neck must have been broken. Standing on a low branch, I reached out to shake the silken rope, to make the body jerk and dance. It was my little brother.

I climbed down. My horse was already clawing at the grass, but I pulled him free, down the slope. There was no space to ride, but in a little while the trees gave out into a grassy meadow. There I swung myself up. Paradise was bright like day, and the horse uneasy, pulling at his rope. At first I thought it was from horsey love of open spaces, until I smelled what it smelled: once again, the smell of death. The grass had been trampled in a muddy track down towards the town, as if a troop of men and horses had passed together. That was unusual enough. But in the middle of it lay the body of a dog, a great noble brute, silver in the gleaming starlight. His silver fur was seething, alive in the shadows of the grass. But he was stone dead, lying on his side, his heavy head stretched out in the mud. I walked my horse around him in a circle.

Farther on, over the next hillside, I found my brother's body, the boy I'd seen that evening, running down the mountain, full of laughing plans for dinner and the love of running.

I got down. He had been shot with an expanding bullet through the back and had fallen with his arms in front of him. I hadn't heard the shot. His stick had broken under him, and the rabbits were trampled in the mud. They had shot another dog there too, shot it in the side and disemboweled it later, it seemed. And again, the boy's face was mutilated, as if they had tried to carve a letter or a sign into his features.

I gathered together my brother's scattered arrows. There was no bow, but that morning I had taken mine, taken my knives and steel slingshot—tools for hunting. When the track of horses broke away uphill again, I followed it up into the fields beneath a mountain slope of red volcanic stone. It was a place I knew well. At one time biters had brought their sheep up there to graze on insects incubating in the snow; they had lit fires and stayed for a long time. I had come, too, with my childish music, or with some childish problem only a biter could resolve—an earache, a hole in my boot.

Now the grass lay thick and white, and it dragged at my horse's feet. His claws got stuck in it, and sometimes he came near to stumbling, for I spurred him hard, driven by my anger, until we broke the crest of a steep hill, and I saw in the valley underneath us, a bonfire.

I left my horse and ran down through the fields. The fire seemed enormous. Close at hand I could only see outlines and shadows, but on the far side, the hot light painted their faces and their clothes. They were barbarians, small hairy men in black uniforms, squatting near the fire. They had heated up some orange mash of vegetables in a metal pot and were eating out of metal cups. I was happy not to smell it close. But I could hear them talking, and I was amazed to realize I could understand what they were saying, though the accents were harsh and ugly, the verbs unfamiliar. There was no music in it, yet even so there was something more than words, for they shouted and laughed and seemed content. I saw that they were drinking. They were drunk. I crept closer. One said, "Even so, you shouldn't have shot the bitch."

"It tried to bite me."

They were talking about the dogs, I thought. I felt a strange thrill listening to their voices, watching their clumsy movements. They were so small, so ugly, with flat, hairy, intelligent faces, full of thoughts and knowledge. Dark skin, dark eyes, dark hair hanging down their backs, gathered at their necks in metal rings.

They finished their food, and they sat drinking, smoking cigarettes, talking about places I had never heard of, things I didn't know. It made a kind of sense. One played the guitar in a way I had no words for. He said, "Let's see if she will dance for us. I'd like to see her dance."

"You let her be. You know what our orders are."

"Our orders are to kill them as we find them. I could report you both for keeping her alive."

One laughed: "That's all right. She's just a girl."

"Yes, that's right. She's a meat-eating bitch. And an atheist. You leave her be."

One laughed: "Admit it, you like her."

I found it hard to understand who was talking. Yet even so it made a kind of sense. There was a fat, older man. He said: "Well maybe she does look more like a woman than some others. I don't care. She still stinks like dead bodies. She stinks like dead bodies she eats."

"I hear they are good dancers," said the one playing the guitar. He plucked out a series of low, peculiar notes. "I find her beautiful," he said.

There was much I didn't understand. But I was fascinated. The older man rose to urinate outside the circle of light. He was a leader, perhaps. He stood facing me, his legs apart, staring outward blindly, and I thought I could puncture his fat stomach like a bag. The other man put down his guitar and got to his feet. Not far away, on the other side of the fire, they had tied their horses in a group. And they had a girl there, my sister, a prisoner. They had tied her hands in front of her, and the guitar man went and got her. I could hear him talking, and she got up from the ground. I saw her shadow cover his. Yet he must have been stronger than he looked, or braver, or stupider. He pulled her roughly by her knotted wrists, down the bare slope from the trees where they had left her with the animals, until she stood in the firelight, humiliated, her shoulders bent. I recognized her, though they had tied a cloth bag over her head. I recognized her body—naked from the waist, her wide hips. Her legs were spattered with mud, and she was bleeding from a wound on the outside of her thigh. Her feet were bare.

They had built their fire in a space between some large rocks, and I was watching their shadows on the uneven surface. At first the flames were high, their shadows long and menacing, but now the fire had settled somewhat. And when I saw my sister with them, they no longer seemed so fearsome. Without thinking, I had thought that there were lots of them, but there were not. Barbarians have names for any kind of quantity; they are in love with numbers. But such things are difficult for us. There, that night, there were not many: the fat man, the musician, and another with a long gun standing up between his knees. I could see the shadow of it on the rock.

The musician pulled the bag away from her face, and I saw her yellow hair, her nose, her heavy lips. He put his fingers to her face and to her hair, catching at the tangles, pulling them back from her forehead. When he forced her face into the light, I felt a surge of joy. I was happy to see her. And if in some part of my mind I was happy to see her conquered by these men, happy to see them dare what I could not, yet I was also happy to see her proud and unafraid, for there was nothing in her eyes but hatred. I could almost hear the song of it, but the barbarian heard nothing. He pushed the hair back from her face, and she let him touch her without moving, touch her bruised cheeks, her torn and broken lips. He said, "Don't be afraid. We won't hurt you. Understand?" She made no movement. "Don't be afraid," he repeated. "Here, drink," and he brought a cup of something to her mouth. She swallowed it in silence. She finished it. "Here," he said, and squatting, he pulled a piece of cloth out from beneath his shirt. There was a plastic bucket on the ground; he wet the napkin and stood up again to clean her face. "There," he said. "We mean you no harm."

One sat on the rocks, fingering his gun. "There's no point in talking," he said. "She can't understand you."

"I think she can. Can you?" he asked her. "Would you like something to eat? You must be hungry." She shook her head. "You see?" he said, gesturing to his companions. "You see? She understands. My name is . . ." something, he said, pointing to himself.

The fat one laughed. He was squatting near the fire, poking at it with a stick.

My sister brought her hands up to her face. I saw the cords had cut into her wrists, "Free me," she said, her voice naked, empty of significance. She thought that otherwise they wouldn't understand.

They stared at her. "Free me," she repeated carefully. "What do you want?"

The man with the gun stood up. "Beloved Angkhdt," he whispered, and even the other one, the musician, took a step back from her uncertainly. And then he smiled and stuck his tongue out of his mouth. "She understands," he said. And then he turned away. "I think it could be done," he said to the fat man.

The fat man laughed. He was drunk.

"No," the other said again. "I think I do. She's beautiful. She's like an animal." He turned back to face her, and showed her his tongue, and said something I didn't understand. But later I would come to recognize that famous verse of scripture which begins, "Oh my sweet love, let us be free as wild beasts, free as dogs, and let us kiss one another mouth to tail, like the wild dogs . . ."

He stuck his tongue out of his mouth. The fat man laughed. "You're repulsive," he said.

"No. Nothing like that. Take what you can find. I think she's beautiful. Look at her. Look at her arms."

"Yes, look at them. Be careful. Female or not."

"She's a female. You'll see."

"Don't be a fool."

The musician shrugged. "I think she's beautiful." And then he paused and smiled, and said to her, "We heard you were a dancer. That's why we captured you."

She shook her hair back from her face and brought her joined hands up to show him. The rope was biting her. I could see it and could hear it when she talked. "Free me." They were too deaf to hear the mixed intentions in her voice.

The musician licked his lips. He was standing in front of her, between her and the fire, looking at her body, her naked legs, her sex. She wore the remnants of a sheepskin shirt, and her arms were bare. And yes, she was beautiful, yes. He said so, and I thought so too. He was a slave to it. He reached to touch her, cupping his palm around the bone of her hip. "We mean you no harm," he said. "We'll let you go, don't worry about that. You're safe with us." He was smiling, and working his thumb into her skin as if to soothe her, staring up into her face. Even in his smile I could see his nervousness; still, he met no resistance when he slid his hand, so slowly, down along the bone of her hip, across her leg, down to the hair between her legs. He plucked at it and curled it between his fingers. And then he brought his hand up to his face, to sniff it and spit from his smiling mouth into his palm, but I could see he was still nervous, nervous when he put it back between her legs, nervous as he rubbed his spit into her sex. He was standing close to me, for I had crept so close. He faced away from me, the fire between us, and I could see the fingers of his other hand gripped tight behind his back, gripped tight around the handle of a knife hung upside down between his shoulder blades, and he gripped it nervously as he was rubbing spit into her sex. The other men were nervous too, one standing with his long gun, the fat one sitting forward, smoking. Paradise was down, and the fire was low, neglected. I also was excited. I knew that she was going to kill him if he freed her hands. I took an arrow from my belt.

She smiled. And this was hard for me to believe: the barbarian went down on his knees in front of her, turning his face to inhale, and then burrowing his face between her legs, kissing and licking her. In a little while she opened her knees, and he passed his hands under her, hidden from my sight, but I felt something just by looking at her face. She had drawn her lips away from her teeth. And she had let her wrists, tied together in front of her, sink slowly down, her fingers stretched, grasping at nothing, until she put her hands onto his head, burying her fingers in his hair. I heard her breathe. And then she let her neck sink too, until she was looking down at him and I could see her eyes. She was crying, making no noise. But quiet tears were running down her cheeks and down her chin, down her neck and into her hair. Crying is not common among us. But she thought she was going to die, and perhaps a little softness is best, at the end. She worked her fingers into his hair. And then she pulled him to his feet, softly, gently, because he was eager, too; he stumbled to his feet and stood in front of her, still smiling, and he passed the back of his hand across his lips. Then she touched him. She put her hands down to touch the front of his pants, and then she looked him in the face, her eyes shining with tears. She smiled. This was the moment, and he hesitated. But she stared at him, the yellow hair around her cheeks, her wet eyes—she was so beautiful. I suppose he must have known it too, in his own way, because again he reached behind his back and loosened the knife there. He hesitated, and then he drew it out, the short cruel blade, and he brought it around between them and tested the cruel edge along his palm. But she was still standing with her legs apart, the dew of some moisture shining on her sex, and she had bent her shoulders to hide the difference in their heights. For whatever the reason, for the sake of his own pride, he pulled the blade under her wrists and cut them apart. The ropes fell away; I had crept close, I could see the marks. And I could see her tense the muscles in her hands, testing the strength, opening and closing her fingers. She slid her hand into his pants. I waited for his yell, even though it took a little while—she was caressing his forearm below the hand which held the knife, running her fingernail along the vein. He had given away all of his power. In a little while he realized it. He had closed his eyes, but then they started open; he cried out and raised his knife, and she grabbed him under the wrist. The others were slow to respond, because they understood the noises he was making in another way at first. But she was squeezing his testicles to jelly. I saw the one who had been standing still as stone, holding his long gun, come suddenly to life. I shot him in the throat, in the chest, in the arm, and he fell over into the fire.

The fat man didn't move, though I was waiting for him. I had nocked another arrow and had pulled it back. Yet he just sat there, his fat stomach in his hands. He was afraid. I came close into the firelight, and I could see him—he was afraid of death, and it made it hard for him to think. He had no weapons, yet he reached for none—nothing, not a movement, though his body was tense. Nothing, only he had opened his eyes wide, opened his mouth, and he had dropped his cigarette. His hands were shaking, grasping stiffly at nothing as I squatted down in front of him. I was not a frightening sight—hungry, barely grown, old clothes, ripped leather, filthy fur. Nothing to be afraid of, except death like the black night around him, and the fire burning low. I stuck my knife into his face, hurting his cheek with the ragged steel. "Holy beloved God," he croaked, "don't hurt me," but it was as if he wasn't paying attention. Maybe it was hard for him to think because his friend was screaming hoarsely, without pause. Not that it mattered, for he was already finished: she had bent his hand back over his shoulder and his knife was useless. Yet still he kicked at her with his feet and hit her with his free hand, with his head, but it didn't matter, he was finished. The hand around his testicles had lifted him up almost off the ground. And in a little while he stopped struggling and started to cry, as she had done, yet different, too, because the pain was different. He had words and no music, and no tears either, just a rhythm of breath and a contorted mouth, and she stood staring at him, trying to understand him, her quiet face so close to him, her tears dry. How could she understand? She made a quick movement, and his knife fell to the stones. She let go of his wrist and joined her hands together on his sex, hoisting him up still farther. And when he hung limp from her hands, she dropped him to the dirt. He curled up like a baby, his shoulders shaking, his face turned to the ground.

Then she danced for them as they had asked, for them and for me, too, on the mountainside, in the white, fragile grass by the dying fire. It was the darkest part of the night. It had gotten cold. The man had curled himself around her feet, and she stepped free of him. Turning her back, she walked a few steps away, and I could see her tiredness in the way she walked. She walked to where the bucket stood, and she stooped to wash her face in it, to wash her arms. She stood up, her back still towards us, and with a simple, awkward movement she let her shirt slip from her shoulders. I could see the firelight on her body, the muscles, the flesh. She pulled her hair back and held it in a knot behind her neck. Then she released it and squatted down again over the bucket, washing herself, scooping up the water and pouring it over her, rubbing her arms. She was using a language of movement that belongs to little girls. The water was cold, I could tell. And I could see it dripping down her back, catching the light, dripping from her legs, scattering in circles when she shook her head. The black night was all around us, and I could feel something opening in my body like an empty hand. I sat cross-legged by the fire. I had taken the gun. The fat man had not moved. At one point he had seemed eager to speak, until I pointed the gun's long barrel at him through my knees and put my finger to my lips. The other had huddled himself together and sat nursing himself, his head bowed, his lips wet. He was watching my sister with pale eyes, so that it was by looking at him and listening to his breathing suddenly change that I first saw a new difference in the language of her body. She was dancing.

Death is the dark mountain where the snow never breaks beneath your feet. To believe in something else, to believe in something after death, that is a savage temptation, and only savages succumb to it. Myself, I would never want to live in a world that had not contained that moment: I watched her a long time. I watched her until she was weak and near collapse. For a long time she kept her back to us, and when she turned around I could see she had been wounded in the side—not much blood now, but the wound was deep. I noticed that among the other things, her breasts, her tangled hair, her beauty, the light painting her body. And the way language vanished from her arms when she saw me—her eyes were partly closed; she opened them and let her head fall forward. I was overcome with tenderness. I stood up and stepped toward her. She was close to falling, and I stretched out my hand. She came unsteadily, like a drunk, accepting my arm around her like a drunk. This was the first time that I touched her. She was shivering with cold.

* * *

Their clothes were too small for us, but we took their riding capes, and in one saddlebag I found larger stuff: a loose red shirt—velvet embroidered with silver thread—and heavy pants. My sister put them on. The rest we left, and left them their lives, too, because they seemed to value them. They squatted near the fire, making no movement when we turned our backs.

It was late when we rode away, near the red dawn. The stars were already dim, covered in a silky haze. My sister was tired, nodding to sleep in the barbarian saddle as we came in under the belltower, down through the heavy gateway of our town. She had not spoken once. I got down and went to help her, but I had hoped too much—she kicked my hand away and slid down to the ground, standing with her neck bent, her hair over her face, holding onto the horse's mane to keep from falling. But in a little while she gathered her strength and set off across the open stones without looking back. Later, when I came into the hall looking for food, tired after loosing the horses and rubbing them down, she was already asleep in her tangled bed, still in her clothes.

Inside it was still dark, in the entranceway among the beds. Farther on in the hearth, I could see a pale fire and hear music. Around me people were asleep. I walked among them down the length of the hall. In winter they had never slept so long. They would have been outside by then, trampling the snow, running with the dogs, but in this strange red thaw it was as if the air was starving us. I walked down through the aisles of beds, hearing some flute music from somewhere, a song called "I don't know." But it did nothing to ease my mind, for I could see the bodies of some children stretched out on the stones in front of the hearth, their faces mutilated in a way I had already seen. I hated that mark. The barbarians had cut a double line across their brows and a hole through their cheeks, as if they were trying to pollute the emptiness of death with meaning. I hated it; I was unhappy and ashamed to admit it even to myself, for unhappiness, too, is a barbarian ritual. It is the enemy of freedom, and to console myself I thought: things happen by chance. But chance had not killed these children and marked their faces.

My lords, you must think we were fools. Now, tonight, it seems so clear—the barbarians had sent soldiers to destroy us. Your bishop had sent soldiers. Even then I knew we were in danger. But we are not easily roused, you can imagine. So I did nothing, thinking that what was clear to me was clear to all. Only I had brought the barbarians' guns, long rifles and belts of ammunition. I threw them down on the stone steps below the stage and turned to go to bed.

I awoke to gunshots. I opened my eyes in stuffy darkness, and for a while I just lay there, listening to the sounds, gunshots and people yelling. I lay there, and in a little while I could see around me and see my sister in the next bed.

The night before, she had taken a silver bracelet from a bag of barbarian jewelry. It had been slaved into a pattern of fighting beasts; now she held her arm above her head, moving her wrist from side to side, examining the effect, not altogether happy. "They mean to kill us," she said, in a voice heavy with sleep. This was something she knew, something she had been told; doubtless the barbarian soldiers had told her, for even in a few notes I knew the mode, and I could hear no self, no speculation in it. I understood she was repeating something she had heard the night before. She continued: "They have a prince . . . A priest . . .who tells them what to do."

These words meant nothing to her, I could tell. And I lost interest. I was more interested in the gunshots, the bracelet, her white wrist. I sat up, rubbing my eyes and saying, "What?" to make her talk again. But that was all. She made an answer, but I could hear a part of her own music in it. So I listened only to the sound. I loved the sound of her. Some of her melodies I can no longer live without. They have become a part of my own music, part of myself, my own heart's music. My lords, why am I telling you this? It is not the place. And if, then, it was part of my thoughts, it was only a small part. I was listening to the gunshots. I thought, I will never see her again. And so my image of her then is a special burden: reclining in the half-light in a pile of dirty blankets, her red clothes already rumpled, studying the bracelet on her wrist, her skin the color of honey, her yellow hair, her yellow eyes. Her dark eyebrows—there was no delicacy in her face, no art.

Death is the dark mountain where the snow never breaks beneath your feet. Yet something in the way she looked made it hard to bear the thought of dying. And I cursed my weakness, for a free man comes to love death as a drunkard loves his bottle. Both contain something, I see now, the thought and the glass. It is painful to have reasons to live. And so I turned away from her, and in a little while I got to my feet and wandered outside into the sunlight.

I wandered towards the gate. Barbarians were there. You could hear them trying to break in, the rhythm of their hammers on the wooden beams, the lash of the whip, the beat of the cursed drum. I closed my eyes and blocked my ears, but even then I could feel the slavish rhythm in my heart and in my pulse, so deep within us runs that barbarian music. Our bodies are not made for the life we want to lead, for freedom, for emptiness—I saw that, I felt it in my body. That drumbeat can't be stopped. Knowing that, it was as if something broke in me, something surrendered. I looked up at my brothers and sisters, perched on the walls and on the roofs of buildings, clutching their weapons and their instruments, watching the soldiers break down the door.

Over me above the gate rose up the ruins of a tower, squat, round, broken, hollow. There was a way of climbing to the top. I had discovered it when I was still a child, a way of scaling the stairless stones up to the remnants of a belfry high up above the town. Belfry, I say—once wooden scaffolding had supported a great bell, silent in my memory, except for when the beams had broken and the bell had fallen with a singing clash, as if waiting for the moment when a man was riding out into the snow, out through the double gate with all the world in front of him. Horse and rider died. Biters had taken days to slave away the wreck, for the bell cut deeply into the frozen ground. I remembered as I climbed the tower, the mass of fallen masonry and metal, the broken horse and man.

As I reached the top, my body full of breath, blood in my head, I could hear music around me. At first it had been part of the air, a low woodwind speaking music as a kind of farewell, and I knew that when I put my head up through the opening, I would be struck full in the face by what the musician saw, the beauty of the sun, the sun glinting on the hills. I heard without listening the melodies for all these things—red light on stone, on snow, the blood-red light, light struggling with sadness. I pulled myself up into the belfry and saw my brother lying in the shelter of the broken wall, safe from gunfire, playing his pipe. He had worked his song around the hammering under our feet, using it as rhythm. He did it without thinking, I suppose, out of instinct for the sounds around him. There was no reason why the swing of that barbarian cadence should mean the same to him as to me. Why should he want to stop it? He was right to lie there with his music. There was nothing to be done. But I stepped over his body to the lip of the wall, and far below I could see the soldiers slaving at the gate, hairy men in black uniforms. I kicked the stones along the parapet, testing them for falseness. They did not move, but I grabbed up a loose one, the size of a man's head, and threw it down and watched it fall. There was no effect. I kicked the hunks of masonry, searching for a flaw, but I was not strong enough to break the stones apart, not by myself.

I worked at it until my face was hot, and still my brother lay there. I cried out for him to help me, and the music changed a little. I tried to find the words that would make him help me, but there were none; he was still free. But his song was changing, there was pride in it, and hatred, and a shadow of laughter. So I bent down to snatch the instrument out of his mouth, and tried to break it on my knee. A pipe made out of black wood strapped with barbarian silver—it would not break. So I battered it against the rocks until it cracked and the reed snapped off. Then I threw it back at him as he sat up astonished, his mouth looking for words. He grabbed at me, and I stepped out of reach, up onto the parapet.

For an instant I stood, balanced on the narrow battlement, in full view, with the mountains and the sunlight and the open air around me. It was so still. The swing of hammers down below had stopped, the drumbeats scattering into silence. And my brother jumped up to stand beside me, violence in his mind, perhaps, but he did nothing. We just stood there, together in the silence and the shining hills, until there came up from the soldiers below us the sound of a single gunshot. And as I jumped down to safety, I saw him press his hand against his ribs, and saw the blood leak out between his fingers, saw the sudden terror in his face, the thought solidifying there that he was going to die not just soon, but then, right then. I could see the pump of his lungs, hear the low music in his throat, and then he stepped backward into the red, quiet air. Leaning over, I was in time to see him dropping like a stone into that mass of slaves.

A boy falling out of the sky—the image seemed to mean something to them, for down below the soldiers left off their work to gather round his body. They were doing something to him, pulling at him, arranging his limbs in some way. A man in red robes—a priest, I can say now—knelt to cut that mark into his cheeks. I wasn't paying much attention. I was watching my brothers and my sisters on the walls and rooftops, because the image of the falling boy had captured their minds too, had seized and shaken them, so that they had put their instruments aside. I heard a shout, chaotic and unmusical, and they began to open fire on the soldiers with the guns that I had brought down from the mountain. They threw bricks and rocks. They shot a drizzle of arrows. We are a peaceful race, and it amazed me to see the soldiers below scuttle back like insects, out of range. One was wounded, and I heard him yell, a high-pitched screaming, full of unconscious music, of double tones and squeaks. He expected to be left behind. But another soldier came running back. Above, the sky was cloudless with no wind, and on the tower top I tried to clear my mind. But I was distracted by the noise outside the gate—the wounded soldier and his friend, one kicking and crying, one scurrying around him in a kind of dance. The man bent down to take his hurt companion on his back. They made slow progress, and I watched them a long time as they labored out of range.

One we captured alive. A boy had opened up the gate to go out scavenging for weapons. Just outside, in a litter of sledgehammers and iron bars, we found a man. At first I thought he had been wounded in the stomach, because he was curled up. He would not look us in the face. And he was praying with fanatic speed; he would not stop, even when my brother lost patience and tried to pull him to his feet. "Sweet love, deliver me. I have done no harm, by the hair of your head, deliver me, by the power of your thighs, by the strength of your thighs. Hold me in your arms, so that I may say, 'Sweeter than sugar is your taste in my mouth, sweeter than sugar is the taste of your ministers . . .'" He went on and on. He wouldn't be quiet. So we dragged him up into the town by his shirt, up to the dancing hall, and left him outside where he lay in a heap.

My brothers and my sisters had no interest in him, for the barbarians did not come back that day. But I was interested. He pulled himself upright, and in a little while I saw him sitting up, supported in the angle of a wall, crooning to himself, his eyes closed whenever I looked at him, open when I didn't.

In the evening I brought him food, a mush of corn in a bowl, and for a while I stood without knowing what to say as he rocked and prayed, one hand clamped on his genitals, the other on an amulet around his neck. It was unusual just to watch someone so closely. Barbarians took no offense. This one sat cross-legged, rocking. He was an old man, his skin pale and spotted, loose and shrunken at the same time. His hair was gray, streaked with white, tied in a black rag at the nape of his neck. It hung long down his back. He had no beard, and I could see his skinny face. There was no meat on it, or on his bone-white arms. His belly was soft and fat.

I didn't know how to talk to him. Old man? Barbarian? Coward dwarf? But he didn't look afraid anymore; he seemed happy, in fact, smiling at intervals, as if at inner jokes. He showed his teeth; they were dirty, but looked strong. "Old man," I said.

He started, and his eyes flickered open, as if I had just woken him. And when he turned to me, I saw in his face and in his eyes a statement I had not looked for, something you see in the faces of small children, a mixture of delight and fear. He put his hand out towards me, and I could see the amulet around his neck. It was molded from heavy plastic in the shape of a man's genitals.

"Old man," I said, holding out the bowl I had brought. "Here is food for pigs and slaves."

He smiled up at me, looking into my face but not my eyes. "Is it . . . flesh?" he asked, almost reverently. "I cannot eat . . . flesh."

"It is not," I said. He looked both disappointed and relieved, but he made no motion, and so I squatted down and pushed the bowl into his face.

"Thank you," he said, words I'd never heard, and the tone made me think he was refusing. But when I tried to pull my hand away, he grabbed the bowl and held it in his lap without looking at it.

"Who are you?" I asked.

"I am God's soldier. And I am happy here. Happy to be here." He looked around. "Very glad to have seen it, at the end of my life."

The sun was down, the sky darkening. Someone had started to play music in the hall behind us. Children came to stand in the bright doorway. One raised his hands and twirled a child's pirouette. "Listen," said the soldier, as if I had no ears. "How beautiful!" I squatted down beside him. I could hear the sound of a wooden flute, played in a difficult and obscure key called "water-bird." In that particular tempo you could see a bird rising from the surface of a pool, fanning the water into ripples with its wings. Usually the bird is small and white, with a long straight bill; the pool is crisp on a bright day, but to-night the musician—a very young girl, I knew her tone—had chosen the lu-minous dark of early evening, a great bird of prey, its wings outstretched, the feathers of its wingtips stretching wide like fingers, circling exhausted over an endless sea. In the alien water it will sink without a trace. The music changed, the bird disappeared into the dark, and you could see the stars com-ing out one by one, a song we called "first stars."

The soldier spoke again. He said, "We only have tonight to listen. My prince is camped under the hill. Tomorrow he will burn the town. He's sworn an oath to level every stone. The priest has already blessed the gallows. This is the last night for you and me." His voice was dreamy, and I was surprised by how much he seemed to understand. Not the bird, not the water, not the stars. That was part of a language only we could hear, the images summoned out of forms and choices meaningless to a stranger. Yet he was responding to the music's other part, the melody, the song of the artist, as sad as she could make it at so young an age. She was afraid of death. Death sang in every note. Like me, she was afraid.

"Why?" I asked.

He smiled as if he were smarter than I. A dog was slinking past the porch, his head down. "He knows," said the soldier, pointing. "Ask him."

This meant nothing to me. Then, I knew nothing of barbarian heresy. I made no distinction between barbarian creeds. But I was interested in the sol-dier. He was listening to the music, which was changing, and I wondered whether he could sense its change. His eyes were full of tears. "I am so happy to be here," he repeated. "Here at the end of all things."

His food still lay untasted in his lap. And in a little while he spoke again: "So happy just to listen. I have heard so much about your music. When I was young, the bishop would have whipped a man for whistling in the streets. Now they are more desperate."

"Tell me," I said.

He smiled. He brought his hand up to his mouth. "This is the last night," he said, pointing towards Paradise, just rising. "Look, you can see the mountain where I used to live, that black spot. Look." He sniffed. "It has been warm here. Tonight it will snow. And tomorrow morning, that will be the end. I think the sun will never rise again. And look." He motioned to the stone table not far away, the statue lying on its back. "The idols are broken. Tomorrow we shall see. False priests and false governors. At the hour of seven-times-ten they shall be overthrown."

I looked around at the gathering dark. Music had started again, one of the many kinds of fire music, boastful, proud, and you could see fire flashing from the empty doorway of the hall. The soldier sat with his own thoughts, rocking and humming, and fingering his amulet. So I settled back to listen, and I watched the stars gather and combine as darkness fell, solitary at first, the brightest, one or two in all the sky. As I watched there were always more, filling up that aching space with light, with stars and patterns, numberless, nameless.

Some children came down through the bright doorway, running and laughing and carrying torches. You could see their faces in the torchlight, dirty, thin, and full of joy. One threw her torch high up into the air, meaning to catch it as it came down; she missed, and it exploded in a shower of sparks. And then they all ran down together across the open stones towards the tower gate, their bodies disappearing in the dark, until below us all that remained were their high, wordless voices and the flickering lights, chasing and spinning, part formless dance, part ruleless game.

The soldier, too, was covered up in darkness. His body had retreated from my sight, and in the long silence I would have let his image go as well, until I remembered nothing. I would have cleared my mind, opened up my hand, and like a timid animal he might have stayed for a while, trembling on my palm until I prodded him away. In the end he would have gone, just as if he had been eager to escape. I would have forgotten him and everything. For that night I was in love. It filled me like a brimming flood, too deep, too painful for joy. I felt it around me as if for the last time. In the cooling dark, I could hear it in the music, in the scattering voices, see it in the children's restless torches, mocked from above by an eternity of stars.

But in time the soldier spoke again. I was surprised to hear the sadness in his voice, for without thinking I had thought that my new ecstasy was filling all the world. "The stars will shine like day," he said. "And in the new light, the earth will blossom like a flower in springtime, and it will need no tending. Stones will move, and fish will speak. Birds will speak. The earth will bring forth all good things, and all men will be free. And Angkhdt will wipe the dirt from our faces, and He will stand up like a giant in the farthest north, and He will say, 'Bring to me all tyrants and false priests . . .'" The old man's voice was sad. "I will not live to see it," he said, turning towards me. I could see the outline of his face.

His breath stank. I reached out to grab the string around his neck, to twist it in my hand until the slack was taken up. I held him at arm's length and shook him once, gently. He went quiet, and I looked up at the stars. "Please," he said, his voice full of fear. "You don't really . . . eat flesh? You are not cannibals . . . As they say?"

I let him go and I stood up. It was too cold to sit. He followed me into the doorway and grabbed me by the arm. Inside the hall, my brothers and my sisters had slaved in from somewhere the corpse of a horse. Some were stripping the skin away from the flesh, pouring off the blood into wooden buckets; some were sawing through the bones, breaking the joints apart; some were building up the fire. It was like a drug, the smell of fresh-cut meat. For me and for the barbarian too: he looked past me into the uncertain light, and at first he didn't understand what they were doing. When he did, the strength of his body failed. He leaned against the doorpost, his eyes wide with fear. His shoulders and his neck fell forward. He raised his hand up to his face. He dropped his forehead to his palm, and then ducked it to his armpits, once to each side, and murmured a little prayer.

I left him and walked down into the hall, looking for someone. The music was saying something to me. It was in a form called "no regret," played with wavering purity on the long horn, a large, difficult, metal instrument, which someone had left behind when all the rest of us were left behind. The boy who had picked it up to make it his still did not possess the lungs for any but the easiest modes. This one, "no regret," he played tentatively, using a melody plainer and sweeter than usual. He knelt wheezing on his bed in the hot firelight, and others squatted near him, listening. And the music told me something too. I thought, if I am going to die tomorrow, I don't have time to wash myself as clean as snow.

My brothers and my sisters were moving towards the center of the feast, to where the butchered horse was thrown onto the fire. Their desires were of the simplest kind. Mine was different. I had no interest in the food, though I was hungry. Instead I turned aside and walked away under the shadows of the wooden arches, to my own bed and the bed beside it. She was lying on her side, with one arm stretched out. She was still asleep, or asleep again, for she had stripped off some of her red clothes and lay part-naked under dirty blankets.

I sat cross-legged on my bed. The song told me not to be afraid. I wanted to touch her, to make some mark on her before time closed its hand. I reached out to touch her on the arm. I touched her with my entire hand. I felt her skin, her muscle, her blood, her bone, everything. I ran my thumb along the bare, sleeping flesh, listening to the music. I ran my fingers all along her arm, from her shoulder to her palm. Yes, it was a beautiful arm, though in some places it was cut and torn. It was rounded and strong, the hair golden and fine along her wrist. I could have done anything to her as she slept, I don't know, I barely knew what it all meant to touch her where I wanted, yes, her sleep seemed deep enough, untroubled by noise, untroubled by the boy's long horn. She had no regret. My brothers and sisters were clanging bells and shouting, and behind that rose the sound of activity around the fire—all of it had not sufficed to wake her. I myself was aware of everything, every noise, every motion.

I sat cross-legged, and she lay beside me with her face pressed against the outside of my thigh, her elbow in my lap. She lay soft and responsive, so I touched her with more force, to press some hardness back into the long muscles of her arm. And as her body came alive under my hand, her spirit coming back from wherever it had been, I thought of all the times I had seen her, every image, every song. And the rest of the room receded into darkness, as if I sat with her alone. So we woke to each other, my fingers suddenly sensitized by memory, her fingers opening under mine, responsive at first, then tight and hard as she woke up. That was the moment. I will remember it. Since then I have dreamed of loving, and all my dreams have been like that, trying to recapture the brittle tension not even of her kisses, but of that one moment, that moment when I held her by the wrist, reawakening to her as if from sleep while she pulled sleepily away. She tried to pull away, and I clamped my hand down on her wrist.

She let me hold her. Without relaxing in the slightest degree, she raised herself up on her other arm and looked around.

Near us, the fire was burning brighter. On a table in the center of the hall, my brothers and sisters had piled roasted joints of horsemeat, high up to keep them from the dogs. A little girl had jumped up on the table's back, straddling the carcass like a rider; with a stick she beat away their snapping mouths, until my little brother reached up for the horse's head, bigger than his own. Holding it up between his hands, he did a dance, grinning from behind its cruel, empty beak. And then he threw it far away into a corner where it rolled along the floor, the dogs skidding and sliding after it, biting at each other. And to the other side he flung the neck, a bucketful of entrails, its feet and claws, and even a great haunch of meat, so drunk he was with generosity. My sister hit him with her stick. But I could see there was enough for all, because the pony was a fat one, a barbarian beast shot in the white grass, and not one of our starving nags.

I squeezed my sister's hand, and she squeezed mine. I turned to look at her, and she looked away and lay back in the shadow of the wall. But even so I could see her naked shoulders and her arms, and her golden hair around her face. I could see her frowning, biting her lips. The shadow cut across her face. I kept staring at her, trying to memorize her. She would glance at me and glance away, holding my hand so tightly she was hurting me. I reached out and took hold of her jaw, and pulled her towards me, and when I kissed her I could feel her tense, hard lips, and feel her teeth clenched tight beneath them. She let me kiss her on the mouth.

I was with her the whole night. When it was almost morning, I left her and walked outside into a snowstorm, to watch the snow falling out of a clear sky, the stars like chips of ice, and Paradise small behind the mountains, circled by a ring of ice. The thaw was over, and some little girls were throwing snowballs. I heard some music from the rooftops, fragile and sweet, a song called "children playing," and when they heard it, the girls stopped and looked at each other, their arms at their sides. One held up her wrist and stared at it, and turned it, and turned each finger in a movement so delicate, so expressive of the music, that it was as if another instrument had joined in, playing in a kind of harmony.

CPSIA information can be obtained
at www.ICGtesting.com
Printed in the USA
LVHW041247121221
705979LV00013B/1855

9 781587 155086